THE MEAN

by

John Arthur Long

This book is dedicated to all those in education who show children the joy that can be found in learning.

In addition, this book is dedicated to every American who would not hesitate to defend our children and nation against those who would try to do us harm.

The author wishes to acknowledge his indebtedness to *THE BOOK OF ANSWERS, The New York Public Library Telephone Reference Service's Most Unusual and Entertaining Questions* by Barbara Berliner with Melinda Corey and George Ochoa, A FIRESIDE BOOK published by Simon and Schuster for many of the "fact and answer questions" used in this book.

THE MEAN © 2017 by John Arthur Long

Published by:

VELLUM PUBLISHING, INC.
PO Box 415
Round Top, New York 12473

ISBN-13: 978-0-9897651-1-4

BOOK ONE

FINDING THE MEAN

PROLOGUE

"Abdul Jehmar has betrayed us," the leader hissed, his fist slamming down so hard on the rough-hewn wooden table where they sat that the ceramic cups and bowls before them jumped in response.

"No, he is the negotiator. They do not take sides," insisted the old one. The language the old one spoke was thick with the accent of those who were of the desert regions.

The leader came to his feet, his chair making a scraping sound as it scooted backwards and toppled to the floor behind him. "Lies!" he shouted harshly at the old man. "How did they know our location? The American Special Forces unit moved without hesitation, firing as they came. There was no doubt. They knew. Only Abdul Jehmar could have told them."

"He would not do this thing. The negotiator seeks only peace. It has always been this way with him," the old one pleaded. "Let us speak to him. You will see."

"ENOUGH!" the leader screamed. His hand emerged from the loose material of the robe he wore, gesturing from the old one to the entrance of the small dirt-floored room in which they had gathered. "Take him from here. The time of words has ended. Abdul Jehmar has betrayed us. Now we must act."

A soldier who stood behind them nodded curtly and pulled the old one to his feet, dragging him from the room as he protested, tears gathering in the crevasses of his ancient eyes. "No, please. You must not do this thing."

Then the objector was gone, and the leader sat again in the chair another had quickly moved to upright. The leader pulled the chair into the table and, sweeping the dishes to the side, folded his hands before him and leaned in towards those awaiting his next command.

"It will be done," he said, his voice quiet once more, hardened with the firmness of conviction. "I have spoken to others who have spoken to others with unending networks of power who will help to assure it will succeed. We know the location of the Jehmar family in America and the school his children attend. That will be our target. It has never been done before to strike within America in a place where children gather to be educated. It will instill fear in their hearts as nothing else can. And when Abdul Jehmar's children die, he will know also that he has paid a terrible price for his betrayal. It will be a great moment for us and those who will help us. America will tremble in response, knowing that no one, not even their children, are safe from the force of our power."

Heads nodded slightly in response to the words, as the leader looked from one to the next. He gestured to the man standing beside him, and the soldier unrolled a large square of Tyvek and placed it on the table. The leader stood, the others moving closer to look at the map that had been spread out before them.

It was a chart with symbols and areas unknown to them. The leader leaned in and pointed to a section that displayed thick intersecting black lines on an accented area that indicated it was a place of heavy population. Many blue and red roads crisscrossed one another as they stretched from west to east, moving along a narrow strip of land, bordered by bodies of water.

"This is the great capital of New York City. We will not strike there where so many expect targets to be located." His long, dark index finger moved eastward, following the patterns of the roads. "Instead, our objective is to the east where those who work in this great American city live with their families and believe they are safe. This is also the location of Abdul Jehmar's family. He is seldom there, but that is of no consequence. It is his children we are after, and they live here on what is called Long Island."

His finger stopped on a large round dot approximately a third of the way along the middle of the narrow land mass. "This is the place where all three of Abdul Jehmar's beautiful young daughters attend school. Central High School it is called. Here is where we will strike."

ONE
THE PHANTOM STRIKES AGAIN

"Mr. Scarlucci, I have a *deposit* in my drawers."

Not really listening, I glanced up distractedly from the computer screen of my laptop, my attention still on the "Lockdown Protocol During Building Emergency" staff memo I was drafting in accordance with the New York State mandate.

"MR. SCARLUCCI!" the voice insisted loudly.

I glanced up. The business teacher standing in my office doorway was elderly, stout, wide-hipped, and perpetually angry, probably about being elderly, stout and wide-hipped.

"I'll be with you in a moment, Blanche," I said.

"Mr. Scarlucci, I said there is a *deposit* in my drawers."

"Okay...What?"

Blanche Turner stepped into my Assistant Principal's Office, moving toward where I sat behind my large mahogany desk. She pushed a loose strand of her graying, not overly-clean wavy hair from her furrowed brow, and her voice dropped to a hushed conspiratorial level. "I said there are feces... in my drawers."

"Feces."

"Yes, SHIT. I have shit in my drawers! I came in this morning, opened the center desk drawer to get my plastic pass which I always keep at the blackboard because I refuse to stop the lesson for bathroom requests...and there it was...in the front tray.

5

Great. The phantom, as we had come to call him, had struck again, this time making Blanche Turner the target.

For years, everyone, including myself, had been urging Blanche to retire. But Blanche was and always had been single, and teaching always had been and still was her entire life. So, in spite of everyone except her knowing that her classroom atmosphere was always somewhere between rude and chaotic, she was tenured and still here. And now she had shit in her drawers.

"I'll see that it gets cleaned up, Blanche. I'm sorry."

"How in God's name could anyone do such a thing? There's no excuse for it. It's just mean, that's all. Just mean!"

"Yes it is. I'm afraid the 'good old golden rule days' aren't what they used to be. We seem to have more and more mean days lately."

"But when could it have happened? I keep the door locked. That means someone has keys." An element of panic entered Blanche's voice. "Why, they could come into my room anytime they want. They could be waiting for me when I come into the room in the morning. We've got to do something! What in God's name has the school come to when a student can leave shit in a teacher's drawers?"

Damn good question! I had to give Blanche that.

I pushed back my chair, coming to my feet and moving to where Blanche had begun to tremble visibly, and I touched her arm tentatively in an attempt at comfort.

"Blanche, you know we have a key problem. And until we can get all the locks changed, we're doing the best we can."

"Well, why didn't the cameras catch him? Isn't that what they're for?"

"Whoever it was taped over the camera in that hallway, and since your room is at the end, the opposite camera could not pick it up. Every system has its flaws."

"Well, maybe if those retired policemen supposedly providing security actually did their jobs...."

I stifled a sigh. "Thank you for reporting this, Blanche. You're not the only one, believe me. Earlier this week, Ms. Madison found a...deposit...in the center of the stage."

The phone on my desk buzzed.

"Excuse me a moment," I said to Blanche, reaching back across the desk and picking up the receiver. "Yes, Betty?"

"Mr. Mordento is here to see you, Mr. Scarlucci."

Swell. First the phantom shitter left a deposit in Blanche's drawers, and now the mafia had arrived. And it wasn't even eight-thirty in the morning yet.

I steered Blanche by her bone-skinny arm back around and toward the door. "Look, I'll have Richie come to your room and clean up the mess. And I'm sorry. We'll get the person responsible, I promise. Now I have to take this appointment."

She stopped at the door. "How could they ever have allowed that Mordento boy back into this school?"

"We can only suspend him for so long. It's a court ruling."

She pursed her lips in disapproval. "After being caught with a loaded weapon in school?"

"Well, Ken Valentine tells me Joey seems to be doing all right in his class, so we'll see. There's nothing we can do except try to make the best of it."

"Oh, if Mr. Valentine says he's fine, I guess we have nothing to worry about," Blanche answered, expressing undisguised disgust. "I'm sure that juvenile delinquent Joey Mordento will get an A, just like all the rest of Valentine's students."

"Blanche...."

"I hope he is being searched each day when he arrives at school?"

"Everyone who enters this building passes through the metal detector. We are not permitted to do a physical search. You know that."

"Well, no detector stopped him the first time. So then we won't know if he has a weapon in school again or not, will we!"

"Blanche, if you'll excuse me, I really have to take this appointment."

"What does his father want?"

"That's what I'm about to find out."

Nodding curtly, Blanche turned once again and disappeared out the door, as I hurried back to my desk and opened the Mordento file.

Joseph Mordento's school record was filled with disciplinary infractions: insubordination, cutting school, fights, and even punching a chaperone, Arthur Brant, at a Friday evening performance of Battle of the Bands. There were, of course, countless referrals, internal suspension assignments, Saturday morning suspension assignments and, finally, the weapon incident, which had led to his arrest and external suspension. Unfortunately, as Blanche had correctly pointed out, we still had no idea how Joey had smuggled the weapon past the metal detector, but if there is one thing I have come to realize, it is that nothing in life is foolproof.

Actually, when he was sent to the Dean's Office for another incident of insubordination with, as fate would have it, Blanche Turner, no one, least of all Ms. Turner, was even faintly aware that the boy was carrying a loaded pistol. However, it was only after she had sent Joey to the Dean's Office that Greg Latch discovered the .38 in the boy's possession.

As is so frequently the case with careless youth, Joey had failed to be thorough with his smuggled weapon, tucking it haphazardly into the back of the boxer-exposed, low-slung beltline of his oversize denim pants, so that when he sat down, the gun fell onto the floor. Panicking, Joey tried to bolt from the room, but Latch grabbed him, saw the gun on the floor, and called in law enforcement.

The police, of course, are not school officials, and when Joey lipped-off to the arriving officers, they promptly did the thing that every teacher and administrator can only dream of doing to obnoxious, insubordinate students: slam Joey

Mordento down and cuff both of his wrists to his chair while they went into the office to get the facts about the weapon possession. However, even the police could not have anticipated Joey Mordento's tenacity. As the officers and Dean Latch spoke, Joey could be seen though the office window running awkwardly, still cuffed to the waiting room chair, his low-slung jeans sliding progressively down his ass. He dragged the chair with him, across the sidewalks and entrance drive that curved around the front of the high school, and up the grassy hill leading to the teacher's parking lot that bordered Central Avenue.

"Holy shit," shouted Latch, and the three of them ran for the front door. However, there was no need for them to hurry in pursuit, as, at that very moment, none other than A. J. Gotz was coming out the front entrance of the high school, arriving for bus duty.

A. J. Gotz was a legend at Central High, unfortunately, not always for the right reasons. Educationally, this somewhat short-of-stature individual was a throwback to the stern, taskmaster days of yore, when an instructor not only adhered unbendingly to the rules, but also enforced them with a vengeance. After A.J. proceeded to teach grammar and sentence outlining during the first three weeks of his English classes, with wailing cries that A. J. didn't know "gatz," students ran to the Guidance Center in droves to transfer out of his classes. Simultaneously, parent phone messages piled in at record numbers to everyone from Sherri Walsh, the

English Department Chairperson, to the next in the command chain, Assistant Principal in charge of discipline Brian Scarlucci, and right on up the line from Mary J. Talley, the high school Principal, to Dr. Francis Farnsworth, the Superintendent of Schools. Over the years, A.J. had been spoken to, then warned, then written up with letters in his personnel file, all to no avail. He seemed to delight in being a pontificating and unyielding carrier of the torch of overzealous academic integrity.

Actually, the hard truth was that basic English skills were being thoroughly taught in his classes, and A.J.'s students probably ended up with a better understanding of English usage than most. However, there were other aspects to the man's personality that were troublesome. A.J. loved to come riding up to school on a Harley Davidson motorcycle and to show students his tattoos. I had no knowledge of what the inked body emblems might be or where they were located, nor did I want to know.

In addition, A.J. supplemented his teacher's salary working as an auxiliary county policeman, and he had gotten caught and reprimanded more than once for bringing his weapon into the school in his briefcase. There was, therefore, a certain amount of irony that, with a weapon violation of his own, it would be A.J. who stepped up to the plate to stop a student trying to escape from the authorities because of a...weapon possession violation.

Still, critics of the infamous A.J. Gotz had to admit that the man took care of business when needed on that bitterly cold November day. As the chair-cuffed Joey Mordento ran coatless across the front lawn of the school, and A. J. simultaneously exited the school through the front entrance for bus duty, the auxiliary police officer within Gotz rose instantly to the occasion.

School bus check-off sheet clipboard in hand, A. J. immediately assessed the situation correctly and sprang into action, hurling the clipboard like a Frisbee with a mighty snap of the wrist as Joey ran clumsily by him. The hard clear plastic board connected with the running boy's legs just below his pants-encumbered knees, and Joey fell in a heap onto the upward-sloping lawn. A. J. covered the distance between them in seconds, grabbing the chair to hold Joey on the ground until the police and a slightly overweight and puffing Greg Latch reached them.

Open-ended external suspension followed the incident with a ruling that Joey Mordento could not return or come within five miles of the school building until he had passed a psychological review that attested to his rehabilitation, which is, to the school administration's complete surprise, what had taken place the previous week. There were those who insisted that Joey's father had rigged the entire review process since, as recognized second-in-command of what was reputed to be one of the most influential organized crime families in the tri-state area, Salvatore "The Gimp" Mordento held considerable influence over the outcome of certain matters when he chose to do so, especially when the matters in question concerned his son. However, as is so often the case with such matters, there was no proof of Mordento coercion. So, Joey was back in attendance at Central High.

I closed Joey's infraction folder, placing it in the center of my desk for quick reference and, after mentally preparing myself for the encounter, buzzed Betty, my secretary, to send in Mr. Mordento. There were really only two reasons he could be coming to see me: either to thank me for his son's being allowed to return to school, or to kill me for being the person who had been responsible for expelling Joey in the first place. Although, the fact that Joey was carrying a loaded weapon definitely weighed in my favor on that particular decision, and I intended to tell Mr. Mordento just that,…if he didn't kill me first, of course.

TWO

SAL THE GIMP

Many thought Salvatore Mordento's infamous nickname was the result of some gangland showdown, where, guns blazing, a younger Sal had taken a stray bullet in the leg as he ruthlessly gunned down all comers. According to those who were supposedly in the know about such things, however, the truth was far less exotic. Sal the Gimp's limp was actually the result of having a foot and the lower portion of his leg up to the knee removed because of the early onset of diabetes, which was slowly destroying his body.

It seemed that from his early teens, and maybe even before that, not only had Sal made it a practice to unhesitatingly kill anything and anyone who irritated him, but he had also consumed staggering amounts of sweets on a daily basis, undoubtedly as a little reward to himself for doing such a good job of killing the things that got in his way. You would think that having a leg amputated when you reached middle age and having to get around with a prosthesis would slow the sugar intake down a tad, but as the corpulent Salvatore Mordento entered my office with a sort of waddle-jerk to propel his body forward, the girth of his form left no doubt in my mind that cream-filled doughnuts, hot fudge sundaes, and lots of fettuccine Alfredo were still very much staples of the Mordento daily diet.

From beneath heavy, fleshy lids, dead unflinching eyes met mine as I stood and shook Mordento's damp pudgy hand.

"Mr. Mordento. Nice to see you. Won't you have a seat?" I offered, with a gesture to the wider of the two chairs flanking the area in front of my desk.

Mordento grunted his response and followed my gestured lead, dropping a little too heavily into the chair.

"So, just so's we're clear here. You're the individual who is responsible for getting my boy Joey expelled, and him having to go through all that psycho analysis bullshit. Is that correct?" Sal said, dead eyes glaring at me.

Well, at least that answered my question as to why he made the appointment to see me. With an opening like that, obviously, he was here to kill me.

I cleared my tightening throat and nodded. "Technically, since I am in charge of discipline here at Central, that would be true; but, believe me, Mr. Mordento, it was a collective decision. I'm sure you can appreciate the reaction a loaded weapon on school grounds might cause."

Sal nodded, his cheeks jiggling. "Absolutely. Don't get me wrong. I know the kid was way out of line. Trust me, Mr. Scarlucci, we had a little discussion about it, Joey and me. It ain't gonna happen again. Ever."

A slight wave of relief passed through me. "Well, I appreciate your saying that, Mr. Mordento. Parental cooperation is always a tremendous help in circumstances like these."

15

"Oh, yeah? 'Bout how many circumstances where the son of a reputed member of organized crime brings a loaded .38 to school have occurred on these premises?"

"Actually, Joseph's actions would be the first such incident," I answered, trying to assess, but having no idea where Sal the Gimp was going with all this. "But I'm happy to report that since his return, Joseph seems to be doing quite well. He's been back in school for several days now, and there has not been one infraction or even a complaint about his behavior. Let's hope this is a new beginning for him. Nothing would make us happier. Our goal here at Central is to assure that every student is able to make the best of the opportunities for learning that we provide."

"No child left behind or some such bullshit. Is that it?"

"We feel strongly that Central should do everything it can to help a child achieve his or her potential, yes."

Salvatore made a wheezing sound that carried with it an unmistakable air of personal disgust. "Can't say I agree with that. Way I see it, there are some kids who'd be better off flushed down the shitter far as learning is concerned, along with their parents who are usually to blame for the kid being such a miserable fuck to begin with. Who's kidding who here?"

The correctly worded form to the question was *who's kidding "whom,"* but I didn't think the moment was right for me to point out the grammatical error to a man who killed people for a living. Plus the question was obviously rhetorical since Sal continued on without waiting for an answer.

"Some of these kids are major fuck-ups and will continue to be fuck-ups, and don't stand a chance in hell of learning shit, no matter what you do. Am I right or what?"

"Well, I...."

"Truth is, I always thought Joey was one of the fuck-up types. Not that it mattered, far as I was concerned. I could always find something for him to do within my organization." Mordento paused a beat before he finished. "You know, like have him kill people for me."

I stared at Mordento, dumbfounded.

One of the reasons I had gotten the Assistant Principal position at Central was because I had a knack for handling people in difficult situations, and Mary J. Talley liked the buffer I was able to provide before problems reached her Principal's desk. However, Salvatore Mordento was a totally different animal. Within minutes of entering my office, he had managed to render me speechless. I frantically tried to think of a response as I watched his eyes come to life with a crinkle of amusement and he snorted loudly.

"That's a joke. Ya gotta learn to lighten up a little, Scarlucci. You want to know how I learned not to be so fuckin' serious all the time?"

I said nothing, giving the man across from me the opportunity to go on. Mordento clearly wanted to talk, so letting him ramble on about how his occupation of extortion, beating the shit out of or actually killing people had given him unique insights into life seemed the best option if I were going to find out why he was in my office.

"I don't know if you noticed," Mordento continued, again without waiting for a response, "but I have a slight limp."

I nodded carefully, masking any reaction to the enormity of Mordento's understatement.

"You know why?"

I shook my head, meeting his eyes and lying to the killer across from me like the best of them.

"Goddamned diabetes is slowly eating my body from the feet up," he said, reaching down and smacking his trouser leg viciously. "This little piggy ain't goin' to market or any other fuckin' place. I've already lost one foot and half a leg to it, and the future don't look all that promising. Well, let me tell you, when they cut your leg off and you have to hobble around like a goddamned pirate, you can either become one bitter miserable son-of-a-bitch about it all or you learn to appreciate a good laugh. So I'm choosing to have a laugh every now and then, 'cause otherwise you're completely fucked...you see what I mean?"

Chancing a quick surreptitious glance at the clock high on the wall behind Mordento, I nodded and cleared my throat. "Absolutely. And I appreciate what you're saying, but I'm not exactly sure why you are here, Mr. Mordento," I replied. "How can I help you?"

Sal shrugged. "The point is I've learned an important thing from this diabetes bullshit. We should always leave room for

18

the possibility that we can be wrong. Man in my position tends to forget that and, as you can imagine, there aren't a hell of a lot of people with enough nerve to point it out to me." He paused momentarily and shrugged. "I was wrong about Joey, so I thought I'd come see you. I would have bet my ass that Joey would always be one of those major fuck-up types as far as school was concerned, the goddamned gun thing being a prime example. And, you don't have to answer, but I know you probably thought the same thing. Well, son-of-a-bitch, but hasn't the little bastard started to prove me wrong. I think you're one of the reasons Joey's seen the light, expelling him the way you did and forcing him to take a good look at his actions and the consequences... and I came to thank you."

"Excuse me?" I said, making no attempt to cover my surprise.

"That's right."

He reached into the outer pocket of the black windbreaker he was wearing. In spite of hearing Mordento's expressed gratitude, I inwardly flinched as I watched the plump fingers of his right hand extract not a gun, but two large bulging envelopes out of his pocket. He looked at the envelopes a moment, smiled and threw them on the desk in front of me.

"Here," he said, with a little wheeze of exertion brought about by the exercise of the movement. "A little something for you and for Mr. Valentine."

Speechless once again, I glanced from Mordento to the envelopes on my desk. One of them had opened slightly when

19

it landed, and I could clearly see several one hundred dollar bills protruding from under the unsealed flap.

I frowned, pointing needlessly at the objects in front of me. "What are these?"

Mordento's smile widened, thickening his lower jowls and exposing surprisingly white, glistening saliva-coated teeth. "Those are dollars for scholars, Mr. Scarlucci."

"Mr. Mordento," I stammered, realizing there must be a great deal of money before me, "I couldn't possibly...."

"By that I mean, the dollars are for you and Valentine because the scholar is none other than my little pal, Joey."

Mordento held up his chubby short-fingered hand to stop me from responding. I shut my mouth and sat there. I mean, I wasn't an idiot. When Sal the Gimp indicates you better shut up and listen, unaccustomed as you may be as the Assistant Principal of Central High to parents giving you orders, the wise course of action is to shut up and listen. Plus, I was fascinated. What the hell was he talking about? If there was one thing the Joey Mordento I knew wasn't, it was a scholar.

"Listen, I know this sounds crazy, but, goddamn it, Joey's suddenly gone smart. Shit, I'm starting to think there may even be a chance he'll graduate high school."

The corpulent crime figure sitting across from me paused for a moment, dropping his raised hand, his eyes suddenly glistening with an influx of moisture. To my continued astonishment, Sal Mordento looked like he was actually getting all choked up. Now I truly was flabbergasted.

"It's Valentine," Mordento continued. "Don't ask me how, but somehow, Joey's English teacher has done something that no other teacher was able to do. He's actually got through to the kid. And, not only has he reached him, he's...I don't know,...he's done something,...somehow tapped into the kid's mind. Joey's not just interested in school for the first time in his life. He's fuckin' intelligent. You hear what I'm saying? The kid's suddenly got brains...and is starting to use them, for Christ's sake. And it's not just in English. The other day, he brought home a paper from his physics class with an A on it. I mean, are you shitting me? Fuckin' physics! I don't even know what the fuck physics is...."

"Well, whatever the reason," I said, "it sounds like Joseph is now on the right track, and the best thing you and I can both do for him is to help make sure he stays on track."

I said this with a concerned smile as I settled back in the chair; however, my mind was registering something entirely different, and it wasn't just about Sal the Gimp's colorful language skills.

It was about Ken Valentine.

Although *this* time, it was a positive report on Mr. Valentine, it still worried me. One of the major agendas on my day's calendar was a scheduled meeting that included Ken and the English Chairperson, Sherri Walsh, to find out exactly what was going on in Ken Valentine's classes. Many parents as well as teachers were up in arms over the grades he was issuing to students and the activities he was conducting during

21

classes. I had to deal with it as soon as possible, if it were not already too late to stop the whole thing from turning into a major problem.

I knew that whatever was happening in Ken's classroom was not going to be easy for me. Ken might have earned the reputation of being the "rogue" English teacher at the high school, but he was also one of my oldest friends. We had started at Central High School some 20 years before as eager young educators, drinking together at social hours, sharing laughs, planning English lessons, and generally becoming fast friends as we evolved into competent teachers. Ken Valentine was one of the first black teachers in the high school, and during his career he had handled his position with such humility and professionalism that he was nominated for District Teacher of the Year three times. But now, I was his boss, and Mr. Valentine was in big trouble. I hoped I would be able to solve things and still preserve our friendship.

"And as far as this 'contribution' is concerned..." I said, frowning with a shake of my head and gesturing once again to the envelopes.

"Stop right there, Scarlucci!" Sal's arms pushed his massive bulk up out of the chair and he leaned against the front of my desk, left hand on the top for support while the right one pointed. "Open that middle drawer there on your desk."

I glanced down involuntarily. "What?"

"The drawer there. Open the fucking drawer," he responded, his voice taking on a hardness that I imagined he used when horrible things were about to happen.

I stood and opened the drawer.

Mordento's plump-cheeked smile returned. He reached across the desk, pushing the envelopes forward one at a time until each dropped with a light plunk into the open drawer.

"Now close the drawer."

I closed it.

He grinned viciously.

"What envelopes?" he said.

"Mr. Mordento...," I protested.

"Look,...Brian. May I call you Brian?"

I sighed, deciding a different approach might work, considering Mordento had given me the opening with his earlier remark. "Mr. Mordento, you can call me anything you want...just don't call me late for dinner."

Mordento stared blankly at me for a moment, then, finally grasping that what I said was a joke, he laughed a hearty wheeze. "Hey, that's better. Son-of-a-bitch. I wasn't sure you had it in you, Brian. Late for dinner. I like that. And you should call me Sal."

Great. Now we were pals. It didn't solve a damn thing, but now Sal the Gimp and I were buddies. Good job, Mr. Scarlucci.

"Now, look, Brian," my newfound friend Sal continued, "I don't give a shit what you do with my little contribution. Give it

23

to the athletic league, build a new fuckin' wing on the school, or keep it for yourselves and buy a couple of nice Beamers. But, don't try to give it back 'cause that would be an insult, and I don't take very well to insults. Your suspending Joey got his attention in a way I wasn't able to do, Valentine opened up his mind so that the kid wants to learn shit, and I've expressed my thanks. That's the end of it. Far as I'm concerned, those envelopes and what they contain do not and never did exist. You have my word on that. And no matter what you may think of me or what you've heard, Brian, my word is fuckin' gold. Got it?"

"Oh, I've got it," I answered.

"Sal," he prompted.

I acquiesced reluctantly. "Sal. But I honestly don't know what to say."

He extended his hand. "Good. You educators talk too fuckin' much anyway. Have a nice day."

I took his hand, knowing there was something very wrong with what had just taken place, but not having any idea how I could have stopped it from happening or what to do about it.

"'Course, you better make sure Valentine gets his share, or you know what'll happen, don't you," he said, the threatening tone returning as he released my hand.

I nodded as I came around the desk to escort Sal Mordento out of my office.

"Yeah, Sal, you'll have to have Joey kill me," I said.

Wheezes of laugher again. "You're all right, Brian...," Mordento responded between gasps for air, "...once you loosen up a little. I'm glad we had this little talk, aren't you?"

Before I could answer, there was a quick knock from behind Mordento's bulk, and then my office door opened tentatively. It was my secretary. Her appearance, however, did not broadcast good news. There was only one circumstance when Betty was instructed to interrupt a meeting, and that was when a critical problem erupted without warning somewhere within the school, and she had no choice.

A heaviness inside me I was all too familiar with tightened once again.

"Yes, Betty," I said, as the elderly woman's gray-haired head poked into the doorway.

"I'm sorry to intrude, Mr. Scarlucci,"

"That's fine, Betty. Mr. Mordento and I were just finishing up. What is it?"

"It's Dr. Driscoll's science lab. I'm afraid there's a problem."

"Thank you for coming in, Mr. Mordento," I said, ushering Sal to the doorway, which Betty opened as she stepped aside so that Mordento could pass. "I'll be in touch if I see or hear of a turn for the worse as far as Joseph's activities are concerned. But, after what you've told me, I am hopeful he'll be fine."

With an appreciative nod, Sal "The Gimp" Mordento shook my hand, waddled out, and I turned to my secretary.

"What's going on, Betty?"

"I know April and Gina are already there, and the ambulance has been called, but since Mrs. Talley is at the Administration Building and Mr. Pugh is not in his office, I think you better get up to Doc's room as fast as you can."

April Stern and Gina Burton were the school nurses. I gave Betty an anxious frown.

"The ambulance. Why? What's happened?"

"I'm not sure," she answered.

Then my secretary uttered the words that a school administrator never, and I mean never, wants to hear.

"All I know is that a student is bleeding...," my secretary said, her expression filled with worry. "...And there's lots and lots of blood."

THREE

DAY OF THE LEECHES

As I hurried, not quite running, down the main hallway of Central High, the first thing I thought of were the leeches. There are, of course, any number of ways students can become involved in accidents while working in a science lab. That is why there are showers placed in readily-available areas of the labs, and why science teachers must go through standardized safety training if there are to be activities within the classroom, such as frog dissection with sharp instruments or the mixing of volatile chemicals, during which accidents could possibly occur.

After several years as an Assistant Principal, I had gained a certain instinct for knowing the cause of a crisis when it occurred before being told the reason. I reached the UP staircase off of Wing A, and took the ascending wall-enclosed hard concrete steps to the second floor, two and three at a time. I don't know why, but every instinct I possessed told me that whatever was happening in Driscoll's science lab, the culprit for this particular crisis was the leeches. Doc was the most likable of individuals, and had given me the most persuasive of arguments for bringing the little blood-suckers into the classroom, but even before I reached the room, I knew I had made a mistake.

Though generally very knowledgeable in all aspects of a particular field, every teacher usually has a specialty that drew

27

him or her to that academic study. Ted Driscoll was a biology instructor and his special interest was Hirudinea, better known to us non-scientific types as leeches. He loved the little suckers. He was even on a first name basis with Dr. Kenneth Renthroe of the Museum of Natural History, and had traveled with Renthroe to remote swamp-infested locations of the world where the two of them had taken off their shoes, rolled up their pants legs and waded into murky foreign waters using themselves as bait to capture exotic species of leeches, the only sure way to collect rare specimens in the field…according to Doc Driscoll.

Not only did he love studying leeches, Doc also loved to talk about them, so much so that students had him categorized in their own special nomenclature as the Leech Teach. In fact, it was often difficult to get Doc to shut up about the slug-like creatures, a personal predilection that had caused several female staff members to move to a different lunch table whenever Doc Driscoll sat down. According to the ladies, there was something about learning that *Dinobdella ferox*, the terrifying and ferocious Bengali leech that will crawl up your nose while you are sleeping to lodge in the back of your throat, that doesn't go that well with eating a chicken salad.

However, those who found the leech discussions interesting mealtime fare remained at a Driscoll lunch table, absorbing leech lore that included some fascinating facts: leeches have three sets of jaws to slice open a wound and secrete an anticoagulant emitted in their saliva to keep the

28

victim bleeding; they undulate like seals and whales to move water over them to absorb oxygen; they have ten eyespots on their heads and possess incredible eyesight, able to track anything that moves across their vision. Leeches are still used today on re-attached fingers and on wounds to speed healing by drawing blood to the wound. There are even special leeches, valuable to researchers for their large bacteria chambers, that can only survive by living on and draining the blood out of the interior lining of the wide center opening of the huge hindquarters of a hippopotamus. The "sucking on the moist inner crack of a hippo's ass" leech information had caused raucous laughter to erupt from the Driscoll table and eye-rolling and tsks of disgust from the females of the table nearby.

Okay, so we finish eating and laughing heartily as a lunch-break bonus, we get up from the table, and I'm in a good mood, and Doc is walking along beside me as we leave the lunchroom and he asks me if it would be all right if he brought a few medical leeches into the lab for the students to observe in a behavioral study?

I remember hesitating in response, an interior Assistant Principal alarm that I had mentally programmed to beep automatically whenever the granting of a request harbored the possibility of problems. However, these were *Macrobdella decora* leeches, Doc went on to explain persuasively, the harmless North American medical leeches with the visually-interesting orange polka dots on the backs. Doc promised he

29

would keep them sealed within an enclosed plastic tub on his desk for observation only, and so I said yes. What could happen?

FOUR

MR. PEE U

Laurence Pugh was the first person I saw as I exited the stairwell on the second floor and headed down the Science wing. Larry Pugh, or Mr. Pee U as the majority of the student body and a few too many faculty members referred to my counterpart in the Assistant Principal slots at Central High, had the major responsibility of handling the business end of running the school. Dealing with a crisis that erupted within the building was the responsibility of everyone in the high school administration. However, I had come to discover that Larry Pugh rarely did so. He was always too busy dealing with "business affairs" to leave his office.

A trait that should be noted about Mr. Pugh and his nickname is that this man of small, emaciated stature and, some would say, rather mousy spectacled features, was that he was a "sweater." By that I mean, regardless of the temperature or season, when in stress, perspiration poured out of the man. And, most unfortunately for someone with the name of Pugh, this excessive flow of moisture carried with it a faint body odor. This was probably because of the excessively thick black hair that grew everywhere on his body, except on his bald pate.

Approaching Pugh's beckoning as I hurried toward Doc's lab, I could see that the perspiration floodgates were definitely wide open. He was jacketless, which meant he had made a

31

hurried exit from his office, and sweat was pouring out of the man.

"Brian, thank God," Pugh exclaimed as I reached him. "I have to go...."

"What's going on?"

"You need to take over here, and do what you can, Brian," Pugh insisted, squirming to leave. "It's bad in there. It's Jerome Stempowitz, the pale quiet one we were told was a hemophiliac. Some kids put a leech on his neck as a joke, and they can't stop the bleeding. Just do what you can until the ambulance gets here. Sorry, but I've got to go."

And with that, Laurence Pugh hustled down the hall away from me. And I was left holding the bag. Inside Driscoll's bio lab there was a kid possibly bleeding to death.

FIVE

BLOOD LAB

"Brian, I...I'm sorry," Doc Driscoll stammered as I came through the doorway into the lab. Anyway, I think that's what he said because his was just one of many strident voices that filled the air. I couldn't hear him any too clearly because of the emotional talking and crying mass of bodies in the far rear corner of the lab.

At the opposite end of the room, across from where I had entered, stretched out on top of the chest-high countertop directly in front of me, lay the limp body of Jerome Stempowitz, the back of his head resting against the metal lip of the deep sink that was installed at the near end of the counter. April Stern, the most seasoned of the two nurses, was applying a pressure pack from the lab's Crash Kit to the back of the boy's neck, while Gina Burton, her younger colleague, held the boy's head steady. A small stream of water flowed into the sink from the round nippled mouth of a metal goose-neck faucet that protruded in a curved arch high over the sink. I could see immediately, it was to wash away excess blood that was continuing to flow from the back of the boy's neck. Not that all the blood had been contained within the sink. Blood was all over the counter top, the face and body of Jerome Stempowitz, and on the clothing and rubber-gloved hands of the nurses who were attending to the bleeding student.

"The ambulance is on its way," I said, moving to the counter.

"The bleeding just won't stop," April said, tilting her head unconsciously toward where she held pressure against the open wound.

"Leeches have an anticoagulant in their saliva that is injected into the wound when they bite," I said, using an unbidden lunch leech fact that randomly popped into my head to ease her concern that it was her fault that the bleeding continued. "When the victim is a hemophiliac, I'm sure it aggravates the condition. Do what you can."

April nodded in response and adjusted the pressure pack on the wound. I moved across the room to where Doc stood with the students, punching in the number of the school library on my cell phone as I moved.

"Doc, take everyone in this class to the library now. I will have both Mary Ellen Drury and John Drake report there immediately. They should be there by the time you arrive."

" Brian, I...," Doc stammered.

I cut him off. "Not now, Doc. Just do it." I raised my voice to the students. "All right. I want it quiet!" The loud intrusion of my "person-in-authority" voice seemed to work, and the vocal noises quieted considerably. "Obviously, this is an emergency, and I know I can count on all of you to cooperate. Please follow Doc Driscoll to the library. No one may go anywhere but the library until either myself or another administrator has cleared it. Mrs. Drury and Dr. Drake will be there for anyone who needs to talk about what has happened."

With his mouth clenched tightly, Driscoll started the students moving, as I called the library to let them know that the class was on its way. The Assistant Librarian at the desk answered, and I instructed her to direct Doc's class into one of the research rooms when they arrived, keeping them isolated from the rest of the people in the library. That done, I dialed the social worker's office.

Mary Ellen Drury answered. I filled in Mary Ellen as quickly and succinctly as I could and told her to contact John Drake and get to the library. Mary Ellen was true to my expectations of her. She didn't even ask a question. Just told me she'd deal with it and hung up.

A passing female student grabbed my arm. She was sobbing.

"I didn't mean to do anything, Mr. Scarlucci. I swear. It was Bobby. He thought it would be funny."

I took the girl gently by the shoulder and guided her forward, catching a glimpse of the broad back and shoulders of the school's football quarterback, Bobby Weiss, hurrying out of the room without looking in my direction. "Dawn, it's okay. I understand. Now go with the others, and we'll talk later. We'll sort it all out, I promise." Angel Jehmar was next to the sobbing girl, and I turned Dawn to her as I spoke. "Angel, will you see that Dawn gets to library okay?"

Angel's eyes smiled at me through her expression of concern. "Sure, Mr. 'Carlucci. Will Jerry be okay?"

"We'll know more as soon as the medics get here."

"Okay. See you later," Angel said, giving me a knowing look as she took the sobbing girl from me and led her comfortingly out of the room with the remainder of the departing students.

I shook my head. Even in the middle of a crisis, as she moved away from me, the image of Angel's revealing cleavage and bare midriff cut into my conscious awareness. Outrageous was the only way to describe the way Angel Jehmar dressed. And that was why she was scheduled to see me yet again later in the day to discuss her inability to follow the guidelines of the dress code, and to decide what action was needed to insure that she would start dressing appropriately in the immediate future.

There had been meetings before, of course, all to no avail. In spite of repeated warnings that included being sent home and told to not return until she could find appropriate clothing to wear to school, Angel Jehmar still showed up to classes day after day dressed in clothing that covered the bare minimum. Round areas of upper breasts would be exposed well into the danger zone, and her butt could be seen swaying down the hall for all lookers with words like "Juicy And Just For You" etched on the back of her low-slung skin-tight jeans.

Angel had learned the tricks of the dress-for-school trade from other girls, and had the switch down perfectly. By switch I mean, that she would leave her home dressed appropriately and with a dignity that in no way would offend her mother. Then, once picked up for school and in the car, she would do the old switcheroo, transforming her appearance from dignified modest young lady to half-naked teen before the car arrived in the school parking lot.

Calls home proved to be totally ineffective. The mother spoke very little English, so communicating the issue of proper school attire to the woman's maternal instincts was virtually impossible, and the father was never available. On the one occasion I had been able to reach Mr. Abdul Jehmar on his cell phone, he told me that I must deal with these situations as I saw fit. That he had not time for he must concern himself with matters of far more import than domestic school issues. Apparently, Mr. Jehmar was some sort of important negotiator in the Middle East, and world issues came *before* family. The Jehmars had two other daughters, the twins Aphrodite and Venus, who were seniors at Central, and dressed appropriately on all occasions.

Angel, it seemed, was determined to "fit in" and be as American a girl as she possibly could, even if she had to go half-naked through the school each day to accomplish her goal.. Though extremely bright with honor roll grades, Angel had earned additional high marks in school on how to dress in order to use her beautifully proportioned body to her advantage by the time she finished 9th grade, and was now well on her way to an advanced degree in Peer Popularity Through Sexuality.

I even had concerns about one of the younger male faculty members standing too close to Angel as he "counseled" her. His eyes strayed over her body as she spoke, and her breast "accidentally" brushed against his arm, without any visible attempt by him to move away. It was the kind of teacher-student touch that could bring no accusations, but both student and teacher were fully aware of what was happening between them.

I say this with a fairly high degree of certainty, having once asked English Chairperson Sherri Walsh, my source of all things female, if a girl's breasts pressing ever so lightly against me as I showed her the marks in my grade book could be just an accident. Sherri smiled with that knowing smile of hers, giving me an unqualified immediate answer:

Not a chance, Mr. Naïve. Trust me, if a girl's breasts, or woman's for that matter, are brushing against a male, she not only knows it, but probably planned it. Run, don't walk, away from the sexy little teen brushing against you as quickly as possible.

So then when I'm showing you a paper, and you lean in to see it and I feel your breasts against me, it's no accident? I smilingly queried in response,

You can count on it, Big Boy, was Sherri's answer, the round swell of her own breasts firmly up against me as she spoke.

38

Oh, the things I had learned over the years that made me an Assistant Principal extraordinaire! Right now, however, I had readily accepted Miss Scantily Clad's help, because there were more pressing matters, like a student bleeding non-stop less than ten feet away.

"How we doin'?" I asked, moving back through the now-empty biology lab where the nurses administered to the bleeding boy.

April answered. "It's not as bad as it looks, Brian...if the bleeding can be stopped. But it better happen...."

She didn't finish her sentence because as she spoke, members of the Central Community Volunteer Ambulance Corps came through the door. They were all business and they were very good. If what they saw when they came in bothered them, they gave no such sign, but handled things with precise cautious efficiency. I allowed April to take charge, and moved to the woman who had come in right behind the four members of the Ambulance Corps. The woman was Mary J. Talley, principal of Central High School.

"How bad is it, Brian?" she asked, her beet-red complexion in defiance of her usual pale white Irish skin, the only visible sign of how truly worried she was.

"April thinks it'll be okay, especially now that the paramedics are here."

She nodded, jaw set, dealing with it. "Family been notified?"

"I don't think so. I just got here a moment ago, and dealt with the students in the class. Some were pretty upset. They should be down in the library by now, and I've had Mary Ellen and John go there to counsel those who need it."

She nodded. "Okay. I'll take care of notifying the family as soon as I know where we stand here. I have Sam and the rest of Security lined up to keep the halls clear until the boy is moved out of the building and into the ambulance. We still have ten minutes before the bell. Hopefully we'll make it before the classes change."

"If not, we'll have to hold the classes," I said, stating the obvious.

"Agreed. The secretaries are on alert in the main office to make an announcement to hold classes if it comes to that. Where the hell is Larry?"

"I'm not sure," I said, not quite lying as I met her gaze. "I came right here when Betty alerted me to the problem."

She did not nod, but looked at me, then looked away again and sighed, continuing to speak to me, but watching as the gurney was spring-released to rise to the level of the counter. Two paramedics transferred Jerry Stempowitz onto the portable bed as another held a new white pressure bandage to the back of the boy's neck. Obviously the bleeding had not stopped, for the bandage was slowly turning red.

"Do we know what happened?"

"Kids being stupid, as usual, from what I can make of it. Bobby Weiss or Dawn Stewart...I'm not sure which one actually handled the leech, probably Bobby, unless he got Dawn to do it on a dare...anyway, one of them put a leech on the back of Jerry Stempowitz's neck. They had no idea the kid was a hemophiliac, of course."

Mary J. was watching the paramedics work as she listened. "Okay, you'll deal with the two of them after we've resolved the immediate crisis. Get all the information you can and then bring them to me."

"I'd say it is what would have been a harmless kid prank that Doc could have easily handled if it hadn't gone bad. How far do you want to go with this?"

"You mean am I going to suspend the school quarterback and the head cheerleader when Central is playing on Saturday for the county championship in the biggest football game this school has seen in years?" she answered, still not looking at me as she spoke.

"That would be one of my concerns, yes."

The flush of her skin color deepened yet again. "Let's just pray the boy comes out of this all right. You find out exactly what happened, Brian. We'll meet in my office in thirty minutes and decide how we're going to deal with all the ramifications. Why do things like this always happen when I'm out of the building." Her frown deepened as she realized things like this particular crisis usually did not happen, and repeated the facts aloud, as if speaking them would somehow help her grasp their reality. "They put a leech on the neck of a hemophiliac. It's unbelievable."

"I know. I don't remember this being covered in any graduate administration education course. Anyway, you're here now, and I'm glad you are. I'm not as calm as I look," I said, drawing the tiniest trace of a smile from my boss as she shook her head slowly back and forth in disbelief. "I'm going to the library to see how Mary Ellen and John are doing, and talk to Bobby and Dawn. You want to see Driscoll?"

"No," Mary J. said. "Let him come back up here and clean up his leeches. And tell him to get that goddamned drawing off the front of the counter."

I glanced over and saw the all too familiar scrawl etched into the white front wall of the counter. I hadn't even noticed it, but the all-seeing principal eyes of Mary J. Talley had, probably because it was a clever caricature of her that had become prominent not only on the walls and in the restrooms of Central High, but on walls of the community as well. Sherri Walsh told me she had even seen one of the drawings on a wall outside of Penn Station in the city.

The drawing was instantly both staggeringly cruel and an expression of creative, albeit pornographic, artistic genius. As any educator will attest, leave it to kids to know how to really hurt you in ways you couldn't even have imagined.

A simple unbroken line that even a non-artist could copy conveyed a sketch of a female's naked stick figure body. The figure was rendered with sagging breasts, hips thrust forward and legs spread wide to reveal a gaping oval opening at the genital area, the line continuing in a raised arch of a finishing artistic accent below the body that said, "TALLEY HO!" District maintenance had sand blasted huge renderings of the "TALLEY HO" stick figure off the front of Central High's building three times in the last month.

The true genius of the sketch was that the simplicity of its appeal had caught on to such an extent that it was virtually unstoppable at this point. I had even been made aware by way of an anonymous phone message left on my office answering machine that a talleyho.com website had shown up on the internet over the past weekend, which featured the infamous Mary J. Talley stick figure in all kinds of pornographic acts. At the rate the appearances were multiplying, it was well within the realm of possibility that the figure would start showing up before long scrawled across the walls in South Central L.A. on the opposite side of the nation. Clearly, the poor woman was doomed to the fame of having a nasty artistic rendering that would leave a legacy no woman would ever want as a remembrance.

"Are we certain that Doc signed off on the nurse's form that he was aware of Jerome being a hemophiliac?" Mary J. continued, tearing her gaze from the sketch with an expression of disgust as she agonized over the worst case scenario.

"I'm certain of nothing. You better check with April about that. God help us if he didn't and the school and he are held responsible."

"I'm not sure how much God is going to help us with this one. We may be on our own," Mary J. answered. She moved

43

closer to me and lowered her voice to almost a whisper. "How about the camera video business that happened yesterday afternoon? Have you spoken to Sherri about it?"

"Not yet. She was busy with grade level leaders putting English midterm exams together this morning. I plan to discuss it with her after our meeting with Ken Valentine this afternoon."

A sort of hiss escaped her lips. "What the hell is going on in that department. First the Valentine problem and now this video surfaces!"

"I wouldn't say either is Sherri's fault," I answered, coming to Sherri Walsh's defense a little too quickly and instantly regretting the knee jerk response of someone who cared more than the relationship of a colleague might have warranted. However, if Mary J. noticed, she let it pass.

"Have you seen the video?"

"No," I responded, happy to be moving out of Sherri Walsh territory as quickly as possible. "But I made sure Sam pulled it and that no one else saw it. It's in my office."

"And he's sure about what's on it?"

I gave her a "not-much-question-about-it" head tilt as I answered. "Sam says the ceiling camera that was in the back hall behind the stage recorded Ms. Madison on her knees in front of a tall male student with her hands on his hips just inside the partially-open stage door. The time stamp was 5:45 p.m., not long after they finished play rehearsal in time for the cast to catch the 6:00 late bus. It was not possible for Sam to

44

ID the male figure from the back, but he's pretty sure it's Todd Hershborne, the male lead in the upcoming school production of *Death of a Salesman*. Apparently, there's no question the kneeling female is Maggie Madison. You want to see the video when I look at it?"

"No. You watch it with Sherri. The woman is a teacher in her department, so Sherri has to be involved from step one. She might as well see the damned thing when you do, then you both can make a collective decision about what's on it. We must be absolutely sure about this, Brian, before any accusations are made. Absolutely positive."

"That goes without saying."

"You've sworn Sam to secrecy, right?"

"He promised me."

She gave me a look. Sam Shapiro, the head of Security, was a talker. I mean, he was a nice old guy and all, but the hard truth was Sam couldn't keep his mouth shut about what went on in the school if it were duct-taped closed, and we both knew it.

"So what are the odds that we can keep a lid on it?"

"I'd say that by now, knowing the way this school works, probably half the staff is already aware that there is a Security video that supposedly shows Ms. Madison in a questionable position with the male lead of this much-anticipated school production."

The principal of Central High grimaced and shook her head again. "I'm sure you're right. Looks like it's going to be quite a day."

You don't know the half of it, Mary J. 'cause the phantom dropped a load of shit in Blanche Turner's drawer, your other Assistant Principal left me in the lurch with this bloodbath for God knows what reason, and Sal "The Gimp" Mordento dumped what looked like close twenty thousand dollars in one of my drawers," was what I thought.

What I said was, "Certainly looks that way. I'll see you in thirty minutes."

I turned and headed out of the room, peripherally watching Mary J. Talley move to talk to the nurses and the paramedics who were preparing to move the bleeding student's body out of Doc Driscoll's science lab. Her eyes were consciously avoiding the pornographic sketch of "TALLEY HO" that glared back at her from the front of the counter.

SIX

THE ANSWER MAN

I actually dreaded going to the library at Central High, avoiding it whenever possible because a trip to the library invariably meant that I must encounter and converse with the Head Librarian, Mr. Harold Billings. Billings made Sam Shapiro look like an inept amateur when it came to boring the pants off you with inane bullshit. Sam was just a congenial old guy who loved to shoot the shit. Harold Billings, on the other hand, was a sick man, and the illness that held him tightly in its unyielding grip was *Talkis Nonstopis*. Not that he was totally to blame. Seeds of the illness were sown on the job he held prior to becoming Head Librarian.

Many people don't even know such a job exists, but Billings's previous employer was the New York Public Library System, and his job was...are you ready?...the Answer Man. According to him, every ten seconds of every 8-hour day except Sunday, people from all over the world called the New York Public Library with questions like, *Why is the sky blue?* These endless questions are fielded by the Telephone Reference Service or Tel Ref. Billings worked in that position for seven years, rummaging through the 1,800 volumes of reference books that occupied the Tel Ref office shelves, as one of the people who answered the questions posed by the unending stream of callers. For instance...*What was Geronimo's real name? (Answer: Goyathlay, meaning "one*

47

who yawns.") I know this answer because, unrequested, Billings told me, as well as an endless string of other totally useless answers to questions... over and over and over.

There's no blame here, you understand. As is the case with many other horrible compulsions that are the result of illness, like say alcoholism, the man could not help himself. People had even insulted him to his face. Made no difference. The Answer Man always greeted people with a useless question and answer like... *Who invented the rubber band? (Answer: Stephen Perry of Perry and Co. in 1845.)*

And you know what my answer is to that, don't you? That's correct. Who gives a good damn? And the answer to that question is... nobody but Harold Billings, the Answer Man.

In addition, I was not in the best of moods because, once again, Laurence Pugh's absence had left me to deal with a crisis, and this time he had even been on the scene and he *still* left. I was having those thoughts and more when he emerged from the men's faculty room at the end of Wing C just as I started down the hall.

"Thanks for your help at the lab, Larry," I said, unable to control my displeasure.

"I'm sorry, Brian," Pugh answered. "Is the Stempowitz boy going to be all right?"

"Hopefully. They're on the way to the hospital now. But seriously, Larry. What was so important that you couldn't give me a little help up there?"

Pugh dabbed at a trickle of perspiration and looked up and down the empty hallway furtively.

"Can I trust you with some very private information, Brian?"

I shrugged, having no idea what to expect from the man. "Of course."

He leaned in closer. "I have IBS," he whispered.

"IBS?"

"Irritable Bowel Syndrome," he clarified, continuing to look both ways.

I nodded.

There were many explanations for Pugh's thoughtlessness that I had considered prior to running into him, but, I have to admit, I hadn't expected that one.

"Ohhh. I see."

"That's right. Sometimes under stress, it causes me…problems. I'm taking medication, of course, but it comes on at unexpected moments."

"And while you were waiting in front of the lab was one of those moments?" I said, helping him through it.

"Yes, I'd had a little accident," he hissed in quick confession. "Now do you understand?"

"Of course. Say no more, Larry. I wouldn't have even mentioned anything if I'd known. It must be very difficult…not knowing when it may be a problem."

"It is." He straightened up with a sigh of relief. "Thank you for understanding and taking over for me. I'll make it up to you, I promise."

I nodded, giving him the old thumbs up. I mean, what do you say to a man who tells you he has IBS? Actually, I could think of a hundred things to say, but they all bordered on the humorous or cruel, and I just couldn't do it to the poor guy.

Feeling as if my day had somehow wandered into a kind of scatological nightmare, I moved hurriedly down the hall and on my way to the library.

Reaching the corner at the end of the hallway, I heard a female voice call my name.

"Bri!"

I turned to see Sherri Walsh at the half-open doorway of the English office. She gave me a quick "come here" gesture and I, of course, did.

"What's going on? I heard the ambulance is here and there's a kid in trouble in the science lab."

I nodded. "Yeah, Jerome Stempowitz...."

"Oh, God. The bleeder. All the chairs were told, just in case."

"Well, just in case has happened. But the paramedics are moving him out now, so we'll see."

"You need any help?"

"No, Mary J. is dealing with it, and I'm headed to the library where Mary Ellen and John are talking to the students in the class. I had Larry helping me for a moment, but he shit his pants and had to run away."

Eyes widening as she gasped in humorous surprise, her right hand going to her mouth, Sherri grabbed my arm with her left.

"WHAT?"

Well, I'm certainly a man who can be trusted with someone's intimate secret, aren't I. How long did I last with that one? Twenty seconds?

I smiled. Only with Sherri could I joke about such things.

"I've got to go. I'll tell you later."

She held on to my jacket sleeve with tightly pinched fingers. "Oh, no. You can't tell me Larry Pugh shit his pants and then leave without an explanation."

I glanced in both directions, leaning forward out of the end-of-hall surveillance camera's range, gave Sherri a quick kiss on the cheek, and pulled away.

"Yes I can," I said with a wave, and hurried away, grinning at the sound of the loudly-whispered "Brian!" that echoed in the hallway as I moved.

Harold Billings was standing just inside the library as I came through the entrance.

"Good morning, Harold. Is the bio class here?"

"Yes it is. Research room Number # 2. And now I have a question for you."

"Harold...."

"Oh, no, don't think some emergency will get you off the hook, Brian. Ready?"

I sighed, feeling anger beginning to simmer. "All right. Get it over with."

He grinned, happy as a pig in shit. "What colors make up the rainbow?"

Suddenly, in spite of myself, I was hooked into Harold's stupid game because I realized I knew the answer.

"Red, orange, yellow, green, blue, and violet," I spat at him with childish satisfaction. "Now if you'll excuse me."

Billings raised his hand and shook his head. "Wrong. You forgot indigo."

"All right. Great. You got me. Now...."

"Oh, no, you missed, so I get another one."

"Harold, I do not have time for this now."

"How can you tell the sex of a cat?"

"I don't know. Look at its crotch, I guess."

"Close, but wrong. Not specific enough. Lift its tail. If you see what looks like a colon punctuation mark, it's a male. If you see an upside-down semicolon, it's a female."

"Great. Next time I'm looking at a cat's ass, I'll remember that."

"One more. Where does the term *last laugh* come from?"

I glared at him.

"The answer is that a bullet shot through a victim's heart sometimes precipitates a final laugh before death."

"Good thing you know that, because if you don't let me get to the research room I'm going to kill you and I will have the last laugh."

Billings chuckled. "That's a good one. How about this? Why does...."

"No," I snarled. "It's my turn. Where do you find the largest bacteria-carrying leech in the world?"

I knew I was crossing over a line that separated appropriate from inappropriate behavior when dealing with staff, but it was a day of leeches and problems, so to hell with it. The Answer Man had it coming. It might as well be now.

Billings frowned, suddenly taken aback. "I don't believe I know that. Sounds like something Doc would know, though. I'll ask him before he leaves."

"No need to. The answer is on the inside crack of a Hippopotamus's ass, and I'm not sure I'm right about this though, so the first chance you get, I want you to go there, stick your head in, and check to see if it's true."

Harold's face took on an expression like he'd just swallowed a mouthful of vinegar, and I walked away from him.

"I bet you don't talk to Sherri that way," he called after me.

I stopped in my tracks. Instinct pulled my head to the library's main desk where both of the women assistants were looking at us.

Uh oh. Dance very quickly and carefully, Assistant Principal Scarlucci.

"Wrong, Harold," I said, slowly turning back toward him. "And do you know why? Here's the answer: Ms. Walsh is my friend, and she would know better than to bother me with selfish stupidity when I was in the middle of dealing with a crisis. Now get over it. Sometimes there are matters that take precedence over your Answer Man crap. Go check your Dewey Decimal System or something."

The ladies behind the main desk smiled, Harold Billings headed to the stacks in a huff, and I hurried to the research room, doing my very best to ignore the red flag that flapped its warning soundlessly inside my head. It was a flag with the names of a very married Brian Scarlucci and a divorced Sherri Walsh and a big fat question mark waving suspiciously over the rumor mills of Central High School.

SEVEN
ANGEL DUST

Well, as it turned out, Mary J. Talley was wrong, and God did seem to be working in our favor on this day of the leeches at Central High. Upon medical examination at the hospital, it seems that there were no traces of leech puncture marks on the back of Jerome Stempowitz's neck. In spite of my instinctual belief that the leeches were the cause of the crisis, this news was actually something that I had suspected, considering the large amount of blood in evidence around the lab counter, even if the victim were a hemophiliac. However, Larry Pugh shitting his pants had left me to deal with the immediacy of the problems rather than having time to consider the improbability of what supposedly happened as opposed to what actually took place. Mary J. Talley had been right. Students putting a leech on the back of the neck of a hemophiliac which then proceeded to bite him so that he bled non-stop *was* unbelievable... because it did not happen.

Once the hospital staff had the bleeding stabilized, Jerome admitted he had injured himself the night before when he slipped and fell backwards against the corner of his bedroom dresser while dancing to some violent rap music. Fearing he would be forced to go to the hospital and suffer through more endless tests and medical ordeals, he had withheld the information from his parents and patched himself up as best he could. The wound had opened of its own accord during his lab

55

class, and things had disintegrated from there. It was possible that the wound had re-opened because Bobby Weiss was fooling around with the boy's shirt collar, dropping leeches on it and all, but that could not be proven, so Central High was given an all-clear on the incident. More importantly for the big game, Bobby Weiss and Dawn Stewart got away with a warning from yours truly.

It was now one o'clock in the afternoon, and I was back in my office. Angel Jehmar was in the smaller of the two chairs in front of my desk, breasts bulging revealingly from beneath a low-cut blouse and short denim skirt riding high up onto firm young thighs, as she sat there with her jiggling legs crossed.

I looked up from her open infraction folder, removed my reading glasses, and cleared my throat.

"Angel, do you know how many times we have had this discussion about your wearing apparel that is not in accordance with the guidelines of the dress code?"

At my question, her gum chewing jaws slowed just a tad. However, the crossed-leg jiggle continued full speed ahead. "How is Jerry?" Angel asked, reminding me how she had helped me in the lab crisis before we got to a discussion of her behavior. She smiled and added a feminine "hair flick" to punctuate her point.

Bad beginning, Angel. I am immune to the feminine "look at me" hair flick.

"Jerry is stabilized," I said. "We've been informed by the hospital that he should be fine in a few days."

"That's good, Mr. 'Carlucci."

Angel had a fascinating accent. Though she had done her very best to acquire the Long Island student speech patterns, Angel had not been able to erase completely the traces of a family-oriented Middle Eastern dialect. For example, *Scarlucci* became '*Carlucci*, the "s" mysteriously disappearing for some reason. Truth be told, however, this strange distortion of the norm in her speech pattern made the girl even more amusingly appealing. And again, there was no doubt in my mind that she knew it.

"Yes, and thank you for helping out with Dawn this morning. I appreciate it."

She smiled a flirty teen smile, leg jiggling away. "No problem, Mr. 'Carlucci. We were a good team, right? And Bobby and Dawn are okay 'cause I hear it wasn't even the letches, which are disgusting, by the way."

Yes, ironically, the little sexpot had said, "letches," not "leeches."

"How do you know that information already?"

"Please, Mr. 'Carlucci. Word gets around, ya know. But they're going to be able to be at the game, right? Dawn and Bobby, I mean. 'Cause the people in this town would have about fifteen hemorrhages if Bobby wasn't in that game and Dawn couldn't cheer this weekend. Bet you're glad it turned out the way it did and you and Talley didn't have to keep them out. Right?"

"First of all, it's *Mrs.* Talley, not *Talley*," I said, correcting her, for which I got a roll of the eyes in response. "And, let's be clear that they shouldn't have done what they did. But a warning seemed to be the appropriate action under the circumstances, which is *not* what I'm considering in your case. Now, could we talk about this, please?"

The gum chewing pace returned, matching the pace of the leg jiggle. "Sure. I changed clothes. Did you notice? I had these in my gym locker, so I switched before I came here."

Actually, I had not noticed. To me, whatever Angel wore had just become one big blur of dress code violations. "And you think what you now have on is okay?"

Angel looked down as if momentarily mystified.

"Yeah. What's wrong with this? You can't see anything…can you?" she asked, smiling and batting her eyes innocently.

I pointed to the folder in front of me. "Let's get back to my original question. Do you know how many times we have talked about this dress code problem?"

She made a little frown and stood, coming around behind the desk to stand beside me. "No, let me see."

That said, Angel leaned in to inspect what was contained in the folder on the desk.

Do not look, Scarlucci! my mind screamed as Angel leaned forward, the material in her loose-fitting blouse falling forward.

And I did not look.

All right, I did look.

But it was a very quick glance, involuntary really, and instant guilt surfaced inside me immediately. Had I known what was coming, of course, I wouldn't have had to bother.

However, the flash of half-revealed breasts was not my major concern, believe it or not. See, Angel didn't even bother with the tried and true breast brush against the arm, for as she leaned in, there was the unmistakable feel of the lower core of her young body pressing up against me.

"Where is the number?" Angel asked, all serious and concentrating on the folder as the pressure increased and the lower portion of her body moved ever so slightly up and down against me.

I pushed the chair back and stood. "Angel, sit back down, please!"

"All right...all right!" she said, arms raised in mock defense as she moved back to the chair. "I just wanted to understand what you were talking about. The truth is I was going to make an appointment to see you today anyway."

I sat down again, control restored...or so I thought.

"Why is that? To tell me you just purchased a new line of clothing with high neck collars and knee length skirts?"

"Nooooo, Mr. Smarty," she answered. The tone carried irritation, but with the trace of a smile. "For your information, I'm being 'talked."

"I'm sorry. What?"

"'TALKED," she said. "You know, followed around all the time."

I suppressed a smile. "Oh...*STALKED.* Sorry, I misunderstood you.

"Yeah, that's what I said...'talked. That's what I wanted to tell you. It's really bad, and I wanted to see if you could do anything about it."

"Well, I don't know," I answered, well aware that Angel was manipulating the discussion away from the dress code infractions. "What do you mean? Is this stalking happening here in school or when you're in the community?"

"Here, in the mall, outside my house...everywhere. I'm telling you, it's really bad, Mr. 'Carlucci."

"Okay. Who is it? A student?"

"Yeah." She made a face of disgust. "Tyler Karidae. He's a new kid that moved here from Queens. You know him?"

Actually, I didn't, which only meant that since arriving at Central, he had managed to stay out of trouble or kept a low enough profile that he hadn't yet come to my attention.

"No, but I can check on him for you. Make some inquiries. Has he done anything to frighten you?"

She shook her head, coming to her feet and moving to the front of my desk. "No, but that doesn't mean anything. I can tell by the way he looks at me all the time. Like I'll come out of class and he'll be standing there, staring. He's such a freakin' weirdo. Ask around. You'll see. And we've been getting hang-ups at home. You know, where they don't answer, but you can hear them breathing and then they hang up. I know it's him. Seriously. There's something wrong with him. He scares me."

"Well, I need a little more than that to go on. Can you think of anything you've done that might have caused him to act this way?"

"No." Her eyes suddenly widened as her head tilted in remembrance. "Except I showed him my piercing once."

Somehow I didn't think seeing Angel's belly button piercing would cause a male student to become a stalker. The way Angel displayed her midriff constantly, there probably wasn't anyone in the school who hadn't seen her piercing.

"I'm not sure that would do it. Belly button piercings are pretty common now. Can you think...?"

"Not that piercing. It happened when we were all drinking and playing a game of truth or dare," Angel said, her hands moving to the bottom of her blouse and yanking the material upward before I could even comprehend the meaning of the motion. "I mean this piercing!"

And suddenly, the girls were out to play!

I found myself staring at Angel Jehmar's breasts, a glistening silver piercing ring hanging from the center of the left nipple.

Oh, that piercing! Holy Shit!

I could not believe it. Angel was flashing me, in my office, no less. However, it wasn't the girl's breasts that I saw before me, but rather fucking prison bars!

"Angel, for God's sake...," I stammered.

61

And then, just as quickly, the blouse dropped and to my stunned relief, the breasts were gone.

"I have another one," she smiled, dare in her eyes as her hands moved to the side zipper of her short skirt. "Would you like to see it?"

I stood again, this time with the force of speed, and leaned toward her, my hands slamming down loudly on the desk.

"NO, I DO NOT WANT TO SEE YOUR PIERCINGS!" I heard myself nearly shouting at her, true outrage in my voice. "I SHOULDN'T JUST SUSPEND YOU. I SHOULD SEE THAT YOU ARE EXPELLED."

"Who are you kidding? I see the way you look at me. You love it," came the challenging response.

"What in God's name is the matter with you, young lady?" I said, finally getting my voice back under control. "I mean, pulling a stupid stunt like that...I'm old enough to be your father."

Angel leaned on the front of the desk, matching my stance and answered with a raised voice of her own.

"DON'T EVER MENTION MY FATHER TO ME, 'CARLUCCI. AS FAR AS I'M CONCERNED, I DON'T HAVE A FATHER!"

And there it was, out of the mouths of babes: The reason.

I could see it hovering in the space between us as we stared at each other as if it were a physical reality: Abdul Jehmar, the father.

It was a simplistic explanation on my part, of course, with obviously far more beneath it all than just an absentee father, as I'm sure Mary Ellen Drury would point out to me. Still, a high school girl acting out in all the wrong ways because she believed she had a father who didn't give a shit about her was a pretty good beginning explanation for Angel's behavior as far as I was concerned.

There was a quick knock, followed by my office door being opened, and, Laurence Pugh, whose office was next to mine, poked his head in the doorway.

"Everything okay in here?"

Oh, now you help me. Thanks a lot, Larry. Yeah, we're fine, thanks. Angel here was just showing me her breasts. How's the underwear?

"Yes, Mr. Pugh. Everything is fine. Miss Jehmar and I are just getting a few things straight about the school dress code regulations. You may leave the door open. Thanks."

Angel, meanwhile, had slammed herself angrily back into her chair and was glaring at me. Larry gave me an "OK" wave and disappeared. I moved around the desk and sat against the front of it, close to Angel, but not too close. She looked away, chewing on her lower lip.

"Want to talk about it, Angel?" I said quietly. "Sounds to me like things aren't going too well right now. You think this Karidae kid is stalking you. You're indicating there's some trouble with Dad. I don't just hand out discipline. I can listen too, you know. Or I could set it up for you to talk to Mrs. Drury?"

Nothing.

And believe me, I know when I'm getting the cold shoulder from a female, young or old. It's an instinctual response, passed down in DNA.

"You know why I became an Assistant Principal, Angel?"

Angel looked up at me.

"Frankly, Mr. 'Carlucci, I don't give a shit why you became a principal," she said.

I pushed myself away from the desk.

"Okay, you may go, Angel. Try to dress in an appropriate manner when you come to school from now on."

She continued to look at me as if not comprehending. "I should just go?"

"Angel, I have a very busy afternoon. You don't want to talk to me, fine. Let's move on. You know the rules. Follow them, please."

Angel started to cry. And it was not in some fake bullshit way, but with real tears and sobs that came from deeply-felt emotion.

"Close the door, please. I don't want anybody to see me crying."

I shook my head. "I don't think so, Angel."

The crying intensified. "Please. I won't try anymore crap, I promise."

I looked at her for a moment, considering the crossroads at which we stood. For what had already happened moments before, I could lose my job if it were taken the wrong way. Then again, screw it. What was life in the hallowed educational halls if you didn't take a few chances, and try to really connect with a troubled student? I moved to the door, closed it, crossed back to the chair opposite Angel and sat down.

"He doesn't care about us. Any of us," Angel said between quick intakes of breath as she attempted to get herself back under control.

"I'm sure that's not true," I said. "I know your father is very busy, and his job could not be more important in that volatile section of the world. I'm not sure I would want the kind of responsibility he carries."

She wiped at her face with the sleeve of her blouse and sneered. "Oh, you mean '*The Negotiator.*' Please. I have listened to this all my life: '*Your father would like to be here, but he cannot.*' Do you know how many times my father has been to see my school on parent's night or to see any of my stupid dance recitals or anything? Never! That's how often. Never. I do not believe any father must be that busy. Everyone has choices, Mr. 'Carlucci.'"

"That is true," I agreed. "Sometimes the choices are very difficult to make, but they are always there. When there are actually lives at stake, I'm sure it is very difficult."

"I know. I know. It is what my mother tells me, that he has no such choices. That we must be grateful that he provides for us and be thankful that he has been chosen to perform such an important job in this world. And you know what I say to that?"

"Don't tell me," I said. "I can imagine."

There was a smile through the tears and she wiped at her face again, smearing make-up, looking very young and vulnerable. "That's right. Excuses do not cut it. Not with me anyway. Aphrodite and Venus, they don't seem to mind, but they've always been the special ones to my parents from when they were born, the first ones and twins and all. But now that we are older, how can he not see we still need him? That his youngest daughter needs him. How can he not know that?"

"He must. I'm sure he knows how much a valuable daughter like you at home needs him."

Angel gave me a "cut the bullshit" look, but I could tell she appreciated the comment.

"Not bad, 'Carlucci," she said. "You want to be my therapist?"

"I'm just offering the possibility that maybe it does hurt him to be away so much. Have you asked him? Maybe you should do that. Find out how he really feels."

Angel sat up straight and dignified, an obvious imitation of her mother. "No, I must not. We do not discuss such things. We must only offer our support and be grateful." Her posture deflated. "Such crap. You know what I wish? Sometimes I wish I had some pixie dust. You know, like Tinker Bell had in *Peter Pan*, and that I could just think happy thoughts and fly away." She stood up. I sensed a little embarrassment on her part that she had actually let her guard down a little in front of me. "Anyway, I think I'm going to go." She paused a beat as if deciding. "But if I did, you know, feel like talking sometime, would it be okay if I stopped by?"

I stood also and smiled. "I'd like that, Angel. Anytime. If you're dressed properly, of course."

"Always the principal, right?"

"It's what I do."

She looked down, embarrassed. "Listen, I'm sorry about that thing that happened before. I won't say anything. I promise."

"What thing?" I answered, thinking for a moment of Sal Mordento's morning visit and the envelopes in my drawer. "I don't know what you're talking about."

Angel nodded in understanding as she crossed the room, stopping at the door. "Do you have any children, Mr. 'Carlucci?"

I was always prepared for it and had spent years steeling myself against the question. However, whenever it was asked, it still hit me with new and unexpected force, re-opening a half-closed wound deep inside that would never heal.

No, Angel. My wife is a paraplegic confined to a wheelchair because of a car accident she had coming to work at Central Middle School the first year we were married. We

67

have not nor will we ever be able to have children, whispered the voice within my mind. *I would give anything to have had a child, perhaps a daughter like you that I could help guide through these difficult years. And, the truth is I don't give a shit how important your father may think his job is, he should have his head examined for not caring enough to see how badly you need him.*

"No, I don't," was what I said.

She smiled a tight little smile. "You would be a good father. Why doesn't it ever work out the way it should?"

Welcome to the adult world you're struggling so hard to be a part of, kid. See, unfortunately, there's a little more to it than music, iPhones, video games, cigarettes, alcohol, drugs, parties and sex.

"I don't know. We all have to struggle a little, I guess," I said.

"I...don't suppose I could have a hug before I go?"

I moved to where she stood at the door. I knew that if ever there were a girl who needed a hug to show someone cared, this was one. However, in today's world, that kind of genuine emotion cannot be expressed from adult male to young teen, male or female. And probably rightfully so, considering the number of unknown sickos prowling around, looking for just such an opportunity.

"I don't think it's a good idea. The school district tends to frown on administrators hugging female students behind closed doors. Let's not push our luck, considering how the day has gone, all right? But, I do have the next best thing to a hug."

I reached into my pocket, extracted a closed fist, and held it over her head, opening my hand and moving my fingers in a fanning motion through the air.

"What was that about?" she said with an amused frown.

"Angel dust. I just happened to have had a little on me. You're all protected now. No harm can come to you. Just think happy thoughts, dress appropriately, and you'll be okay."

Angel shook her head as she opened the door. "Really, 'Carlucci. That was so childish."

But I could tell by the wide smile and sparkle in Angel Jehmar's now dry eyes that "childish" was just what she had needed, and she loved it.

As soon as Angel was gone, I placed a call to Mary Ellen Drury. Her response to the name Tyler Karidae consisted of two words: *Bad news!* Other students had already complained to her about the new kid. Her best guess from what she been told was that a flow of readily available drugs, the best seller being heroin, had come with Tyler Karidae from Queens, and that he was setting up ways to stake out a flourishing business at Central High. Very smooth operator, however, who knew how to stay out of trouble. Definitely one to be watched.

I thanked Mary Ellen and hung up, determined to make it my business to look deeper into the activities of Tyler Karidae. If I were able to keep my job after what had already happened, that is. So far, I had accepted illegal funds from a member of

John Arthur Long

organized crime and seen a student's naked breasts, and the day wasn't even over yet.

Actually, I wasn't really all that worried. I could deal with it. At the moment, I felt good about the connection I'd been able to make with Angel Jehmar. She had proven what I always knew to be true and, though Angel had rejected hearing the explanation, it was the reason why I had taken the job of Assistant Principal when it was offered to me.

Here is the truth about kids: Though they look like adults, these hormone-charged, explosively energized students who roam our school hallways are really still children in adult bodies, fighting their way blindly forward through the winding maze that, through no choice of their own, forces them to leave the innocence of early childhood behind and enter into the land of adults. And our job is not to show how superior we are, or tell them how rotten they are, or punish them endlessly for making mistakes and taking some wrong turns in the maze. All too often these kinds of ego-bruising reactions to the behavior of a developing child in the name of education are really nothing more than a weak adult's desperate grasp for some kind of control. Once out of the maze as adults, how quickly we forget that we were rebellious and loved being outrageous. We made the same kinds of mistakes when we were fighting our way through it all. It's what kids do! Our job is to help them get through the maze without screwing up too badly and come out the other side into the land of adults with at least a fighting chance of making it. Sure, they need some

70

rules and structure so the maze doesn't crush them as they pass through it. But mainly they're looking for someone who, rather than constantly "telling," knows how to "listen." That's all. Frequently, no action or advice is required, just someone who will hear what they have to say while they try to sort it all out. *(Why isn't this educational doctrine not on a plaque at the entrance of every school in America?)*

That's what Angel Jehmar needed, and the need for attention was so acute, that she had resorted to sexual display as a way of coping. When all she really wanted was a dad who cared enough to be there once in while so he could listen to her say, "This is me, Dad. This is what I'm doing, and saying, and becoming." As is the case with most kids, they don't even really need or want an answer, as long as there is an adult who cares and is willing to truly listen.

Okay, enough with the wonderful proselytizing Scarlucci educational insights. If this new Karidae kid was truly stalking Angel, now that the two of us had made an honest connection, I could not let her down. I needed to make sure she was protected. I had given her a promising sprinkle of protective Angel dust, after all.

A frequently repeated phrase to students is that soon they will be out in the "real world." However, sometimes even the cocoon-like, semi-secure environment of school cannot keep the real world out. Sometimes it comes calling when you least expect it, riding in on the blazing shoulders of hatred, with the sole purpose of hurting everyone and everything as much as it possibly can.

What I didn't know then, of course, was that protecting Angel Jehmar was going to be the most difficult task I would ever face.

EIGHT
THE MEAN FACTOR

Ken Valentine was one of my oldest and closest friends. He was my drinking buddy in the early years, and our relationship of social camaraderie as well as friendly support when needed is something that goes without question. Since he was my confidant, I asked him to be my best man. And, on that horrible day that the word came in that my wife Evelyn had been in a terrible car accident and was on the critical list in intensive care, it was Ken Valentine who was there for me. He met me at the door of my classroom to be with me when I got the news. He took me to the hospital. He stayed with me through the nights and days that followed. He helped me plan Evelyn's move to the rehabilitation facility where, after months of endless therapy, it was concluded that we should not give up hope, but the reality was that her shattered body would probably never be able to function properly on its own ever again. He helped me re-design our home so that It was handicapped accessible. And most importantly, since we adults – surprise, surprise – need the same goddamned things as kids…he listened.

I was in very bad shape during those horrible days and months, and Ken Valentine was one of the main reasons I made it through. There was no possible way to explain what I owed him. In a way, he had saved my life.

Oh, and just so it's clear that I'm not all that noble, in addition to wanting to help kids, there was another significant reason why I took the job of Assistant Principal: I needed the money and the benefits.

In spite of the school having a more than adequate medical plan for its employees, the cost of surgeries, therapy, and round-the-clock care for my wife went far beyond any insurance compensation. So, even though I knew I was not the typical ass-kissing type one usually found in such a position, here I was, having kissed my own fair share of ass to keep the job, sitting behind a desk where I was more than likely going to have to make an assessment regarding the teaching performance of my best friend.

The only consoling factor to the situation was that I was not alone. Sherri Walsh, Ken's present English chairperson, one time lover, and still good friend, was also sitting in on this meeting to assess Ken Valentine's competence in the classroom.

Knowing how to break the ice when there's a chance that tension is on the immediate horizon, I started things off with a good laugh. In other words, I told my two friends about Larry Pugh shitting his pants and grabbing at his ass as he ran down the hallway.

Sherri was laughing so hard, I thought she was going to soil her own silk panties, and Ken found the information hysterical as he paced the room. Finally, Ken cleared his throat, took in a large gulp of air and exhaled.

"All right. Enough. I'm good," he said, though sounding none too sure of himself. "Let's talk about why we're here. That ought to take the humor out of things pretty fast. Since you two are my best friends and we talk about everything, obviously, I'm in trouble, or the two of you would have talked to me about this before this meeting. Right?"

Sherri and I exchanged a quick glance of guilt.

"Okay, so, lay it on me. I'm a big boy. I can take it. And just so you both know, I have a totally clear conscience in all things. I know exactly what I have done, what I am doing, and will answer all comers."

I looked at Sherri, and she nodded back to me.

Take it away, Brian.

"Okay," I said. "What have you been doing?"

"You mean the iPad listening, I assume."

I nodded. "Among other things. I want to be as up front as possible with this, Ken. It isn't just the iPads. There is also a voiced concern about how many of your students are getting grades in the high 90's on their report cards. I mean, I checked and we're talking about 80% here. That's not exactly a bell curve."

"86.4 percent to be exact," Ken said quickly. "And the answer to those who voiced concern is that the students are being given those grades because they are earning them. I'll be more than happy to show the records to prove it."

"Ken, we know you. Of course you can back it up. We're not floundering beginners here. That's not the issue. I'm just

75

telling you what's going on. I actually thought of recusing myself from this because of our friendship, but on reflection, I decided it might be better if I did handle the initial meeting so that we'd have an inside track and be able to head things off at the pass, if necessary. And remember, I'm just the messenger here. As you know, I do my very best to make sure I can't be held responsible for anything, so don't take offense."

"I am well aware of how much of a chicken-shit you are when it comes to shouldering the blame, so have no fear of that. Start with whatever you wish," Ken confirmed with a characteristic grin.

"Okay, actually, I think the iPads are a good place to start since, according to school policy, it is forbidden to play iPads or any other MP3 player in the classroom, except for instructional purposes, and I am told that every one of your students has been listening to music on school-owned iPads while in supposed 'meditation time' while your class is in session…with your permission."

"That is true. Actually some use their own iPhones or iPads to listen. But I don't want to start with the iPads."

"Didn't you just tell me to start whereever I wanted to?"

"Yes, but in order for what I'm going to tell you and Sherri to make sense, I have to tell you about the Mean."

I tilted my head quizzically. "What do you mean?"

"Cute, Bri," Ken answered, "Ever the clever punster. Irritating, but clever. All right, here's the deal. Has either of you ever heard of a physicist named David Bohm?"

76

I looked at Sherri. We hadn't, and both looked back to Ken.

"All right, according to Bohm in his book, *The Implicate Order*, reality is a matter of implicate enfolded order and explicate unfolded order. Explicate is what we can see or rather what is called manifest reality and implicate is what we can't see or all that exists in an unmanifested state, the two of these making up the whole of reality. The fact is we see less than 1 percent of reality. It's all there, we just don't see it."

"Like we're pretty sure there are other dimensions. We just don't see them?" I put forth as an example.

"We're not pretty sure. There *are* other dimensions, Bri. But, yes, exactly. See, that's why I like you," Ken said. "You get it."

"No, according to Mary J. Talley who is speaking for Superintendent Francis Farnsworth and the Central Board of Education, you're the one who's going to get it if this isn't a damn good explanation, so please continue. And this better lead to why you're using iPads during non-curriculum meditation sessions in the manifest reality of the classroom 'cause so far it sounds like so much razzle-dazzle intellectual bullshit to justify going against school policy."

"That's pretty harsh for someone who's just the messenger." Ken looked at Sherri, gesturing toward me. "Can you believe this? And this guy is supposed to be my friend."

Sherri nodded. "I know. Very insensitive. I don't think I would continue such a friendship if I were you."

Okay, let me explain something here. The three of us have been together for a long time...years, to be precise. And over time, this little game of repartee has developed to the point where we just sort of fall into it naturally. It does not mean we are not well aware of how serious a situation may be. On the contrary, when it happens, the three of us know only too well that the stakes are usually quite high, and each of us knows that the other two know also. It's just our way of coping as we work our way to a solution, if there is one to be found.

"Or perhaps he just has trouble with weightier things like quantum physics," Sherri continued. "I understand what you're saying, of course, but maybe if you put it in simpler terms for Brian."

Ken shifted back toward me. "Well, I could simplify it for those of us who are having trouble following if you wish, but it will take even longer."

"Hey, simplify schmimplify, but try to finish the explanation sometime before the Board of Education meeting next week, so we'll be able to give them a logical explanation that will save your sorry ass, okay?" I said.

"I'll go before the Board," Ken said proudly. "Bring 'em on!"

I held up my hand, calling out, "Question, Mr. Valentine."

The teacher in Ken responded immediately. "Yes, Brian?"

Called upon, I put my hand down. "Okay, before you delve any deeper into the, and I use the term loosely here, 'scientific explanations' of why students are justified in playing iPads during supposed meditation sessions, which is against school policy, let's establish this: Are you going to have them stop doing it?"

"No," was the answer without an ounce of contrition.

"And exactly how far are you willing to take this?"

"To the pain, as they say in *Princess Bride.*"

"You realize the people in that old movie don't really exist and cannot lose their jobs, right? See, the guy in *that* fantasy is just pretending he can't move. He really can move because he's just acting. This, on the other hand, is real life, so I wouldn't be quite so fast with the 'to the pain' if I were you."

Sherri looked at her watch. Always the practical one, frequently it was Sherri who cut to the chase to move things along. "Guys, we have to get somewhere here. Let's have it, Ken. What's your reason for the iPad crap in the classroom? That's all we need. If it's justified, I can handle it with an explanation that an exception is being made for lesson plan reasons of a unit concept."

"Not bad," I said to Sherri. Then to Ken, "Okay, go on, but keep it simple for me."

Ken pushed ahead. "Dr. Bohm feels that the holographic view of the universe is a good place to begin to understand the implicate enfolded and the explicate unfolded orders because every piece is an exact representation of the whole. Are you with me, Brian?"

"Actually, yes," I said. "I get that. If you grasp a piece of it, you grasp everything."

"Exactly. Now, how do we grasp it? That's the question. And the answer is it's all a matter of vibration."

"And, ignoring the fact that you just sounded like that most tedious of talkers, Head Librarian Harold Billings, with your question and answer response, I assume you have devised a way to give them *Good Vibrations*, as they say in the Beach Boys song."

"Yes, in essence, that is exactly what I have done. See, the totality of reality is all here.   We just have to elevate our consciousness to perceive it."

"To explicate the implicate, as it were," I summarized.

"Exactly. Now, let's transfer this to mental networking."

"Fine. Let's. Because I get that too," I said. "It's like we can only tap into a very small portion of our unlimited brain power. It's all there, but we don't know how to utilize it."

"Right. You get it once again. Bravo."

"Hey, no dullard, I. But I'm telling you, Mr. Wizard, and I know I'm repeating myself. You're the one who's going to *get it* from Superintendent Farnsworth if we can't give him something better than that. Give me some provable results and concrete reasoning, please." I turned to Sherri. "You know, I saw this coming. Years ago, when he arranged the chairs in his classroom in a circle, and put a statue of Buddha in the corner of the room with that self-contained flowing water fountain next to it and had incense burning, I knew it would come to this."

Sherri shifted in her seat, no longer amused, which frequently happened when she was pressed for time, and I was starting to get on her nerves.

"I'm serious now. We really don't have time for these asides, Brian" she said, understanding that her saying it wouldn't really make a bit of difference where I was concerned. "Go ahead, Ken. What have you been able to do?"

Ken hesitated slightly. "Well, here's where it gets a little sticky...."

"Ah ha! Just as I suspected," I said. "Ken, I love you, but the La La Land aspect of your thinking has never ceased to amaze me."

"Brian, let him talk...please!"

I knew that tone and gave Sherri a zipped-lip gesture. Though as I listened, I have to tell you, it was all I could do to contain myself. I mean, seriously now, listen to this:

"According to a man named Tom Kenyon...and I have his lectures on CD if you'd care to listen to them...there exists in all of us a coherent energy pattern, represented by the ethereal layers of the heart. See, the heart has seven ethereal layers shaped like doughnuts. When there are good vibrations happening within us, the rings open, and when there are bad vibrations the heart rings close."

Knowing me all too well, Sherri glared at me threateningly, and I suppressed at least five really good snack cake quips that surfaced unbidden in my mind.

"Transferring this concept to the mental networking," Ken continued, "it has been discovered that anything that creates the correct vibrational pressure can open the mind. Sound communicates from cell to cell by pressure, so...."

"Here come the iPads," I put in, unable to contain myself.

Both of them gave me a look, then Ken went on.

"So, the opening of the brain can be accomplished by applying pressure through tones. This is not performing, you understand. It is just creating resonance. And the tone must be free of ego. The vibration must be pure."

"Which eliminates all songs by Snoop Dog," I added.

Ken went on, ignoring me. "Remember my trip to Tibet last summer?"

"Who could forget it after that three-hour slide show you subjected us to," I said, backsliding horribly in the keeping-my-mouth-shut department. Then I remembered. "Oh, I know what this is! It's about the balls, isn't it?"

"Yes, it is. The Tibetan balls. Only I don't like the way you say balls. Let's call them gongs."

"No, they're balls. You called them balls and you should know because they're your balls. If we're going to talk about your balls, let's call them balls."

"BRIAN!" Sherri said.

I know, sometimes it's inexcusable and childish, yet again and again, as you may have already noticed, I am unable to suppress my urge to be a wiseass. Trust me, I still have no idea how I've been able to hang onto my job for all these years with this crucial flaw in my personality.

"Okay, the truth is I actually went to Tibet for the Tibetan...balls. They are very rare and hard to find. I was extremely lucky. The balls are made by an order of Tibetan monks, and they only make six over an extended period of time, all according to astrological configuration, first gold, then silver, and so on."

"And so what you're saying is that you are having students listen to your balls on the iPads?"

"That's right," Ken said, so into his explanation at this point that all double entendres were wasted on him. "When they are sounded in a specific sequence, they raise the vibration level to the ratio of 1.618. Do you know what that is?"

"The golden mean," Sherri said.

"That's right," Ken exclaimed, looking at her impressed.

"How the hell do you know that?" I asked Sherri.

"Never underestimate me, Brian. I'm not just a pretty face."

"Actually the precise number is 1.6180339887499, represented by the Greek letter *phi* that arises out of the basic structure of our cosmos. *Phi* appears clearly and regularly in things that grow and unfold in steps, and that includes all *living things*," Ken went on, the excitement of his explanation carrying him now.

He reached into his briefcase and pulled out his phone, clicking the screen to life and handing it to Sherri. She looked at the visual on the face of Ken's cell and passed it to me. On the front of his iPhone, a strange symbol filled the screen. The thick golden capital "P" curved to a point and circled back, almost like a clef of some kind, but it had to be a Greek letter.

"That is the symbol for *Phi*, the Golden Mean," Ken said as I gave him back his phone. "You understand the significance here."

"I understand it must be pretty important to you if you keep it as wallpaper on your phone," I answered.

"Exactly," he said, with a wide smile. "The golden mean is one of the core building units of the universe found in sequentially built and developing things. It can be found in the structure of the Greek Parthenon, in entire galaxies, in the DNA spiral, and even in the ratio of the emotion Love. And when things vibrate at 1.618, the DNA becomes stronger and healthier, and on and on.

"And here is the payoff: The wave frequencies caused by the sounding of the Tibetan balls are esthetic forms that, in the right combination of sounding, vibrate at a 1.618 ratio, which in turn creates a pressure that lifts the vibration level of our mental circuitry and opens the human mind."

There was a silence in the room for a moment as we all just kind of looked at one another. I cleared my throat.

"So let me get this straight."

Ken stood up. "No, I will not let you get anything straight. And that is exactly why I didn't tell you about this before. You understand perfectly well what I'm saying. Sorry, Brian, but

84

this means a great deal to me and, for once, I don't want to hear you make light of it."

"All right, Ken, I'm sorry. I'll restrain myself. And I don't doubt your sincerity, but please tell me you don't really expect us to report to the Central Board of Education that you are having the students in your class meditate with iPads, listening to the sound of Tibetan balls, and it is opening up their minds. First of all, classroom meditation is against school policy because is smacks of religious practice, and we know where all schools stand on that issue. Secondly...no, forget secondly, one is enough to hang you, for Christ's sake. Listen to what you're saying, please."

He shook his head and moved to the front of the desk. He bent down, reached into his briefcase and took out an iPad Mini, along with thin wiring that ended with tiny earbuds wrapped around it. After looking at the small iPad for a moment, he placed it in front of me on the desk.

"No, you listen," he said. "Knowing precisely what the Scarlucci reaction to this would be, I brought you a present. I will not discuss this any more until each of you has listened to the audio track that I have created. I don't care which of you goes first, but when we meet again, I want you both to have listened to it. Then we'll discuss this further. I've got to go to my ninth period class."

"I think that's fair. We should all know what we're talking about," I said. "Sherri?"

"Fine with me. You go first, then I'll take it."

85

"Done. I'll listen to it tonight because I'm telling you, we have to move quickly on this," I said, opening the center drawer of my desk and starting to place the iPad inside as Ken headed for the door. Of course, the first thing I saw when I pulled the drawer open were the envelopes from Sal Mordento, and I shook my head in realization.

"Hold it," I said, slipping the iPad into the drawer and extracting one of the envelopes. "Hold everything! There's something I forgot to tell you."

Sherri frowned at the envelope in my hand, and Ken crossed back to my desk. "Make it fast, Bri. I've got a class. What is it?"

"Looks like it is a day of presents because a corpulent parent of one of your student converts stopped by this morning, Ken, and he left you a present." I held up the envelope. "This is from Salvatore "The Gimp" Mordento. It's a present for you because Joey has suddenly started using his brain and Sal wanted to thank you. I got one too because I suspended Joey which, according to Sal, helped the boy see the light. Is Sal right about Joey getting good grades now?"

Taking the envelope from me, Ken just looked at. "Well, yes, but what...?"

Sherri came out of her chair, voicing her own astonishment. "You're kidding about this, right?"

"I am not kidding."

Ken turned the thick envelope in his hand. "But what is this?"

86

"It is cold hard cash to do with as you wish. Sal suggested perhaps you might want to purchase a new Beemer."

"What!" Ken said.

"Brian, seriously now, what is this?" Sherri said.

"I told you. Money."

"Well, how much?" was her next question, probably for want of something else to say as she stared at the envelope.

"I don't know. Several hundred dollar bills slipped out of one of the envelopes when, wheezing with the exertion of the simple effort, Sal threw them on my desk. My guess is probably thousands of dollars in each envelope."

"What!" Ken said for the third time. He dropped the envelope back on the desk as if it were red hot. "I don't want it."

"Brian, how could you have accepted this? This is unbelievable."

I joined the two of them by standing. "Yes it is. But he told me if I didn't take it, he would be insulted and that he didn't take very well to insults."

"So you took it," she said in disbelief.

"Well, what was I supposed to do?"

"Say no, obviously."

"Sherri, it wasn't that easy. Trust me. You weren't here staring into the threatening eyes of a crime figure whose reputation is based on the large number of people he has either killed or had killed. It was...I don't know. He just made me an offer I couldn't refuse."

Ken shook his head. "I've got to go to class."

I took his envelope and placed it back with the other one, closing the drawer.

"So does that mean you're giving me your share?" I called after him as he moved to the door.

Though his exit had a tiny tick of hesitation in it, my good friend didn't answer. He just left the office.

Sherri looked at me without speaking.

"I know. I know," I said.

"Well, what are you going to do? You can't keep it."

"Well, I can't give it back. He'd probably kill me. Come on, sit back down."

"I can't. The day's almost over and I've got about a hundred things I have to do."

"Yes you can because I promised our boss, Mary J., we'd do this one last thing, so you're going to have make the time. I know we're already headed into ninth period, so let's get this over with as quickly as possible. I need to be out of here before the release of school, too. There's a new kid named Tyler Karidae I want to get a look at. You know him?"

"No. What else is there to discuss? Mary didn't say anything to me."

"I know. Since we were having the meeting with Ken anyway, she left it for me to show you." I grabbed the supposed incriminating evidence from my desk, and crossed to the stand with the television and player in the far corner of the room. "This is a Security video. We have to watch it to see if

Maggie Madison is giving not just acting advice, but blowjobs to her lead actor," I said.

"What!" Sherri said, echoing once again a response that had come in pretty handy during the last five minutes or so. "I'm sorry, Brian, but this is not funny. Maggie and Todd Hershborne? That is way out of line, even for you. What in God's name would possess you to say such a thing?"

I shook my head and slid the Security footage into the machine; then I crossed to the wall switch and doused the lights.

"Give me some credit here, Sherri. It may not appear so at times, but I know precisely where the goddamned line is, all right? I didn't say it. Security did, and we need to see if it's true. Now sit down so we can find out."

Clearly not very pleased with me at the moment, Sherri shook her head and sat down. I pointed the remote control at the machine in the corner and pushed the little *play* arrow.

NINE
FREE WILLY

Fast forwarding by means of the digital clock in the lower right hand corner of the video, I found the sequence in question and we both sat in silence, watching as the scene unfolded on the television screen. It didn't last very long. The stage door swung closed after slowly coming partially open to reveal the two figures behind it. Yes, you could see two people from a side angle. And yes, it looked like one of them was Maggie Madison since the female figure could be seen from the side through the opening on the door. And, yes, it appeared she was on her knees or at least stooping with bended knees in front of a male figure, but that was it. If Mary J. wanted absolute certainty, it wasn't going to happen.

I hit *stop*.

"You know, I asked Richie to fix that back stage door latch about a thousand times because it won't lock. If he'd done what he was told instead of sleeping in the teacher's lounge, we wouldn't even have to deal with this. You want the lights?"

I saw Sherri shake her head from where she sat across from me in the darkened office.

"No, play it again."

"I don't think that's a good idea. I'm getting turned on."

"Brian...."

I punched the back arrow.

"Okay, but you want my snap judgment? You can't see shit. You could not possibly prove anything with this. So what if she's on her knees. Maybe she's just fixing the zipper on his costume or something. As far as I'm concerned there is no way to tell if Maggie's is trying to free Willy and do a job on it."

"Play it again, Brian, please."

Finding the appropriate sequence, I backed the video up a little and hit *play.*

"Can you slow it down?"

"Yes, I can."

I held down the reverse arrow button and first *slow x2* appeared, followed by *slow x4,* then *slow x8,* and the scene inched slowly forward on the screen. The door slooowly opened, a side view of the two figures appeared for a few moments, and the door sloooowly closed. The end. Not the best of plots for a movie, that's for sure.

"Okay, hit the lights," Sherri said, standing.

I crossed to the wall switch for the lights, and then moved to the machine, ejecting the Security video, and moved back to Sherri, dropping the disk on my desk.

"Well?"

Sherri did not smile. "I'll talk to her."

"What do you think?"

She shook her head once more. "I don't know. It's too short. How the hell did they even see such a brief thing?"

"It's Sam's job to make sure the videos are reviewed at the end of each school day."

Sherri looked at me, a little inquisitive light coming into her eyes. "Who reviewed it yesterday?"

"Ahhh," I said. "Good question. Interesting. Anthony Galli, perhaps? You think they're after her?"

"In this school, anything is possible. And there is definitely cause to wonder, isn't there."

Sherri was referring to the fact that at the beginning of the year, as Ms. Maggie Madison was exiting the building, one of the Security guards by the name of Anthony Galli had made an obscene genital gesture as Ms. Madison passed by him and another Security guard. Blanche Turner – yes, that Blanche Turner – happened to be leaving the building at the same time, saw Galli making the "disgusting" gesture, told Maggie, and Ms. Madison screamed sexual harassment, threatening to bring the man up on charges. The matter was finally resolved by Mary J. by having Anthony apologize to Ms. Madison in a closed office session.

However, Anthony Galli still held a grudge about what had happened, since he let it be known that he had been prosecuted -- I'm pretty certain he meant persecuted -- unfairly, and "the stupid cunt" didn't know what she was talking about, protesting that he had just been "itching a scratch, and nothing else, for Christ's sake." I decided Anthony Galli's attitude was completely out of line. I informed Mary J. what Sam had informed me Galli was saying around the school, using somewhat different terminology, of course and, equally appalled, Mary J. had tried to have the guard replaced or at least transferred to the Middle School. However, the union had stepped in and SGuard Galli was still with us, itching and bitching his way through the school day, now more pissed off than ever.

"Well, Maggie has to be told, that goes without saying."

"Mary J. said she wants absolute certainty on this before anything is said or done," I warned.

"Brian, Maggie is on my staff, and this is a horrific accusation. She is going to know about it, whether I tell her or not. You think Security is going to keep quiet about this?"

"Sam gave me his word."

"Yeah, right. You tell Mary that I am going to speak to Maggie in the morning. Once we hear her side of things, we'll take it from there."

"What? Do you think she's going to admit it?"

"I only know she has to be told what's going on before she hears it from somewhere else."

"Okay. But if it is true, Maggie's the one going down, no pun intended. If the two of them are swapping spit, the kid will not be blamed, no matter what the circumstances. We've seen enough female-teacher-with-male-student stories in the news lately to know that."

"Do you have to say, *swapping spit*?" Sherri protested. "It's so crude. Couldn't you say, *kissing*?"

"All right...*kissing*. The point is that if they are *kissing* on the sly, *nobody dast blame this man*," I said, quoting from *Death of a Salesman* for English chairperson Sherri Walsh's benefit...who let the quote pass by totally unappreciated. "I mean, if she did come on to the kid, I can't see him resisting. Let's not forget, Maggie is still a pretty hot number, after all."

"You should know," she answered pointedly, a reference to a former dalliance on my part with Ms. Madison that had gone on for several passion-filled months in years past. "What the hell is it with the sex thing in this school? You'd think people could exert a little more control."

"Basic instincts, I guess. Hard to fight. I mean, let's face it. That must be what it is with Mary J. and Larry Pugh. And then there's that couple in the math department."

She smiled in amusement. "You have absolutely no shame, and with poor Larry right in the next office." And after a beat..."What couple in the Math department?"

I shrugged. "I just made that up to see if you were listening." I slid my arm around her waist. "Will I be seeing you tonight?"

"It's Tuesday night, isn't it. What did you tell Evelyn?"

"The usual. That there was a PTA meeting, so I'd just grab a quick bite to eat and go straight there. That it looked like it was going to be a long one, so not to wait up for me."

She nodded. "And you'll listen to the sound of Ken's balls before I get there."

I smiled. Though not sardonic as I was sometimes wont to be, in many ways the two of us were from the same mold. "Yes."

"Okay. I'll bring the wine. Then maybe we can listen to it together and decide what to do."

"Fine. But first...."

Sherri moved close to me, kissing me hard, wonderfully soft portions of her body against me while her hand reached down, searching and then finding Mr. Scarlucci, Jr., who, roused from his mid-afternoon nap, lifted his head in definite interest.

"I know," she said. "But first we free Willy."

TEN

I'M NO SUPERMAN

Having checked on the boy's schedule and file-enclosed photo in Guidance, I posted myself at the end of Wing C near room 124 so that I would not miss Tyler Karidae when he came out of his ninth period class. The bell rang, doors opened, and students filled the halls, sound erupting into higher and higher decibels as they moved to lockers, shouted to one another while plugging into and talking on cell phones, and just generally mixed and tormented one another in end-of-the-day release.

Tyler Karidae came out through the classroom doorway alone, attempting to talk to no one. He had longish, unwashed wavy brown hair, and wore the standard baggy pants with assorted side pockets, which I had come to learn usually held all sorts of legal and illegal paraphernalia. Since cell phones are allowed at the conclusion of the school day, as was the case with many of the students exiting the room around him, earbud headphones sprouted from Tyler Karidae's ears with the wire running down into one of the side pockets of his pants, where I assumed he kept his phone. However, I was fairly certain it was not the sound of Ken Valentine's balls that Tyler Karidae was listening to as he exited the classroom. His eyes, set in deep sockets on his lean angular face, flicked to the side and front, tracking the movement of students, but he clearly preferred isolation to general socialization.

96

Hmmmm.

Then, as Tyler Karidae reached the middle section of the hall, a student came up to him, and they slapped hands, twisted thumbs, and hit fists or what ever the hell the latest coded-greeting movements were at the moment. Tyler removed one earbud, and the two moved to the side, leaning against the row of lockers, talking as they watched students move past.

Hmmmm.

I say *Hmmmm* once more because the student talking to Tyler Karidae was a troublemaker named Lewis Grimley, and Lewis Grimley I knew only too well. In fact, based on my instincts for such things, Lewis was my top choice for the secret identity of the phantom shitter, which should give you some idea of what kind of kid we're talking about here. If there were ever a student who had both the hatred and the nerve to shit all over the school to express his contempt for it, Lewis Grimley was the kid.

I know I said that we had to give kids a chance as they moved through the maze, and idealistically, that's true. However, and this is not something I would ever admit publicly as Assistant Principal Scarlucci, but years of experience as an educator have taught me that there are also the kids who cannot be helped. You could counsel, cajole, and discipline the student until the end of time, and the kid would still turn on you. You can forget "no child left behind" in such a case, as my new pal Sal Mordento had correctly pointed out to me earlier in the day, because this kid, for whatever reason, *wants* to be left behind and there is not a damned thing you can do about it. It is simply not his time to be saved.

Lewis Grimley was one of those students determined to prove to all comers that he was a bad seed. From elementary school on, he had been involved in petty robbery, drug dealing and insubordination with just about every authority figure he ever encountered, including the police.

An example: we were at the homecoming dance and Lewis, little shit that he is, bumped into Principal Mary J. Talley, *accidentally* spilling his entire drink down the front of her outfit. *"Oh, sorry,"* was his response, grinning as he walked away, high-fiving admirers as he joined his crowd in the corner, knowing there wasn't a damn thing she could do about it since it was an *accident.* This kid was so bad that if a fortune teller read his palm, her response about his future would undoubtedly be *JAIL, WITH NO CHANCE OF PAROLE.* And now he was having a talk with his new pal, Tyler Karidae.

Hmmmm.

Okay, Tyler. We'll be keeping an eye on you, Mr. New Student.

When I got back to my office, Laurence Pugh was waiting for me. He closed the door behind me as I entered.

"Brian, you didn't tell anyone about the...problem I had this morning, did you?"

I crossed to my desk, indignant. "Larry, what kind of person do you think I am?"

"Oh, I know what kind of person you are," Pugh responded, moving to the desk after me. "That's why I'm asking."

"You know, I'm really offended by that."

"Well, did you?"

I looked him. A small trickle of perspiration was inching its way down the side of his face to the corner of his eye and he blinked it away.

"No, Larry," I said. "I did not tell anyone. We have to support each other, you know. That's what this is all about."

He held my gaze for a moment and then nodded.

"Okay. Thank you." He turned and crossed to the door, turning back to me as he opened it. "I appreciate it. I owe you one."

Oh, no you don't, Larry 'cause Brian is a liar, liar, pants on fire, and used your unfortunate accident as a tension reliever for the amusement of himself and his two friends at a meeting earlier today, my conscience hissed inside my head.

I obliterated the internal reprimand by busying myself with end-of-the-day work. In addition, I didn't feel so bad about lying to him when I discovered a maintenance requisition form on my desk to be filled out and processed for the building's air conditioning system. Pugh must have slipped the form on my desk while I was out on my Karidae reconnaissance mission, and I was livid that he would try such an underhanded move.

The air conditioning system that had been installed in Central High School was one of the hot controversial issues of the district.   Over the last several years, one of the more active parent factions in the community had been lobbying for the high school to install an air conditioning system in the building.   They argued that during testing periods, which extended into late June because of New York State exam scheduling, when scores on tests were often critical to students' grade point averages, the building was frequently so hot it was unfairly affecting test score results. Truth be told, they did have a legitimate point, as anyone knew who had been in a classroom and seen students sweating through 90-100 degree heat as they took three-hour exams.   Such conditions had to have an adverse effect on student test results. Whether it was worth the exorbitant costs of installing air conditioning in the entire building was another question. Many in the community felt the answer was a resounding NO! However, political strength frequently falls to the most vocally active in a school district and, to the surprise of many, the bond issue for air conditioning passed by a fairly large percentage.

Okay, great. Central High got air for the hot days of early fall and late spring.   Except, after months of delays and construction setbacks involving the duct work and blah, blah, blah, the system worked wonderfully for exactly three weeks and then, two days before testing week, promptly broke down.

Memos flew, phone calls mounted, articles appeared in newspapers, board meetings were flooded with protests and complaints and, finally, a separate consulting firm was called in to assess the system. Resulting report: faulty vacuum pumps. The construction company doing the installation had cut costs and installed pumps that were not sufficient for the size and volume of the duct work, and the system could not function properly until new pumps were installed, for an additional cost of thousands.

The district put out bids, took the lowest submission, and the new pumps were installed.

And the system still did not work.

Threatening to sue the newly-acquired firm, the district was able to get consultants to work with the company and fix the problem... or so they said. That was what the maintenance form was all about. It was to be completed and submitted so that a check and trial run could be made of the system to be sure it worked properly.

Pugh, sneaky little bastard that he is, had passed the hot potato on to me, which meant that if anything went wrong during the June exam week, it was Brian Scarlucci who was supposed to have made sure everything was taken care of and ready. If it didn't work, of course, it would then be Scarlucci's ass that was grass, not Laurence Pugh's. And I realize the man has his fair share of ass problems already, nevertheless....

I threw the form in my already full *TO DO* box on the left side of the desk.

Okay, Larry, I'll take care of it.

Then, after finishing up the day's paperwork, I told my secretary goodbye for the day, and headed for the parking lot, two cash-stuffed envelopes and an audio track of my friend's balls secreted away inside the inner pocket of my briefcase.

I always park all the way at the far end of the faculty parking lot, away from the other cars to prevent door dings from those thoughtless fellow workers who throw open their car doors. Mine is not a fancy car, but I keep it as pristine as possible for re-sale value. As I said, my money situation is not what it should be for a man in my position...not that I'm complaining. I have always done and will continue to do all I can and need to do to make my crippled wife as comfortable as I possibly can, and if that has meant struggling with debt because of in-home round-the-clock care for her all these years, so the fuck be it. Not that I'm in any way bitter about how fate has a way of leaping out of nowhere and kicking you squarely in the nuts when you least expect it, you understand. Just because Evelyn and I were able to achieve such happiness during our first year of marriage, only to have the rug ripped out from under us when the future looked so peachy.

And, while we're on the topic of my wife, before any judgmental moralists who are without fault start looking around for a sharp-edged stone to hurl in my direction, let's deal with this: Yes, I am having an affair with the chairperson of the English department and I also have a crippled wheelchair-bound wife at home. And, yes, I have anguished over this more than you could possibly imagine. And, damn it, yes, I know it demonstrates a certain weakness of character...and yet I still do it.

For years, I was the paragon of virtue as far as dealing with my *personal needs* – if you get my meaning. But then, one fateful alcohol-drenched Central High School Faculty Christmas party night, the opportunity presented itself, and...well, I slipped. I slipped because I was not only drunk, but, after years of abstinence that found only partially satisfying relief from Pamela Palm and her five sisters, I was horny enough to screw one of Santa's reindeers. No, let me re-phrase that without the typical Scarlucci fallback on humor. I slipped because, goddamn it, I'm human.

Please understand, I love my wife, and I will always love her, and I also know there are those who, in a comparable situation, would not do such a thing. I know that in spite of physical needs, there are those who would be unfailingly devoted wives or husbands to their invalid mates for a lifetime. I'm just not that guy.

Though it is something I am certainly not proud of, I found I was not able to do that. And once I strayed, I knew that I would stray again...and I have. And if that makes me a lesser human being, then I have to be able to live with that...and I have. I guess, what it comes down to is this. Though I try to do what I know is right in caring for my paraplegic wife, I cannot be perfect when it comes to suppressing my own needs.

I'm no superman.

I am having an affair because I need a relationship that has moments of fun-filled casual good humor, comfortable tenderness over a glass of wine and, yes, sex. Now before the guilt that has taken up permanent residence inside me forces me to spout any more self-justification for my actions, that's it. I am what I am.

However, when I exited the school building, I was not exactly overjoyed to see that the female who was involved in that first post-Christmas party affair was standing by my isolated car in the far corner of the faculty parking lot.

"Where's the goddamned video, Brian," was Maggie Madison's angry greeting to me as I approached my blue several-years-old, four-door Volvo sedan.

"Hello, Maggie," I said, reaching the driver's door where she had stationed herself, presumably to stop me from getting in and driving away, "and hello to you too. My day is fine, thank you. And yours?"

"Don't give me that shit, Brian. You know damned well what I'm talking about. Where's the fucking Security video?"

And then, in a fit of anger, Maggie Madison raised her foot and kicked my car as hard as she could.

Are you kidding me? I park in the corner of the faculty lot without getting a single door ding for years, and she kicks my goddamned car, putting a huge dent in the door with the Wildhorse leather toe of her Dr. Martens Dana loafer.

I was beside myself. "What in the hell do you think you're doing, Maggie. Jesus Christ, are you kidding me? You just kicked my fucking car. Look at the dent! *God Damn it!*"

And then she was crying...wailing actually, to be precise.

Heads turned, of course, craning to see what was going on at the far corner of the parking lot since damn near the entire faculty was exiting the building. By the custodian's rear entrance to the school, I thought I could make out the personage of one Anthony Galli staring in our direction also.

Clicking the unlock button on my key ring, I grabbed Maggie and hustled her around the front of the car to the passenger side, shoved her inside, slammed the door, and rushed back to the driver's side, getting in and closing the door after me.

I started the car, and shoved it into reverse.

"Goddamn it, Sherri told me she was going to wait until morning to talk to you about this," I said, backing out of the parking space and heading across the lot.

"Sherri didn't say anything," Maggie growled between wails. "It was that damn bastard Galli. He came up beside me as I was leaving and whispered to me in the back hallway, 'Got you now, bitch. Got you on video doin' dirt with your lead actor backstage, and I heard Scarlucci's giving it a look-see. Now we'll see who's leaving this school, you cunt.' What the hell is he talking about?"

Then she saw the Security man by the custodian entrance as he lifted his hand and waved in the direction of my moving car.

"Look, there he is! Let me out of here. I'll show that son-of-a-bitch...."

The passenger door opened.

I grabbed at Maggie, stopping her exit by holding onto her sleeve.

"Maggie, the car is moving. Stop it! Close the door! I mean it."

She yanked the door shut, and I drove out of the parking lot, catching a glimpse of Sherri Walsh, staring in our direction, her hand holding the car key raised toward the lock of her green Saturn's driver's door, but motionless as she watched my Volvo pull out of the parking lot, Maggie giving the finger through the back window to a waving Anthony Galli.

Starbucks was my destination of choice for two reasons. One was that it was near the school, and the other was because when we *were* a *number,* Maggie and I went to Starbucks during our free periods, so since I was with Maggie, I went to Starbucks. Not inside, considering the fact that Maggie was still seething, but rather to the drive-thru window.

After paying for coffee, I pulled into the Starbucks parking lot. Coincidentally, I was parked in the far corner once again, not that it mattered ding-wise anymore, and Maggie had calmed down a tad...but just a tad.

"Okay, I'm all right," she said, sniffing loudly and sipping her skimmed latte with one Splenda. "What's on the Security video?"

I took a sip of my own black Grande. "You tell me. I haven't looked at it."

I know. Liar, liar once again. I learned it from Michael Carleone in THE GODFATHER.

She shrugged angrily. "How the hell should I know? What did Galli say was on it?"

Truth time, to see exactly which way the wind blows. "He said it shows you on your knees in front of a male student with your hands on his hips, and that it appears the student is Todd, but it was impossible to make a positive I.D. because the camera angle is from above and to the side through a partially opened stage door that swings shut, blocking out the view"

Maggie stared at me, latte sipping coming to an abrupt halt. "Are you shitting me?"

"I am not shitting you."

"And when was this?"

"Yesterday afternoon, after drama rehearsal had finished."

She shook her head. "Unfuckingbelievable! This guy is really out to get me, isn't he."

"It would appear so."

"Well, no one's taking this seriously, are they? I mean, I was probably fixing the kid's costume or something."

"That's exactly what I thought. The angle makes it impossible to tell what's going on."

John Arthur Long

"Wait...I thought you said you didn't see it. How do you know about the camera angle?"

Oops. In movies they never get caught in a lie.

Maggie stared at me, not getting an answer.

"You lied to me. Told me you didn't see it just to find out what I'd say?"

"Maggie...."

She opened the passenger door. "Fuck you, Brian. I mean, if I can't even trust you, after all we've been through...Jesus Christ!"

Once out of the car, Maggie slammed the door as hard as she possibly could and, as she walked away in a huff, a Shakespearean adage did come to mind: *The lady doth protest too much, methinks.* However, what really grabbed my attention was the fact that the cup of latte Maggie had placed on the dash in front of her fell forward from the jarring impact of the closing door and spilled its entire contents all over the worn but spotless leather passenger seat of the Volvo's interior.

Damn it!

ELEVEN

ON THE MONEY

I have a place other than my home. It's a little studio apartment, a couple of towns over from Central along the North shore of Long Island. Not too far from the school and not too far from where my home is located, but not too close either.

The place is nothing fancy. Just your basics, and I can barely afford that, so it's pretty tight financially, but I make it work. Sometimes I go there to get away, and sometimes...for other things.

Tonight, after a stiff shot of Johnny Walker Green – my one extravagance –which I keep in the place along with a few assorted glasses, a couple of cups for coffee, and not much else in the cabinet above the quote-unquote *kitchen* sink, while waiting for Sherri, I used the place to listen to my friend Ken Valentine's balls.

And do you know what I heard?

Tibetan balls.

That's right. Tibetan balls and only Tibetan balls, gonging away.

Don't get me wrong. They were very nice, as far as Tibetan balls go, if that's what you're into. You know: Gong...echo....echo...echo. Gong...echo...echo...echo...and so forth. Nice timbre...nice vibrations...I guess.

But that's it.

Sorry, Ken. I don't mean to get your balls in an uproar, but I'm not hearing it the way I think you want me to hear it.

School-wise, I wasn't at all sure what we were going to do about that, which is why I had a second Johnny Walker Green. Not that I intended to tell Sherri my conclusions right away, which I knew would drive her crazy. I mean, isn't tormenting the other person in a relationship half the fun? And to my slightly tipsy- on-Johnny-Walker delight, the wait came to an end. Someone was at the door, and it had to be none other than the chairperson of Central High School's English department since it was now the appointed hour of our tryst, and she was the only other person who knew I had the apartment.

We are all creatures of habit, and Sherri is no exception. The first thing she does when she comes through the door, after closing it behind her and kissing me passionately, of course, is to toss off her shoes, leaving them where they fall. Then, talking to me as she moves, Sherri takes the wine she has brought with her, moves to the quote-unquote *kitchen* counter, and takes down two wine glasses from the overhead cabinet. Then, she uncorks the wine, usually a nice dry Chardonnay, and pours it into the two glasses. Then we toast. Then we take each other's clothes off and fuck our brains out.

Tonight, however, after the toast, Sherri seemed to have decided to *be* an exception and continued talking, not appearing to be in any rush at all for us to take each other's clothes off, which did not bode well for the much-anticipated *fuck our brains out* part of the evening.

"All right," she said, taking another drink of post-toast wine, "Before anything else, I have to know two things. What the hell was that scene with Maggie in the parking lot and, probably more importantly, what happened when you listened to your good friend's balls?"

"Does that mean we're not going to take each other's clothes off...?" I asked, leading her toward the queen-sized bed that sat invitingly on the far side of the studio in the quote-unquote *bedroom*.

"Oh, have no fear. If all goes well, you will see my naked body before the cock awakens to even think about crowing, but I should warn you, if you fool around and lead me astray with your information, as you know I know you might be tempted to do, you may end up having to resort to a less than satisfying conclusion to the evening with your old girl friend, Pamela Palm."

I took my own drink of wine, which as always, was quite good. The woman knows her wines.

"First of all, I am sorry I ever confided in you about Pamela Palm. It was during a weak moment when we were divulging old romances, and it was clearly a mistake since you are obviously jealous of the group sex Pamela, her five sisters and I have had, or why would you continue to throw it in my face at every opportunity? And secondly, didn't anyone ever tell you the harm it does to a relationship to use sex as a weapon. Besides, I've had my fill of naked female bodies today."

She gave me the look. "You better not mean that svelte body of Maggie Madison."

"Please. Old news. No, I meant that Angel Jehmar showed me her breasts today." That stopped her. I smiled. "Now about Maggie...."

"You saw Angel's breasts?"

I took another drink of wine. "Ummm. She flashed me in the office to show me her nipple piercing. Grrrr. I mean, doesn't getting that done have to hurt like a mother? I disciplined her severely for her actions, of course."

"Oh, of course. What'd you say? Something like, *Bad Angel! You put those breasts away. Right now!*"

"Exactly."

"Did you tell anyone?"

"I'm telling you."

"So what. You've seen my breasts too, and I sure as hell am not telling anyone. What do you want me to do?"

"Flash me the way Angel did, obviously."

"Brian, seriously now, she showed you her breasts?"

"It's all right. We came to an understanding."

"I'll bet, considering those breasts. Poor little tight-breasted Maggie Madison didn't have a chance after that."

"I did not fool with Maggie Madison, Sherri. Don't you have any trust?"

"I would never doubt you, even though I watched you pull out of the parking lot with Maggie in your car. So what happened? Someone told her about the video, obviously."

"Right."

I unbuttoned the top button on her blouse.

"Ah, ahhh…easy, big boy. A little more info first."

I pulled her down to a sitting position on the bed. "Anthony Galli told her. Whispered to her as he walked along beside her in the back hallway, ending the information by once again calling her a *cunt*."

"Something's got to be done with that man. Mary must be told. I don't care what's really going on with Maggie. There's no way she can let him get away with that."

"I'm on it, don't worry. First thing tomorrow, along with a few million other things."

"And Maggie went crazy? I couldn't help but notice she was giving everyone in sight the finger out the back window of your car as you pulled away."

"Crazy is putting it mildly. She kicked my car, for God's sake."

Sherri gasped through a suppressed smile. "She kicked your car? Badly?"

"Put a goddamned huge dent in the lower left door panel. I put a call into Dent Wizard Repairs on my way over here. A rep is going to meet me in the parking lot tomorrow to fix it."

"Whoa. She dented your car! No wonder you didn't get it on with her for old time's sake. Where were you headed…Starbucks?"

"Where else? I had to get her the hell out of the parking lot. I can't wait to hear what goes through the Central High rumor mill tomorrow after her little temper tantrum at my car. Did you see Galli over by the custodian's entrance waving at her, that prick? That's what prompted the finger."

"But you calmed her down…."

"Not exactly. I lied to her about viewing the video to see what she'd say, and then let it slip that I had seen it, and she left in a rage, slamming the door and spilling coffee all over the front seat of my car."

"Oh, my God, your poor car."

"I know. So then you feel sorry enough for me to take off your clothes now?" I said, undoing a second button on the blouse.

"Maybe. Tell me about the balls. And don't lie! Did you listen to the recording?"

"Yes."

"And…?"

"Ask me a mathematical question?"

"Like what?"

"I don't know, …like the square root of three hundred and sixty. Let's see how smart it made me."

"You're kidding, right?"

"Right. I had plans to lead you on about this, but just the thought of seeing you naked has me so turned on that I can only tell the truth which is that Ken's balls did absolutely nothing for me. But I've always suspected as much. I'll tell you this, though. I don't know what we're going to do, but like I said this afternoon at the meeting, whatever it is, we've got to do it soon. If something happens because kids are listening to that audio track, the shit is going to hit the fan."

"What do you mean? What could happen?"

"I don't know. It's just a feeling."

"Ah, yes, the Scarlucci instinct for trouble that serves you so well. All right, what are we going to do?"

"Take our clothes off. My information days are over."

"Brian, I'm serious."

"So am I. We have a truckload of things to discuss and decide about, but first things first." I set my wine glass on the floor and undid more buttons. Her blouse fell open as, placing her own glass on the nightstand next to the bed, her hands worked on my shirt buttons. "And do you know why?"

"Why?" Sherri said, leaning in and kissing the bare skin of my chest as she opened my shirt.

"Because I have a surprise. Stand up."

She looked at me in amusement, dropping her blouse as she stood with me and I pulled back the bed spread. A veritable plethora of crisp one hundred dollar bills covered the sheets from the headboard to the foot of the bed.

"Oh, my god! The money! Look at it. How much is there?"

"According to my count, each envelope contained twenty-five thousand dollars, and I'm no math whiz but I think that makes a grand total of FIFTY THOUSAND DOLLARS!"

"FIFTY THOUSAND DOLLARS!" She reached down, touching the money in cautious disbelief, and then looked up at me. "Brian, fifty thousand dollars…?"

I smiled. "I know. And since I can't decide how to proceed, I thought we might start by sleeping on it, which is just a euphemism for what I really have in mind, you understand. Now take the rest of your clothes off."

The look again. "You're kidding."

"Why don't you ever believe me?"

"You want to have sex on this money?"

"You bet your bottom dollar I do. Think what this new twist in our sex life will do for that nagging separate climax problem we've been experiencing lately. This time we should be right on the money."

"But it seems so…I don't know."

"Then you don't want to do it," I teased.

She reached for my belt buckle. "Absolutely I want to do it. Drop those drawers and let's get to it."

"Of course, we may end up staining a few hundred," I said as my buckle opened and she lowered my zipper, "so we have to try to keep the wet spot off Ken's share. Some of it's his, you know."

116

"You do understand what a sick human being you are, don't you?" she said, stepping out of her neatly-creased slacks as I dropped my pants and did the same.

"No more talking," I answered, unhooking the front clip of her bra and slipping it off her shoulders as I kissed each breast lightly, grazing my teeth across the instantly-hardening nipples.

Sherri sank to her knees and pulled my boxers down, her hands grasping my hips. "You know, to really understand exactly what took place on that video, we need a reenactment of the crime." She took the very hard part of me in her hand, looking up and meeting my eyes as her head moved closer. "What do you think?"

"Who's the sick puppy now?" I queried, not really caring.

And then my cell phone rang.

Sherri stood up.

She said nothing and moved to where her glass of wine sat on the nightstand. The phone rang again. I moved to her, holding her, kissing her neck softly. The phone rang again.

"I'm sorry. I have to get it."

She took a slow sip of wine. The phone rang again.

"Oh, I know you do. Go on, Brian. It's all right."

I had made it a very clear understanding from the beginning. If the phone rang, I had to answer it because it might mean there was a problem with Evelyn. It had happened before more than once, but always during work, never when Sherri and I were together. However, there was always that chance, and ignoring a distress call concerning my wife could not happen.

I grabbed the phone from the inner pocket of my jacket that hung on a hook by the door, my eyes watching Sherri, totally at ease with her nakedness, watching me as she sipped on her wine by the bed.

"Hello."

Seconds ticked by as I listened.

Something about my demeanor must have broadcast the devastating impact of what I was hearing because Sherri put down her wine and moved to me, her face filled with concern.

"All right, I understand," I said into the phone. "I'll see what I can do. I'll call you if I learn anything more."

Stunned, I ended the call, unable to speak. Sherri moved close to me, her hand touching my arm.

"Brian, what is it?"

"That was Mary J.," I said. "Laura Silverman committed suicide today. Her mother found her in the bathroom a few minutes ago when she arrived home from work. Laura had severed a main artery while cutting herself, and bled to death."

Laura Silverman was a student we both knew. She was a troubled girl. We had a special *watch list* from Mary Ellen Drury on such students. In the case of Laura Silverman, the girl had been placed on the list because she was a cutter, which means that she was so emotionally numb and unstable she would take a knife and cut herself repeatedly so that, through the pain, she could feel something... anything.

Recently, however, Laura had been showing signs of improvement, and had sort of found a home in the English department as a student aide, more specifically as a student aide for Ken Valentine, who had taken her under his protective wing.

"Oh, how awful," Sherri said, moving closer to me for comfort at the news.

"Oh, it's worse. I'm not finished," I said, shaking my head, feeling a horrible numbness of my own clamping down on me from what I had heard. "She committed suicide while listening to Ken Valentine's audio track of the Tibetan balls on her iPhone."

"Oh, God no!"

I shook my head, still unable to accept what I had heard, speaking with absolutely no intention of going for humor, just a dazed Brian Scarlucci talking his talk.

"Goddamn my instincts. Why can't I be wrong once in a while?" I said. "The shit *has* hit the fan."

TWELVE

AS I LAY DYING

"Thaaat youu, Bwiiiin," my wife's voice called to me as I came through the back door.

"Yeah. Be right there," I said, throwing my jacket on a kitchen chair and, cell phone in hand, moving to the hallway. I had tried both Ken's home phone and cell phone several times. No answer at either. Where the hell was he? It was imperative that I reach him before we all gathered in Mary J. Talley's office at 5:30 in the morning to decide how to handle the situation. I tried his cell again as I stood in the hall prior to entering the den, but it went immediately to voice mail.

Shit.

As always, my wife's wheelchair was by the sofa, facing the television. Joyce, the female attendant for the evening, sat on the sofa nearby, dressed in the requisite white outfit of top, slacks, and sneakers. I gave her a hello wave as I crossed the room to Evelyn, who shifted her eyes towards me since she could not move her brace-supported head.

"How waaasss youuur meeeeeeetinng?" Evelyn asked.

"Same old, same old," I said, leaning in and softly kissing what had once been my wife's flawlessly smooth-skinned forehead, but was now just part of her deformed and partially-crushed skull area.

There had been several operations, but the results had not been too successful. The car crash had been a head-on, the
120

other driver crossing over the grassy median and into the oncoming traffic. Evelyn had been in the passing lane on the opposite side, accelerating beyond seventy-five miles an hour to pass a slower moving vehicle when the impact occurred.

Surgeons had done what they could, meaning my wife could move her eyes and her toothless twist of a mouth and not much else. Her breathing apparatus ran to a portable machine on the platform at the back of her wheelchair. What remained of her shrunken, shattered, skeleton of a body was covered by a powder blue quilt of delicate-winged angels who carried flowers. I had given the quilt to her as a present on her last birthday.

"And how we doin' tonight?" I asked, kneeling beside the wheelchair.

Her eyes narrowed, trying to smile to me. "Okaaaay."

I smiled, placing a tender hand on the quilt, and turned my head toward the sofa. "Is she telling a little white lie, Joyce?"

Joyce smiled and answered quietly. "She's a little tired."

"Pain meds taken?"

Joyce nodded. "Right on schedule. "

I looked back to my wife. "You're up late tonight, you know. Ready for bed?"

"I waaaittted uup foor youu," Evelyn said. "Wiiilll youu carrrwyyy me iiiinn?"

"Nothing would make me happier," I said, surreptitiously changing the ringer on my cell phone to vibrate and slipping it into my pants pocket as I stood to lift her.

They had given me training on the proper procedure for lifting and carrying someone in Evelyn's condition, so I knew what to do. Supporting her head with the removable brace and sliding my other arm under her body, my own knees bent against the movement, I lifted my wife's body gently into the air and, nodding to Joyce, headed toward the bedroom, amazed at how light her broken frame had become. It seemed that every time I lifted her lately, she weighed less than the last time, and it frightened me so much I refused to dwell on it.

Once she was in bed, covered and hooked up to the machine that was on a bedside cart along with a wide supply of needed medication and emergency supplies, I turned off the light and bent to kiss my wife goodnight.

"Wiilll you lii wiithhh meee fooor a wiiillle," her voice asked softly.

"You're not too tired?"

"Nooooo,"

I went around to the foot of the bed, kicked off my shoes and crawled in beside her. Though I always hoped these moments of closeness would last longer, I knew from experience that she would be asleep almost immediately. The medication had long since dulled her responses.

Snuggling in next to her, I stroked her head, humming a little tune that had always been one of our favorites without even thinking about the fact that I was doing it. *Where Have All The Flowers Gone?* by Pete Seeger.

"Briiin?" she said in the darkness.

"Yes."

"It'sss awllriight."

"What's all right?"

"Whaaaatevver youu doo, awwaaay froom meee.   I waaaant youu tooo knooo. It'sss awllriight."

"Evelyn...."

"Noo. Donnn't taalwk. I kooww I saaaid iit beeafowre buut I mean iit. It'sss awllright. I understaaaand."

Hating my weaknesses, I stroked the thin wisps of loose hair that remained on her head and listened.

"Sommetiiimes as I laay heeeree dyyying, I thiinnnk...."

"Evelyn, please don't say things like that...."

"Your'ree noot liistenniing, Brwiiiiin," her teasing voice disciplined me in the darkness.

I stopped talking.

"Sommetiiimes I thiink abowt wheen we uuused to goo toow thaa Plaanting Fieelds aannd haave a piicnicc, reemmbeember?"

"Of course I remember."

"Reemembeemer hoow beeeuteefuuul thaa floowweers weere?"

"Yes."

"Alwaaays haave flooowweers on myy graavee, wiiill youuu? I looove floowwers."

"Evelyn, I'm serious now. Stop talking like that."

"And remmeember weee maadee looovee thaattt tiime aand I wass scaared sooomeonne would caaatch ussss,

123

anndd remmmemmbeeer hoow youuu heellld mee affterwaaards aand wee laay theerre loookiiiing aat awlll the preeety flooowweers arouuund uss?"

"Yes, of course I remember," I whispered, unwanted tears suddenly collecting at the edges of my eyes and sliding down my cheeks. I turned my head away in the darkness so that she would not know.

"IIII lovvedd that," her voice said.

And then she was asleep.

And I lay there next to my sleeping wife, my arms holding her tiny broken wasted body, and cried like a baby.

The vibration of my cell phone brought me out of it. I carefully moved from the bed and out of the room. Once in the hallway, I took out the cell and checked the number display in the window.

It was Ken.

I answered, aware that we had come full circle, he and I.

It was now *my* time to do whatever I could to save my friend.

BOOK TWO

WITCH HUNT

PROLOGUE

"Do you have the money?"

The one in a turban and flowing white robe who spoke was very tall with long, slender hands that reached forward as he asked the question.

"What precisely do you bring me?" said the leader.

The tall one smiled, revealing gaping holes among dirty, yellowed teeth. "What you requested," he answered. "It has many names. O-isopropyl methylphosphonofluoridate. GB. The name you know for the nerve agent is Sarin."

"And what is the quantity?"

"Enough." He looked around the hot crudely-furnished room, his eyes going from the wooden table and chairs in the center of the dirt floor to those who stood near the leader. "Do you have the money?"

The leader answered with another question. "It cannot be detected, this Sarin?"

The slender hands waved in denial. "The vapor is colorless and odorless. No one will know until it is too late."

"And this vapor. It can be propelled through the round air passages that have been constructed for air conditioning within the walls of a large building?"

"Oh, yes. It will move easily through such forced air ducts."

126

He glanced back at the entrance behind him. The door had been closed.

"I need to see the money," the tall man said.

The leader looked at the man for many moments, saying nothing. Then he nodded to one of those with him. A package wrapped in newspaper appeared from among those standing with the leader. It was handed to the tall one in the robe, who grinned widely, almost caressing the package that had been given to him.

"How long?" asked the leader.

"How long?"

"Before the vapor released in the air ducts produces a result."

The man shrugged. "A very short time. Almost immediately after exposure."

"And the effects?" asked the leader. The man frowned. "Shortness of breath? Nausea? What is the reaction to be expected? When exposed to the vapor, what will happen?"

The tall man's blood-veined eyes widened in understanding and he nodded, his smile once again revealing the broken, yellow teeth.

"People will begin to die," he said.

THIRTEEN
EMPTY SUITS

Daylight was seeping into the bleak, cloud-covered morning as I pulled into the faculty parking lot of Central High School. The few cars parked in the lot were ones I knew, and they gave me a quick overview of who was to be in attendance at our early morning meeting.

Richie the custodian's car was there, of course. He was always the first to arrive in the morning to open the building; however, he would not be attending the meeting. Richie would have first looked at his list of things to do for the day, and then, without doing any of them, he would have gone immediately to the teacher's lounge where he would be asleep, snoring away.

I saw Ken Valentine's Ford Explorer parked by the Art Wing entrance, and pulled up next to it. Mary J.'s black Lexus was already in the lot, as was Sherri's Subaru. And, just to make things complete, next to Mary J.'s Lexus sat Laurence Pugh's Volkswagen Beetle, with the vanity license plate WETEACH glaring from the bug's rounded backside bumper.

Ken was still sitting in the front seat of his car, and I got out of the Volvo and crossed the dark lot to where he had parked, knocking on the driver's door window. He had been sitting with his eyes closed, but I knew, unlike Richie, Ken was not catching up on his sleep. I doubted that Ken had slept at all. He turned his head, opening tired sad eyes to look at me through the glass. Then the window lowered.

"Okay?" I said.

"Not really."

I smiled a soft friendly smile. "I'm with you all the way on this. I know I don't have to tell you that, but I wanted to say it aloud."

"Thanks. Brian." His eyes clouded. "Jesus, it's so horrible. That sweet innocent kid. She seemed so much better lately. How could I have missed the warning signs?"

"It's more complex than that, and you know it, Ken. The girl was dealing with issues that have nothing to do with being your school aide or responding to the ways you were trying to help her. You cannot blame yourself in any way, shape, or form about this, and I have no intention of allowing you to go anywhere near there." I grabbed the door handle, released the catch, and pulled the car door toward me, holding it open for him. "Come on." I nodded toward the other cars in the lot. "They're probably already inside waiting for us."

He agreed and slowly climbed out of the car, suddenly looking much older than his usual granola-filled vegan behavior always indicated. "No matter what you say, since Laura was listening to the audio track when it happened, I'm going to have trouble with this, aren't I."

I closed the door after him. "Let's go inside and talk this out before we start making any assumptions," I said, knowing he was absolutely correct, and knowing he knew I knew it.

There is a specific type of strained hushed silence that occurs when you come upon people and the conversation has obviously just abruptly stopped because it was about you. That kind of silence filled the interior space of Mary J. Talley's office when Ken and I entered the room. Sherri Walsh, however, came to her feet, speaking as she moved to Ken, in an attempt to fill the embarrassing void by welcoming him.

"I'm sorry, Ken," she said, taking his hand. "I know how hard you tried to help Laura."

Ken nodded and allowed Sherri to guide him to one of the unoccupied seats that surrounded Mary J.'s large mahogany desk. I nodded to Mary J. and Larry Pugh, who had situated himself in the side chair nearest to his boss, as I took the only remaining chair on the opposite side of the desk. Ever thoughtful, Mary J. had provided containers of Starbucks coffee for each of us in a multiple cup holder at the front of her desk, and I took one with a smile of thanks to her as Ken sat down next to Sherri directly in front of the school principal.

"Good morning, Ken," Mary J. Talley said, putting her own container of coffee down on the desk and folding her hands in front of her. "Thank you for coming in early so that we can discuss how we intend to handle things. Sherri has told me about your attempts to help this girl, and I want you to know that your efforts are appreciated...."

The sentence stopped rather than ended, and I knew her opening words were only a prelude to a "however ."

"However," Mary J. continued after a beat. "I'm sure you also understand the seriousness of the situation. The problem we're facing is twofold: first, we must deal with the suicide of a member of the student body...never an easy situation. I contacted our two social workers, and both Mary Ellen and John will be available all day in the Counseling Center along with any counselors who happen to be free at any given time for students who feel the need to talk. In addition, I alerted Richie when I arrived this morning, and he is preparing a memorial board in Laura's name that will be positioned in the main lobby and will be available so students and staff can place flowers, poems, personal thoughts, and any other materials there in her memory. The board will be moved to the lobby following my general announcement, which I will make at the beginning of first period. At that time, I will explain in the most general terms that a member of the student body, Laura Silverman, has passed away and ask for a moment of silence in her memory. Then I will explain that anyone who feels the need may be given a pass to the Counseling Center, and that teachers should honor such a request, and finally I will explain about the memorial board we are making available.

"That takes care of the immediate problem of informing the student body and staff about the tragedy. Now, this is even more difficult because, as you know, tonight is Parent/Teacher Conference night, which means the school will be loaded with parents asking questions and spreading rumors. I have spoken with Superintendent Farnsworth, and the decision is that the conference will go on as scheduled. I'm going to call a brief faculty meeting immediately after 9th period to make sure teachers are aware of how to field questions from inquiring parents."

Mary J. paused again, and looked specifically at Ken.

"...Which brings us to the second aspect of our problem. I don't want to mince words here, Ken. The fact that the girl was listening to something you had prepared for her at the time of her death makes the situation very, very serious. This is especially true since it is my understanding that what she was listening to is related to an activity that has been taking place during your class lessons. Further, I am told this activity is against a stated school policy and involves not only the use of iPads for a non-curriculum activity in the classroom, but also for some degree of guided group meditation, something this school district policy absolutely forbids taking place within the classroom environment."

"Mrs. Talley...," Ken said quietly.

"No, not now," Mary J. responded, cutting him off. "I intend to hear everything you have to say in this matter, but first, we must be very clear about our actions and public responses in the immediate future. First and most importantly, should the press be informed about what has happened, and we have reason to believe that it is going to happen, no one, and I mean no one, is to talk to anyone in the news media about this. All questions and queries are to be directed to my office and only my office. I will make that crystal clear at the faculty meeting."

Mary J. paused once again, drawing in a long breath before she spoke. Her pale complexion deepened in a flush of color. Her unwavering gaze stayed on Ken.

Uh, oh. Big trouble.

"Secondly, Ken," she said, "Dr. Farnsworth does feel that, considering the circumstances surrounding Laura's death, it would be best if you...."

And that was as far as Mary J. Talley got, because, without a preceding knock, her office door opened, and the Superintendent of Schools, Dr. Francis J. Farnsworth, followed by Assistant Superintendent Arnold Federly, came into the room, and we all stood up.

The Empty Suits had arrived.

Now I don't wish to take credit for maliciously humorous creativity that is not of my own invention, so I want to make clear that the term "Empty Suit" used in reference to either or both of the head administrators of our school district is not mine, but rather has been used by unknown sources from within the high school staff since before my appointment. However, once established, the term stuck to the two who had just made an unannounced entrance to Mary J. Talley's office like dog shit to the sole of a shoe.

Not that the term was necessarily true. It just had a nice malicious ring to it. As far as I could see, there was plenty going on inside those administrative suits. It was just that most

133

of it was not of the highest intellectual level, and almost all of it involved self-preservation and advancement of salary and self, rather than a concentration on the advancement of student education.

Dr. Francis Farnsworth was a major player in the game of Superintendent Roulette that is currently sweeping the country's educational systems. Superintendents in the game get a doctorate degree in *Education*, where the curriculum is one of busywork and business administration instead of one with true intellectual content as would be found in say *a real doctorate degree.* The said Doctor of Education then proceeds to move from district to district, always at a higher salary than before, on the wings of a wide, ever-present white-toothed smile, an unending stream of glad-handing bullshit, and a snow white reputation consisting of often needless innovative publicity touting educational changes. In the case of the Central School District, Dr. Farnsworth had even convinced the district to hire a public relations firm that would assure such good publicity took place.

Dr. Francis J. Farnsworth was a master of the game, and had moved through four previous school districts before coming to the Central School District with sterling credentials for a salary that was reportedly in the six figures, in addition to having a district car at his disposal and assorted bonuses.

Arnold T. Federly had followed a different route. A master "numbers pusher," aka staff reducer, which means teachers lose their jobs because of budget cuts, Federly had been in the district for years as Business Manager. He continued to hang on through the shifting of superintendents by taking care of business in the hopes that, someday, rather than bringing in fresh Doctorate roulette blood, the Board of Education would, in its wisdom, realize the superb professional they had in-house who had over the years saved them bundles of cash by cutting staff and increasing class enrollment numbers. They would then promote him to the head job without his having to move his family all over the country playing Superintendent Roulette.

Unfortunately, Long Island school systems had recently come under the scrutiny of state auditors with a neighboring district's business manager facing a possible prison term for embezzlement, and poor Federly spent most of his waking hours living in fear that auditors would pounce on his business practices and find some horrendous monetary oversight before he had been able to move into the coveted position that Farnsworth still occupied.

In both cases, if further advancement were to be on the horizon, one thing could never happen: BAD PUBLICITY. Public education is by definition, just that: Public. And bad publicity and public education were like oil and water; they do not mix well and are to be avoided at all costs.

In addition, public school districts are all too often run by members of a board of education who have all-encompassing power usually reserved for a position like that of a ship's captain. However, unlike a ship's captain, who knows virtually everything about the vessel and the crew under his command, board of education members usually know next to nothing about running a school district. They are able to bitch their way onto the elected board by publicly complaining to anyone who will listen about the inadequacies of their community's school system and, once in the positions of authority, they become addicted to the power and recognition that the positions provide. Since they have no experience and don't know a damned thing about how to improve the student educational process in the district, which is what they've been elected to do, the most important job that falls to board of education members is choosing a superintendent who can do the job for them. Therefore, it is absolutely critical that they only choose Superintendent Roulette winners to run the school system, and winners do not get bad publicity.

That is why the aforementioned Empty Suits had arrived in Principal Mary J. Talley's office. No one who stood as they entered thought for a second that the team of Farnsworth and Federly had arrived at this dawn meeting because they cared about poor Laura Silverman, Ken Valentine, or even how the tragedy affected the student body.

These Suits cared about only one thing: Containment. Any bad publicity must be minimized at all costs.

If that meant someone had to hang to set things straight, so be it. They would unflinchingly lead that someone to the scaffold, where the executioner stood waiting, rope in hand. And we all also knew that in this particular *containment*, Ken

Valentine was going to be the one standing over the scaffold's trap door, the hangman's rope tightly affixed around his thin throat.

"Gentleman, would you like some coffee?" Mary J. asked, gesturing toward the containers on the front of the desk.

Farnsworth spoke, no white-toothed smile, no glad hand, all business. "No thank you." He looked at Ken Valentine. "Mr. Valentine, would you mind stepping out of the office for a moment please?"

Ken met the Superintendent's gaze, standing and actually taking a step toward the man. "I would prefer to stay," he said, his voice strong and clear.

"That is not an option, I'm afraid. We'll call for you in a few moments."

Ken held Farnsworth's gaze a moment longer, and then, after a quick glance in my direction and catching my briefest of nods, without another word, he moved past Farnsworth and Federly and out of the office, closing the door behind him.

Farnsworth crossed to in front of the principal's desk, where he changed his mind and took a container of coffee. He then waved a finely-manicured hand to the rest of us.

"Let's all sit down."

We all sat down.

Farnsworth took the chair vacated by Ken Valentine. Federly stood by the door, I assumed to guard it in case Ken changed his mind, and came bursting back into the room. Farnsworth took a sip of coffee before he spoke.

"I have decided to temporarily have Mr. Valentine relieved of his teaching duties," he said. "And I wanted to attend this meeting so that there will be no question that this is my decision, rather than Mrs. Talley's. In fact, should he ask, you may inform Mr. Valentine that Mary here spoke very highly of his performance as a teacher, and voiced her objection to his being taken out of the classroom. Ultimately, however, such a decision rests with me, and although I took Mary's objection into consideration, I have decided that, for the moment, this course of action is best...until matters can be clarified, of course. For the time being, he will be assigned temporarily to a desk job in the administration building. Let's let him take the day off and have him report first thing tomorrow morning."

"Who will be taking over his teaching assignment?" Sherri asked.

"We'll use the permanent substitute who serves your department, Sherri. Gene Knickerbocker I believe his name is. For absentees, we'll bring in substitutes as needed." Sherri nodded. "I'd appreciate it if you'd take care of the arrangements, Sherri, and inform Knickerbocker of his duties when he reports to school this morning, explaining to him that this is very open-ended, of course. And tonight, I would like you to simply post a sign on Mr. Valentine's room stating that he was not able to attend the Parent/Teacher Conference, and parents who wish can leave a phone number or contact him by email."

Sherri nodded again. "Understood. I'll take care of it. But I want to go on record here by saying that I know for a fact Ken cared a great deal about helping this young woman. We all did. That's why she was a student aide in the department."

I cleared my throat, taking the cue from Sherri. Ready or not, it was time for Brian Scarlucci to step up to the plate.

"I would like to state my objection to Mr. Valentine being relieved of duty," I said.

Dr. Farnsworth took another sip from the coffee cup he held and turned toward me. "Your objection is noted, Brian, but I'm afraid the decision stands."

"Then let me add support to my objection," I continued, all too aware that I was not supposed to do such a thing. "It seems to me that relieving Mr. Valentine of his teaching duties sends out the message to both the school and the community that he is guilty of something. Otherwise, why is he not continuing to teach his classes? Wouldn't the better course of action be to assume he has done nothing inappropriate, rather than fan the rumors with such an action? Let him continue teaching, at least until there has been time to establish exactly what has taken place and why."

"We know what happened," Arnold Federly said, taking a couple of steps into the room. "A girl is dead."

"Laura Silverman was a very troubled girl with a history of mental problems, none of which has anything to do with Ken Valentine," I shot back at Federly.

I was willing to tread a tad softly with Farnsworth for the moment since he was the one most responsible for my becoming an assistant principal at Central High, but Federly and I had never seen eye to eye. More than once in the past, he had questioned my spending practices in supplying school inventory. He never openly stated that there was impropriety involved in my spending of funds, but the implication was always there, and it came after I had put in hours upon hours of hard work to make sure every single expenditure was backed up and accounted for to the last dime. I, of course, had verbally responded to his insinuations about my spending practices by telling him that perhaps he should spend more time verifying the credentials of the people he hired to install the faulty high school air conditioning system instead of questioning the hard work of others. That hadn't exactly enhanced our working relationship. Bottom line: there was no way I intended to take any sanctimonious shit from Arnold T. Federly.

"If Ken is guilty of anything, it is only of trying to help that girl," I added. "I hardly think reaching out to a troubled student warrants having him taken out of the classroom."

"There has been talk of inappropriate actions on the part of Mr. Valentine and this girl," Federly countered. "Are you aware of that, Mr. Scarlucci? And the fact that Mr. Valentine is black makes the matter even more sensitive."

Farnsworth gave Federly a hard "I'm handling this" look, and the Assistant Superintendent stepped back again.

Instinctually sensing the worst, I stood and went after Federly, more than ready to take care of business with Mr. Business Man after he had had the audacity to drop the racial card.

"Ken Valentine's being black is in no way relevant to this situation, Dr. Federly. What is that supposed to mean anyway...*inappropriate action*? What kind of inappropriate action?"

"I would say accusations of pedophilia justify the steps we've taken," Federly answered, his accountant eyes narrowing in hostility. "And the fact that we have a black male teacher accused of making inappropriate advances toward an underage white student is *very* relevant, Mr. Scarlucci. The news media will eat us alive when this gets out."

I glared at him, and he adjusted his glasses, actually taking a tiny additional step back from me. In the background, Laurence Pugh coughed nervously.

"Yeah, well I'm telling you that is bullshit, Dr. Federly. Every bit of it! Are you hearing me? That is unequivocal and unadulterated bullshit! I know Ken Valentine better than any person on this earth, and I will not listen to you defame his name and degrade him as a human being with such a disgusting slur on his character. Are you telling me someone made such an accusation since yesterday when this girl passed away?"

Mary J. spoke up. "Brian, sit down, please. Getting emotional is not going to help. Let's please try to discuss this rationally and without...."

"No, I'm not going to sit down, goddamn it. This is bullshit, and I will not stand for it! You make the poor guy leave the room, and then, noting he is a black man, accuse him of being a pedophile, going after one of his white students who has just committed suicide. Christ! This is unbelievable."

"Brian," Superintendent Farnsworth said, firm of voice and ever-in-charge. "I know this matter puts you in a difficult position. I am aware that Ken Valentine is your friend. However, I assure you, we are not acting on some wild suspicion, but at the request of Laura's mother who has seen some of the girl's emails, and, according to her, the content of the email communications with Mr. Valentine is questionable. Later this morning, all school email records of Ken Valentine's will be turned over to the authorities as will Laura Silverman's computer so that any communications between Mr. Valentine and the deceased can be examined. If, after such an examination and further investigation, there is no evidence of impropriety on the part of Mr. Valentine, I will put him back in the classroom. How does that sound?"

"Frankly, it sounds like shit, sir," I answered. Clearly, a man who was not accustomed to people responding to him in such a manner, Dr. Farnsworth's mouth actually opened in surprise, and he instantaneously closed it again, traces of anger seeping into his otherwise calm demeanor.

Peripherally, I could see Sherri Walsh trying to catch my gaze, her eyes filled with nervous warning. And somewhere far in the back of my head I could hear an interior voice telling me to cool off; I had a job at stake here and a handicapped wife at home who continued to need very expensive care, but I was in the zone of no return, defending my best friend, and so I pushed on toward the abyss.

"Look, get Ken in here and ask him, and stop all this behind-the-back bullshit!"

"Brian!" Mary J. interjected, cutting me off. "I would appreciate it if you would stop swearing. It is not helping!"

"Oh sorry," I replied, correcting myself. "Let's stop all this behind-the-back *crap*, and ask the man, for God's sake. We are all innocent until proven guilty, remember? Here's my take on it: The mother is understandably an emotional wreck and grasping at straws so that she can justify her daughter's horrific actions, not have to blame herself, and pin it on an innocent teacher who also happens to be a black man, which gives her accusations an even bigger inflammatory punch. Well, I'm telling you, Mr. Ken Valentine is not guilty, and I will not allow this situation to turn into a witch hunt with Ken Valentine as the scapegoat. The girl was a known cutter, for crying out loud. She was on our Watch List. Maybe she wasn't attempting to kill herself. Maybe it was an accident. Maybe she was...."

"Brian," Farnsworth cut in, his voice increasing ever so slightly in volume. "I want to remind you that you are an administrator in this building. You might want to pause for a moment and do some serious reflection on exactly where you stand."

There was a long beat of silence as I looked at Dr. Francis Farnsworth. Again, Laurence Pugh coughed nervously.

"You mean as in *if you're not with us, you're against us*?" I asked. "Are you threatening me?"

"Not at all. I am advising you," Superintendent Farnsworth responded, coming to his feet. "Just because the man is your friend does not mean he is innocent of these charges, and I'm *advising* you that as an administrator in this district, your job is to do the right thing *for* this district, which is exactly what I'm doing. If Ken Valentine *is* guilty of these charges that have been brought against him by the mother and I knew about them and left him in the classroom, I would be remiss in my duties, and that, Mr. Scarlucci, is not going to happen, because I do what I've been authorized to do without allowing my emotions to hinder my actions. Furthermore, there is no *behind the back crap* as you called it going on here. All of the things you're suggesting as possible scenarios will be examined, I assure you. I merely wanted the administrators of this building to be aware of the situation so that they would have an understanding of my decisions before I spoke to Mr. Valentine. Now my decision is that we are going to find out the true facts of exactly what is going on in this case, and then we will act on those facts. And until then, Mr. Valentine is assigned to desk duty in the administration building. Is that clear?"

"Crystal clear," I replied.

Ignoring me momentarily, Farnsworth turned his attention to Federly. "And let's be very clear about this also. Dr. Federly spoke unwisely, I'm afraid. Race has absolutely nothing to do with this, and I do not want to hear the fact that Ken Valentine is black mentioned by anyone in this room in connection with this case ever again. Is *that* clear?"

There were nods all around.

"I'm sorry, Frank. I was just thinking about the press," Federly replied contritely.

"I know precisely what you were thinking about, Arnie. Next time, think before you speak. As far as we're concerned, race is not an issue in this situation, but if it should become an issue, it cannot, under any circumstances, come from anyone connected with this school district. Are we clear?"

"Yes, we're clear," Federly answered quietly. "Sorry."

That little potentially explosive issue settled for the moment, Farnsworth turned his attention back to me.

"So, my question to you, Mr. Scarlucci, since any further discussion on the matter of how I am handling the Ken Valentine situation has come to an end, is this: As an administrator of this building, what do you intend to do?"

"Serve this school in every way I can to the best of my ability, sir," I said, the two of us now face to face. "Just like you hired me to do. And I will also tell you what I'm going to do as Ken Valentine's friend. I'm going to go out that door and take my friend to breakfast. And, I'm going to tell him exactly what went on in here and what he is being accused of behind closed doors, including the reference Dr. Federly made of his being black, so that he knows precisely what he's up against and can have an opportunity to defend himself. What time do you want him to be at the administration building tomorrow?"

"Eight o'clock sharp!" Farnsworth answered a little too loudly, his jaw muscle twitching noticeably.

"Fine. He'll be there," I said. Then, I added, after a beat. "How about me? Should I come back, or is expressing a difference of opinion not an option with this administration?"

Farnsworth exhaled heavily, and sat down, speaking without looking back in my direction.

"By all means, go look after your friend, Brian," he said. "Just be back here before the start of the school day to assume your duties. This is going to be a very difficult day, and I'm sure Mary and Larry here can use your help."

And that was it. No one else spoke, although Pugh did continue his nervous coughing into the pulsating silence that followed Superintendent Farnsworth's words.

Without looking at Sherri Walsh or anyone else, I turned, brushed past Federly with a movement that was close enough to make him step back awkwardly, and left the office.

….And maybe my job.

FOURTEEN
BREAKFAST AND BAD NEWS

Ironically, Ken was far calmer than I had been when hearing about the accusation. After getting him out of the school building as quickly as possible, I told him to meet me in front of IHop, and away we went. Once we had both pulled our cars up in front of the restaurant, however, I jumped into his Explorer and ranted on and on until Ken shouted me into silence.

"BRIAN," he said, grabbing my arm.

"What?" I answered. "Aren't you appalled that The Suits would do something like this? And how about the business of you being black, for Christ's sake. It's fucking unbelievable."

"Well, I am black, you know."

I gave him a look, and he capitulated. "All right, yes, of course I'm appalled. But I also know you, and why you're so unhinged at the moment. You need to eat. Am I right?"

Hey, what can I say? The guy knows his friend. Some people can function on nothing more than coffee in the morning. However, I have never been one of them. I can skip lunch, but I've got to have breakfast in order to deal with the day. A nice Hungry Man breakfast such as bacon, egg, and cheese with salt and pepper on a roll and I'm ready to face all comers. So, after getting next to no sleep, rising in the pre-dawn hours, and having an early morning showdown with my bosses without so much as a frosted Pop Tart in my tummy,

147

Ken probably did have a point about absence of morning nutrition affecting my temperament. Not that I was ready to admit it under the circumstances, you understand.

"I think this is a little more important than food, Ken," I objected.

"So if you don't want to eat, why did you have us come to a breakfast place?" he asked.

"Yeah,…well, I *could* eat, I guess."

He opened the Explorer's driver's door.

"Come on," he said, smiling in the satisfaction of knowing me so well. "Let's get some breakfast. Things are bound to look better after we've had some food."

And they did.

After plowing through a plate of blueberry pancakes smothered in maple syrup, four crispy brown grilled sausages, and three fried eggs, sunny-side up, I found I was noticeably calmer as I sipped my third coffee and watched Ken finish his whole grain muffin.

"So, how should we handle this? What do you want to do?"

Ken took a sip of his green tea to wash down the remnants of his muffin, patted his lips with his napkin, and set the cup back in its saucer.

"First of all, Mrs. Silverman's accusations are nothing new," he said. "The woman is a lunatic of the first order, and has been twisting my attempts to help Laura into something foul and nasty for some time."

148

"How did you handle it?"

"I ignored it. To me, helping Laura Silverman seemed worth taking the mother's abuse. She also came on to me a couple of weeks ago when I took Laura home from a literature magazine meeting. She put the move on me as soon as Laura excused herself to go to the bathroom, so who knows what my rejecting the woman did to her psyche and whatever sick motivations are rolling around inside her disturbed little mind."

The fact that Laura Silverman's mother had made a play for Ken Valentine did not particularly surprise me. It wasn't the first time a woman had made a move on the man. The fact was, although he humbly waved off any such talk, Ken Valentine had Denzel Washington good looks. In fact, the finely-chiseled Jamaican aspect of his features made him even more attractive than Denzel. Women of all races and ethnicities simply could not resist looking at him. Whenever and wherever Ken Valentine passed by, female heads turned.

"How about the email?" I queried. "Can they do anything if they try to twist lecherous meanings into it?"

Ken shrugged. "Probably. I spent a lot of time trying to build up the girl's self esteem. You know, telling her that I liked her. That sort of thing. And telling her that what was more important than my liking her was that she like herself and realized how wonderful a person she was. Sure, you could probably twist that around if you were bent on making something disgusting out of it."

I shook my head. "Well, shit. That's not exactly what I want to hear, you know."

"Brian, there's no changing what is. And sadly, that is most true for poor Laura. I wish I had done and said more, both in emails and to her personally. Maybe she would still be alive."

"Ken, I don't mean to be insensitive about this, but right now, you've got to start concentrating on what we can do for you."

He stared at me a moment with a look of resignation that I found unsettling. "Whatever happens happens," he said. "I'll just have to deal with it the best way I can."

Before I could answer, our waitress came over to the table. She started to remove the dishes, but stopped momentarily as she gave Ken the once-over. I thought it was just the usual good-looks Valentine magnet that caught women's attention, but when she spoke, we both knew it was something far more serious.

"Hey, you're that guy."

"What guy?" I said, asking for both of us.

"The one whose picture was on the news a while ago...the teacher that's involved in that high school girl's suicide. Jeez, you better go. I think they said you're going to be arrested or something."

The girl hurriedly piled the remainder of the dirty dishes from our breakfast on the large tray she held and hurried away. Ken and I looked at each other.

150

"Well, fuck. You want to go?" I asked.

"No," Ken said. "I want to finish my tea."

"Where do you think they got a picture so fast."

"Found one in a yearbook probably."

"Okay. If it comes to it, I'll post your bail, you know."

"Yeah, how? Where you going to get that kind of money?"

I grinned mischievously. "I've come into quite a sum lately."

"Oh, shit, I forgot. Sal Mordento's gift. What are you doing about that one?"

"I have no idea. Let's deal with this right now. First of all, you're going to need a lawyer. You got one?"

Ken shook his head. "No one that I can think of at the moment."

"Okay, so that's one thing we have to put on the to-do list. I'll ask around. I also think you should contact John Hill, the teacher's union president, although my guess is you'll hear from him sometime today once the word gets out. When you talk to him, find out about the legality of them removing you from the classroom."

"If I'm arrested, I think it's a moot point."

"I still think you need to talk to him. Now what *about* bail money? Can you dig up the money if you have to?"

He nodded. "I think so. I've got some cash in savings, and I could take a second mortgage on the house."

"Okay, What else? I can give you the day if you need it, you know. Allow you to have some time to figure things out."

151

"What do you mean you can give me the day?"

I hesitated, but only for a moment. I knew where telling my friend about my second residence would lead, which was why I had never told him about my little secret studio apartment before, but it looked like the time had finally arrived.

"I have a place where you can stay for the day where no one will find you."

"You have a place?"

"Yeah, a little studio apartment on the north shore not far from here. I'll give you the key."

He thought about it for a minute.

"Okay, I'll take it. I need some time. Sounds like it may be the last that I'll have for a while. Come get me later this afternoon. Laura's wake will probably begin around three or four, and it's important to me that I go."

I shook my head. "That is not a good idea, Ken. After your home and the school, that's the third place the cops will look,

"I wasn't asking you if I should do it, Brian. I'm accepting your offer of seclusion because it will allow me to do it. Does your having this apartment on the sly mean what I think it means?"

I met his gaze. "Yes."

He nodded. "No judgments, Brian. That's what makes this such a good friendship. Can you tell me who it is or is that the reason you haven't told me? What is it? Do I know her?"

"Yes, you know her," I said, making a point of not looking away or dropping my gaze.

And then, suddenly, he knew. I could see it in his eyes. He tried to hide the realization, but his self-control wasn't fast enough.

"I see," he said, aware that I had seen his shock of surprise. "Well, that's something, isn't it."

"Ken, it just happened. Neither of us planned it. And we didn't tell you because...well, just because. I mean I didn't know how you felt about Sherri after all this time, and whether it would upset you. Shit. I should have told you. I'm sorry."

"You don't owe me any explanation. Sherri and I are good friends. We didn't mix right as a couple and we both knew it. We were something we fell into after her divorce from Bruce, but we both knew almost immediately that it wasn't going to work. It's okay. And I mean that. I'm actually happy for both of you. God knows, you deserve some moments of happiness and so does Sherri." He shook his head as the realization sank in. "Man, you two are pretty good, though. I had no idea. I thought we were all just pals."

"You would have caught on sooner or later, trust me. It's getting more difficult."

"Anyway, I'm glad you told me. We shouldn't have those kinds of secrets between us. And...I guess that means I should level with you also."

Suddenly it was my turn to be caught off guard.

"What does that mean?"

Ken looked at me. "How do you feel?"

"What?"

"How do you feel now that you've had breakfast? Have you calmed down a little?"

"Yeah, I guess."

"Okay, 'cause this is a biggie, Brian."

I frowned. "Bigger than what's happened already today?"

"I'm afraid so."

"Holy shit, Ken. Okay, let's have it." I tried to steel myself for whatever he was going to tell me, determined to take it in stride, but never could I have prepared myself for what my friend was about to tell me.

"I'm dying, Brian," Ken said quietly.

And I said nothing. I knew my friend far too well to think he would joke about such a thing. I listened to the restaurant noise of the early morning diners...the clattering of dishes coming from the kitchen beyond the swinging doors at the rear of the dining area that the waiters and waitresses moved in and out of with steaming trays of food. I watched as the waitress who had taken our dishes leaned in to the waitress at the counter and whispered to her, nodding to the TV that was mounted above the counter as the two of them stared in our direction. I looked back at my friend who sat across from me and I said nothing.

"It's testicular cancer," Ken volunteered finally. "The doctor found it a few months ago when I had my last physical. I'm told black men have an above average susceptibility to this

154

particular form of cancer. They did all the tests, of course. There are two types, one being pretty harmless. As luck would have it, that is not the one I have. I have the glandular type of testicular cancer which means it spreads more easily. It had already spread into my lymph system when they found it. I've taken several series of radiation, but none of it has had any effect. The cancer has continued to spread, and now it has reached the point where the doctors tell me there is nothing else that can be done." He paused a moment, and then added. "So, you might want to back off a little on the jokes about Ken's balls from now on."

I knew he was trying to be funny to lessen some of the impact of what he was telling me, but it didn't work. I was so devastated that I was unable to speak, and I found the information had caused a heaviness to form in my chest that was so severe I thought my heart was going to crack in half.

"Now you understand why the meditation of the Tibetan balls was so important to me. And I know you have your doubts, but it *is* working, Brian. Students are finding their minds opening up and grasping information in ways we wouldn't have thought possible. This discovery was to be my legacy. My gift to learning." He frowned momentarily, his composure slipping ever so slightly. "And now...Jesus, now it's become something that...."

"We're going to clear you on this bullshit, Ken," I said, finally finding my voice. "I give you my word."

He nodded doubtfully. "We'd better leave. But will you promise me a couple of things before we go?"

"Of course," I said.

"Promise me that you will not tell anyone about the...illness, and that includes Sherri...and Evelyn, of course."

"Okay."

"I mean it. I will not have any kind of unwarranted sympathy interfering with the reality of what takes place in my life while I still have one."

"I said I promise, Ken."

"Okay, and there's one more thing."

"Fine. Let's have it.

He smiled a knowing smile. "You might want to reconsider before you answer so quickly."

"Bullshit. You name it, I'll do it."

"Okay. I want you to continue listening to the audio track I made for you. Will you do that?"

"...Sure."

I had tried not to hesitate, but he saw right through me.

"No, Brian. I know you. Don't just tell me yes, and not do it. I want your word as my friend on this one. Promise me you will take the time to sit in a quiet place, calm your mind in meditation, and listen to the audio track of the Tibetan balls every day."

I frowned. "Come on, Ken. *Every day?*"

"Yes, every day. *You name it; I'll do it.* Those are your words. You're not going back on your word, are you, Mr. Scarlucci?"

I took out my wallet and threw money on the table.

"All right, all right, I'll do it," I said. "I'll listen to the hallowed sound of your goddamned balls every day, I promise. Man, talk about taking advantage of a situation."

Ken's smile widened, and in spite of everything that had happened to him in the past twenty-four hours, and in spite of what he had just told me about the cancer that was consuming him, I could see genuine happiness in his eyes.

"Thank you, my friend," he said. "And I promise *you*, you won't regret it. Now let's get out of here before the police come rushing in. I can't wait to see this secret little love nest of yours."

FIFTEEN
MR. PUGH GETS TANKED

After dropping Ken off at my *secret little love nest*, as he put it, I extracted a final promise from him – to call my cell at the first sign of trouble. Then I headed back to Central High, where things were already humming. In spite of what I had promised Farnsworth, it was well into first period by the time I got back to the school, so I knew Mary J. would have already made her announcement. In fact, a quick glance out the front plate glass windows that faced the main lobby confirmed it because the memorial board for Laura Silverman was already in place. Several students and a couple of faculty members were gathered around it.

Pretending not to notice the surreptitious secretary looks that came my way as I passed through the main office, my first stop was to see the Principal and make sure I still had a job to come back to. I apologized to her for being so emotional at the dawn meeting, and though she purported to understand under the circumstances, there was a new coolness to her receptivity.

Hey, the guy's my friend, lady. Deal with it.

Thanking her for her understanding and offering to help in any way I could, I asked if there was anything else that I needed to know, and she gave me the old good news-bad news punch. The good news was that after hearing from Sherri about Anthony Galli's action toward Maggie the previous afternoon, she had been able to convince Farnsworth to have the Security guard transferred to another building. My response to the news was positive, but I told her we should keep an eye out. My instinct told me that the guy was most definitely a loose cannon and that we should continue to expect trouble from Mr. Galli. Unable to stop myself from mentioning the irony of the situation, I told her that I would alert Security about the Security guard. She did not smile.

Principal definitely pissed off at Assistant Principal.

The bad news was that I had been ordered to attend the drama rehearsal after school in the auditorium on some pretext that would allow me to assess the relationship between Ms. Madison and her lead actor, Todd Hershborne. I knew Maggie would go ballistic over this little administrative chaperoning development, but at least it would be a piece of scenery, not my car that she kicked, and considering my morning track record, I figured I better do it, and agreed to the assignment without a whimper. The final nail in the bad news coffin was that someone – best guess being Mrs. Silverman – had already alerted the news media about the supposed teacher-student affair slash suicide which I knew, but also that what we had heard in the restaurant was true: Ken Valentine was going to be picked up by the authorities for questioning, although at this point, it was all just "routine."

Oh, yeah. And did I know where he was at the moment?

I explained that after filling him in on the accusations and transfer from his teaching assignment, we had parted company and I had no idea where he had gone. Then, *liar, liar, pants on fire* once again, I headed on down the hallway and into my own office, closing the door behind me.

Almost immediately there was a knock on that door, so I hurried to my desk, sat down, and shuffled some papers around as I called out a "yes, what is it?"

My secretary opened the door and stuck her head in.

"Good morning, Betty."

"Hi, Brian. How is everything? All right?"

"Couldn't be better, Betty. Thanks for asking. Just do me a favor, though, and let me know when the wolves are coming toward my door."

As you might imagine, Betty knows me pretty well, and responded with a sympathetic look of understanding. I didn't have to ask what she knew in terms of recent developments. She was a secretary. Of course, she knew everything.

"You got it," she said, giving me her best smile of support. "And I'm not sure if this is a wolf or not, but Joey Mordento is asking to see you. He says it's about Mr. Valentine."

I blew out a soft whistle. "And so it begins. That didn't take long."

Betty nodded. "Joey is in Ken's first period class, and seeing that Gene Knickerbocker was the substitute, he asked for a pass and came right here."

I sighed. "Okay, show him in."

While waiting for Sal's boy, I glanced over at my answering machine, doing a double take at the blinking message window: 132 messages since yesterday afternoon.

Holy shit. Usually there were ten or twelve at the most. This was not going to be easy.

I did not even have a chance to begin dealing with whatever horrible pending circumstances the dozens of unheard messages might portend, however, because Joey Mordento stepped into my office, presumably without a loaded .38 stuffed into the back of his belt.

My pal Sal's boy was a bundle of tension and compact muscle. Short curly black hair, tight facial features, and the kind of well-toned-from-daily-workouts-with-the-weights body that could easily beat the shit out of someone like me in about, say, twelve seconds. Cocky tension backed up with muscle, looking for trouble. At least that was the way I remembered Joey Mordento. However, the boy who now stood before me in my office was different somehow. Oh, the muscled body was still there, but the tension had eased. It wasn't something I could put my finger on exactly.

Joey Mordento was just different...calmer.

Inside my head, Ken's voice said, *Promise me you'll listen to the audio track of the Tibetan balls every day, Brian.*

Hmmmm.

"Could I talk to you a minute, Mr. Scarlucci?"

I stood up, and gestured to in front of my desk. "Sure. Come on in, Joey. Have a seat."

161

Joey took a seat.

"I spoke to your father yesterday, Joey. He's pretty pleased with how you're doing lately."

Joey's steady eyes held my gaze, and he nodded.

"So what's the story with Mr. Valentine? And no bullshit either, all right?"

Okay, so much for Dad is pleased with son talk. Let's get right to it, eh, Joey? Maybe he hadn't changed all that much. Maybe it was just smarter tension looking for trouble.

"Mr. Valentine will not be in today," the Assistant Principal in me answered. "Mr. Knickbocker will be taking over his classes for now."

Joey looked at me. "You heard me ask you not to bullshit me, right?"

I pursed my lips and looked at him a moment. "Joey, it's a difficult situation."

"Yeah, we know." He stood up. "All right, I guess I knew what to expect. It ain't like I haven't been here before. Anyway, I wanted to say that I'm the representative of the group, and we'd like to be kept informed."

I frowned. "What group?"

Joey shrugged. "You know, Mr. Valentine's group. And they wanted me to tell you we're going to have a meditation for Laura after school this afternoon in Mr. Valentine's room before we go to the wake. We'd like you to tell Mr. Valentine for us. You're invited to attend if you like since Mr. Valentine said you were starting to listen to the audio track now, too."

162

"He told you that?"

"Yeah, he mentioned it at our session yesterday afternoon. He seemed really pleased about it. You know, happy that you might become a part of this. Oh, and the whole thing about Mr. Valentine and Laura?" I waited through Joey's pause. "Total crap! Some of us are talking about going to the board meeting later this week. We're more than ready to become Valentine's Vigilantes if we have to, and do whatever it takes. We're not going to stand for it. We thought you should know."

I nodded.

Good for you. Go for it.

"Thank you for telling me, and for the invitation to the meditation. I'm committed to another obligation after school and won't be able to make it, but I think having a session in Laura's name is a very thoughtful thing to do. I'll convey what you've told me to Mr. Valentine and I'd appreciate it if you'd keep me informed as to the group's actions."

Joey's defensive demeanor eased a little.

"So what's the deal, Mr. Scarlucci? Word is you guys are pretty tight, so I figure if anyone knows the deal, it's you. Is Mr. Valentine going to be all right or what?"

"I certainly hope so," I said. "I'm going to do everything I can to make sure he is."

Joey thought my words over and nodded. "So that's it then. You keep me informed, I'll keep you informed. Deal?"

I stuck out my hand. "Deal."

Joey shook it, and stepped back, shuffling awkwardly.

"Yeah, things are a little better between me and Pops. I have Mr. Valentine to thank for that, and I'm not going to let him down. Pops said he likes you, you know, and he doesn't like a whole lot of people. Guess you impressed him somehow."

"Always good to know I can still make a good impression," I said.

Especially when the person I need to impress can have me fitted with cement shoes. Oh, and did your Killer Pops happen to mention that he dropped fifty thousand dollars on me before he left yesterday?

"Anyway, I better get back to class," Joey said, turning and heading back to my office door. However, before exiting he turned back to drop one last little bombshell on me. "Oh, and you don't need to worry about Angel and that new scumbag, Tyler Karidae. I've got it covered."

That brought me around the desk.

"Whoa, wait a minute. What does that mean, *you've got it covered*, Joey? I'm not sure I like the sound of that."

"It means just what I said. Angel Jehmar talked to me about it, and I've got it covered. She shouldn't have to worry. Angel's a good kid. I like her. We're going to start working out together. She's in pretty good shape, you know."

I didn't feel an answer was called for, although I certainly did know.

And with that, Joey Mordento turned and left...except he didn't get too far because right outside my office, he stepped into a rush of water, pouring across the carpet.

"What the hell is this," Joey exclaimed, quickly sidestepping the flow of water coming down the hallway in order to protect his brand new white unlaced high-top sneakers.

Simultaneously, a tremendous crash came from inside Laurence Pugh's office, followed by a cry of "Oh, my God," and as I reached my doorway, I saw the sloppily-clothed body of Lewis Grimley emerging on the run, hotfooting it through the rush of water that poured out of the entranceway to Pugh's office, heading directly toward me.

I stepped in front of Grimley's charging body, but it was the strong, muscled arm of Joey Mordento that stopped him.

"Not so fast, Lewis," Joey said. "What's the hurry? This goddamned water better not be because of you, 'cause if it ruins my sneakers, I'm not going to be too happy about it."

"Eat me, Joey," was Lewis Grimley's reply as he squirmed in Mordento's grasp.

Joey lifted his muscular arm and threw Lewis to the waterlogged carpet, but by that time, Greg Latch had come out of the dean's office, and together, he and I lifted Lewis to his feet.

"I WANT HIM SUSPENDED," Larry Pugh shouted from his office doorway. I looked over. Pugh was soaked, and the water stains were so excessive it had to be more than just his usual abnormal perspiration problem. The answer to the dampness to his person was immediately evident to me as I looked beyond him and into the room's interior. Beautiful, multi-colored fish of various sizes and shapes flipped, flopped and splashed among the collecting pools of water and broken glass that covered Pugh's office floor.

Uh, oh! The crashing sound had been the sound of the destruction of Laurence Pugh's pride and joy: his salt water fish tank. Lewis Grimley had destroyed the poor guy's two hundred gallon office wall fish tank.

"Hey, it was an accident, man!" Lewis protested over his shoulder, as Dean Latch led him down the hall and into the Dean's Office waiting room.

By this time, several of the main office secretaries had gathered in a clump behind us, as my own secretary rushed past me with an empty wastebasket.

"Oh, no, the fishies. The poor fishies," Betty sputtered, hurrying by Pugh and attempting to gather up as many of the flopping fish as possible.

I had a notion to point out that there is no such plural as fishies for fish, but thought better of it. Pugh, meanwhile had rushed to help gather the loose fish, speaking as he scooped them into his tiny hair-covered hands.

"That little creep. He deliberately turned and smashed his books into my tank. The blow caused it to shatter instantly. Oh, my God, look at them. Poor babies. Thank you, Betty. Oh, thank you. It's okay, my darlings. Daddy's got you."

I was afraid that if I continued to listen to Pugh, nausea would flood through my body, but luckily Mary J. came out of her office saying, "What in God's name is going on out here?"

"Lewis Grimley smashed Larry's fish tank," I explained.

"Oh, for heaven's sake. What next," was Mary J.'s response as she turned to go back into her office.

Unfortunately, in her distraction, Mary J. half-missed the doorway, and walked into the wide array of "Talley Ties" that hung from hooks on a long rack mounted at shoulder height next to her door.

See, Mary J. Talley was somewhat old school when it came to her feelings about the proper dress for teachers. Standards of dress might be easing in other sectors of public education, but it was not going to happen where Mary J. Talley was principal. And this applied to both men and women on the staff.

In terms of female dress, her big complaint was with jeans. As more and more of the female teachers started showing up in jeans, Mary J. let it be known that such dress was absolutely unacceptable. Most of the women understood and conformed, but not all. The worst offender was a member of the English department – I know, why is it always the English department? – named Suzy Shiftlet, who commuted from New York City, and, truth be told, did dress a bit like a swinging city single in loose, skimpy tops and tight-ass jeans that covered her long, sleek frame. Still, even Suzy eventually gave in after some cajoling from Sherri and only wore her tight-assed jeans to work on occasional dress-down Fridays.

Surprisingly, with the male faculty members, it was a different story. Proving that you never know where rebellion will surface within the workplace, the men of the staff refused to knuckle under, and many who had worn ties regularly prior to Mary J.'s proper dress edict, actually started coming to work with open collars. Never one to give in without a fight, Mary J. fought right back and had Richie the custodian build and mount the Talley Tie Rack outside her door where she proceeded to place dozens of ties on the rack below a sign that read: Take A Tie And Be A Real Teacher.

And then one fine morning, Mary J. came to work, and the Talley Tie Rack with its wonderful assortment of ties was *gone*! Ripped right off the wall, leaving only broken chipped holes where Molly bolts had once held the rack in place.

And no one knew who did it.

No one, that is, except *everyone* but Mary J. Talley; and Laurence Pugh, of course, who could not be trusted not to rat out the perpetrator. I happened to know who the terrible Talley Tie terminator was, but not wanting to gain the reputation of being a rat like Mr. Pee U, I kept my mouth shut.

The actual culprit was our very own high school band director and music teacher, Quinton Bellerio, or Mr. Q or just plain Q, as he liked to be known. Mr. Q was a jazz trombone player who worked gigs on weekends and absolutely refused to wear a tie to work. *It ain't happenin' man,* Q would insist.

You dig what I'm saying? I don't dress up for gigs and that includes this one. Hey, she can fire me, baby, 'cause it's no tie for the Q-man. Let her say, 'oh me oh my, she might as well not ever try, 'cause before I ever wear a tie, this is one dude who'd rather die.' And having said that, the Q-man would sneak outside the band room door, and proceed to grab a quick butt, another thing forbidden on Central's smoke-free campus.

Mary J. Talley was not one to be trifled with, however, and at the beginning of this very week, a new Talley Tie Rack had appeared mounted at shoulder height with an even nicer array of tie choices hanging in a display outside her office door. In addition, a freshly inked accompanying sign hung above the newly installed rack that read: DON'T EVEN THINK ABOUT IT, with a wide arrow beneath the lettering that pointed to an additional surveillance camera that had been installed in the ceiling at the far end of our office hallway.

It was the new tie rack that Mary J. stumbled into, knocking a number of hanging ties askew and off the rack as she turned back toward her doorway. Never missing a beat, the woman picked up and re-hung the dropped ties, straightened the display, turned to those of us watching with a calm nod, and disappeared back into her office.

Betty, meanwhile with a frantic Pugh at her side, came charging by us with the wastebasket full of fishies flopping away in a small pool of vile-looking salt water in the basket's bottom.

"I'm headed for the pet store with my babies," Pugh gasped, fresh sweat dripping down his face. He took the basket carefully from my secretary. "Cover for me, Brian. And call Richie about the mess in my office."

Joey Mordento, who still stood beside me, spoke up, catching my eye and smiling as Pugh disappeared from view around the corner of the hallway. "Well, I'm going to be getting back to class. You know, I might start coming here even when I'm not called to the Dean's Office for being a bad ass. It's a lot more interesting than I thought it was."

Grabbing some tissues out of the box that sat on Betty's desk, Sal The Gimp's newly intelligent boy, newly elected meditative group representative for Ken Valentine and newly self-appointed protector of Angel Jehmar, brushed off his water-spattered sneakers, gave me a quick wink and left. The parting wink meant that now, both Sal and his son were my good buddies, of course, but I wasn't at all sure that my new father and son pals were particularly good things.

SIXTEEN
OBSERVATIONS TO BE NOTED

Central High School has two types of teacher observations that administrators must perform and write up to be placed in the teachers' permanent files during the course of a school year. One is the standard classroom observation that each teacher is subjected to three times during a year, twice by the department chairperson and once by a member of the school administration.

The other type of observation is one that is given to teachers who have worked in the district for a period of three years and are therefore tenure candidates. Two observations during the course of that teacher's tenure year are regular chairperson observations. The third observation is the Observation of Note, during which both the chairperson and a member of the administration are present so that they can make a collective assessment of the teacher's skills before tenure approval is put before the Board of Education. These types of observations are not randomly performed, as are the chairperson observations, but rather scheduled in advance so that the teacher will have ample opportunity to prepare. Unfortunately, in the middle of what was quickly becoming one of the most hectic days I could remember, at the beginning of fourth period, I was scheduled to attend an Observation of Note with Sherri Walsh for the tenure assessment observation of Molly Lakeland, a member of the English department.

171

Mary J. and I had been fielding calls from both the press and community all morning, and I offered to cancel the observation, but as she answered yet another call about the Valentine situation, Mary J. waved me off and, notepad in hand, I made my way to Molly's classroom in Wing C. That was why I noticed that there was no teacher in the room next to where I was to make the observation, in spite of the fact that the forth period bell had just rung.

I saw Sherri hurrying down the hall toward me, her own observation pad in hand, and crossed over to her as she reached Molly Kirkland's classroom.

"Whose classroom is this?" I asked, pointing to where the students were lounging around and talking just inside the neighboring hall doorway.

Sherri rolled her eyes. "Mitchell Bright's."

"Of course."

"Hey, Mr. Bright is in Social Studies, not English, and not my problem. God forbid I say anything about someone in another department."

"Yeah, well, I can sure as hell say something. Go on in. Tell Molly to start. I'll be there in a minute."

"How is everything?" Sherri asked quickly, as she paused a moment, clearly wanting to say more to me. I, in turn, wanted to share everything with her, but it would have to wait. I shook my head.

"He's at the apartment." Her eyes widened and I nodded. "That's right. Our apartment. And yes, that means I told him. I'll fill you in later."

As I spoke, I watched the hulking figure of Mitchell Bright come through the doorway from outside the school and head down the Wing C hallway toward us. The man was sweating profusely and barefoot, his socks and shoes in his hands.

"Okay," Sherri said, rolling her eyes once more at the approaching teacher. "See you in a minute. But don't be too long. Molly is a wreck about this observation anyway, and if you come bursting in while she's in the middle of teaching, it may throw her."

I nodded. "Two minutes."

Sherri opened the classroom door, closing it behind her as she went inside. I got a quick glance of a very nervous Molly Kirkland looking toward where Sherri entered, and then I turned my attention to Bright as his strapping barefoot, six-feet-eight-inch, two hundred and eighty pound muscled body stopped next to me.

"Sorry, Brian. I lost track of the time."

"Mitch," I said, watching him lean his back against the hallway lockers and pull on first his socks and then his shoes. Several students from his room were looking out the classroom door and smiling. "This has to stop. What if something happened in the class and you weren't there? They'd fire you. You have a family you have to think of, right?"

"I know. I know. Sorry. Just trying to keep in shape. These are dangerous and wondrous times, Brian. We must all stay in shape so we are ready. I got into it and took a few extra laps around the track. It won't happen again, I promise."

Here's what Mitch means about *being ready*: Mitchell Bright of the Central High School Social Studies department thinks the end of the world is coming – that's right, the Apocalypse, the return of Jesus, rapture of the saved, the whole deal – and it is going to happen any day now. And every day, Mitch goes out during his free period, when he is supposed to be preparing lessons and grading papers, and runs laps around the track to stay in the best physical shape possible so that he is ready.

Why does one have to be in top physical shape to be *ready* if, in ascension, one is going to leave the physical body anyway?

I don't know.

And why doesn't he run in the early morning before the start of the school day or perhaps in the cool of the evening to stay *ready*, you may ask?

I don't know.

He likes the school track, I guess. All I do know is the man has not been singing with a complete hymnal for quite some time.

An example: Last year during the school district's holiday break, Mitchell Bright loaded the flatbed of his four-wheel-drive Ford truck with all the essential human possessions he, his

174

wife, and family of three small children owned, piled the family into the double door two-seater cab of his truck, and drove through a snow storm to the mountains in upstate New York. Reaching the designated observation lookout area at the highest location in those mountains, Mitchell and other members of the religious group called The Disciples of Revelations, of which he is a master deacon and senior member, stood in the blinding snowstorm, arms raised in prayer, waiting to be ascended into Heaven as the world ended.

Following several hours of this Praise-God-And-Bring-On-The-Four-Horseman prayer session, the storm finally subsided, Mitchell loaded his frozen family back into the truck and drove home again...because – surprise, surprise – the world did not end.

I know. It would appear to those of us who are purportedly sane that Mr. Bright is not...too bright. Well, Mitchell may not have the best of all grasps on reality, but here's what the man does have: TENURE. And that is why, after innumerable reprimands, Mitchell had license to finish tying his shoes, wipe the sweat from his brow and, with a final apology to me, walk into his classroom, late and ready to Praise The Lord.

God help us all!

Shaking my head, I quietly opened the door next to me, and slipped to the back of the classroom, sitting near Sherri in one of the two desks that Molly had placed behind the last row of students for the observation. Molly Kirkland stood in front of the class, using the board to write notes -- Good -- and calling on various members of her tenth grade class, both those who volunteered and those who didn't -- Good. She was smiling, encouraging, and nicely in charge -- Good.

It occurs to me that, based on descriptions so far of teachers at Central High, there may be questions about whether there are any normal teachers on the staff who care about their students and do an excellent job of teaching. The answer is an emphatic YES! Sherri and I were in the process of observing one of them. Molly Kirkland was a superb teacher who truly cared about helping the students in her classes, and I wanted nothing more than to give her an excellent Observation of Note. Although, she wasn't precisely what I'd call normal, as far as that goes, but, hey, who is?

Molly Kirkland moved out of normal when it came to the *With It* category of human behavior. The woman was just plain scatter-brained; there was no other way to explain it. Yes, she taught the Honors classes with aplomb, but she carried all her school supplies and teacher records from class to class and around school in a cardboard box because she couldn't keep track of shit. In the past year, she had lost her key ring, which contained not only her car keys, but also the key to her classroom, forcing me to have new keys made over and over, approximately 15 times.

Here's another example: Molly got a new car, drove it to school all proud, and at the end of the day when she rushed out to drive home, it wouldn't start because it was *broken*.

176

Several sturdy males attempted to help...no deal. The car was dead. The tow truck guy took the new *lemon* away, only to call Molly shortly thereafter with the news that she had failed to put gas in her new car.

True stories.

Molly Kirkland's lesson for the day was a summary of the book *A Separate Peace* by John Knowles and an analysis of the book's themes. After a thorough question-and-answer review -- Good -- Molly had the students open their books to a reference page near the end of the novel.

At the same time, Sherri passed me a note.

The note read, *I was proud of you this morning. I love you. Is Ken okay?*

I read the note, scribbled a reply and passed it back.

The reply read, So far. *Now stop passing notes in class. I love you, too.*

Smiling, Sherri tore the note into pieces and slid it into the side pocket of her jacket.

I lifted my notepad, and pointed to a scrawl on the top of the desk.

The writing said, *Mr. Wallington sucks cock.*

Sherri's smile widened as she shook her head. I wrote on the observation form, Room Maintenance -- Needs Improvement.

Meanwhile, at the front of the room, Molly was drawing conclusions about why the author had seen fit to have one of the characters in the book die at the conclusion of the story.

"Everything was fine," Molly said to the class, leaning on her desk. "The two boys, Gene and Finny, had made their peace. The author could have stopped there, but he didn't. Why? Why did he have the main character die?"

Not a hand went into the air. The students just sat there and looked at their teacher. They were taking notes. They were listening. They cared. They just didn't know the answer.

Molly glanced quickly back to where we sat, and made her decision, and it was the absolute right choice because sometimes students need to be guided. That's why they are there. They can read the books on their own. The teacher's job is to guide them to the insights and help them to see the truth.

"It's because in society," Molly told them, moving around the room as she connected with her students, "often those who have the purpose of showing what true goodness is within that society cannot survive. This is true whether it happens to be within the microcosm of the school in *A Separate Peace* or in the book's macrocosm in which WW II is raging. Gene realizes his flaws and makes his separate peace with what he is as a human being. But Finny has no such flaws. He is so innocent, he cannot even understand at first why Gene would have such impulses of jealousy and enmity. Remember that vocabulary word? Enmity. What does that mean?"

Some fourteen hands went into the air -- Good.

A student named Hung Wang, president of the student/faculty advisory committee answered, "Hatred."

178

"Right. Very good, Hung. Finny didn't understand hatred because he was incapable of feeling it. He was just a person made up of goodness and innocence. We see examples of this throughout history with beings who become true prophets to humankind. Figures like Jesus and Mohammad. These great figures in history could not and did not survive the mean days in which they found themselves...."

A hand went up. "Are you saying that Finny is like Jesus?" Molly took the question, and masterfully turned it back. "No, but what do you think I'm saying?" – Good.

The girl who had asked the question thought for a moment and then said, "Is it that such a purity of being sometimes sets an example for us, but cannot exist in a world so full of hatred?...That it's almost as if those people are destined to die?"

And I don't know how Molly Kirkland answered the student, because...I suddenly went away.

It wasn't a thing I had control over. It just happened. One minute I was listening to the student in the third row respond to Ms. Kirkland's query, and the next moment, I was gone, listening to Ken Valentine speaking inside my head.

I'm dying, Brian," Ken's voice said. And the sorrow I'd managed to put away earlier in the restaurant suddenly welled up within me in a rush of emotion so overwhelming I had to reach for Sherri's hand and hold it tightly to keep from crying.

Sherri stared at me with concern, but I fought for control, finally finding it, and released her hand.

John Arthur Long

I took several deep, slow breaths, and then forced my attention to the observation pad on the desk in front of me. I moved my pen to the bottom of the form and filled in the blank at the end of Molly Kirkland's Observation of Note: Overall Performance – Excellent.

Tenure Recommended.

SEVENTEEN
TAKING IT STEP BY STEP

Blaming my little spasm of emotion on strain and lack of sleep, I congratulated Molly Kirkland on a good job, and left Sherri to fill in the details of the observation as I hurried away to the cafeteria, deciding I'd use the old tried and true method of food intake to help get myself back under control. I got my chicken Caesar salad – I figured I better ease up on the cholesterol intake after my mega IHop breakfast – and at that moment, the President of the Teachers' Union walked in, cell phone pressed to his ear and, seeing me, gestured in my direction. I crossed to where John Hill stood waiting for me. We moved to the corner of the room, out of earshot of those eating.

"Brian," John Hill said, lowering his cell phone.

I nodded, deciding to dispense with any needless small talk. "Can you help him, John?"

He pursed his lips and looked at me for a moment. "Yeah, I think I can. Guess who that was on the phone just now?" It was not a question that expected an answer, so I waited. "First, I have to ask you a question. You know Ken better than any of us. Is there any truth to the accusations." I looked at him, saying nothing.

Hill was a bit of a bullshitter, but I knew he sincerely cared about what he did and making sure teachers got a fair shake. I wanted him in Ken's corner, so I let the slur of doubt just hang there. He shifted uncomfortably. "Sorry, but I have to ask."

"Who was on the phone, John?" I said.

He nodded. "Okay, that's good enough for me, Brian. Tell Ken the union is behind him one hundred percent. Better yet, what's his cell? I'll tell him. I need to talk to him anyway, better sooner than later."

I gave him Ken's cell number.

"I assume you know where he is."

"You assume correctly," I said.

"And what's his plan?"

"You have his cell phone," I answered. "I'm sure he'll tell you. Who was on the phone?"

John Hill smiled. "J. D. Booker." His smile widened at my look of surprise. J. D. Booker was one of the more famous high profile lawyers in the country. Everyone knew his name from the cases he had defended and won. "You heard me correctly. *The* J.D. Booker. He wants the case. He tells me he'll waive his fee and have Valentine back in the classroom by the end of the week."

"So what does he want out of it?"

Hill shrugged. "That I can't tell you, but I'd say it's pretty obvious since the man seems to have an unquenchable appetite for publicity and media exposure."

"Okay. Call Ken."

Hill hesitated. "Is he going to surface today? They plan to take him in the minute he shows his face, you know."

182

"Call Ken, John," I said.

"Okay now, shifting gears, what's your take on the Maggie Madison thing?"

I waited a beat. "I don't know yet."

He nodded. "Mary says you're doing an observation of the drama rehearsal to do a little analysis of the situation. Will you call me if you feel there's anything to tell me? I value your opinion, Brian."

"I'll call you."

His cell phone rang. "I've got to get over to the Middle School. Thanks, Brian. I'll speak to you soon."

And with that, Hill was heading for the hills, absorbed with his incoming call.

I started for the doorway, but a hand grabbed my elbow and I turned. Karen Wuant stood next to me. "See you this afternoon, right, Brian?"

I winced. I had completely forgotten, probably because I wanted to forget the fact that this very afternoon was my first scheduled rehearsal for Dancing With The Teachers.

Do not ask me why the hell I ever consented to do this, but in a weak moment, I'd let Karen talk me into being a part of a teacher dance contest. I mean it was for charity, and she caught me at a weak moment on a Friday afternoon drinking session at The Black Stallion, a local bar where Central staff members gathered to relax at the end of the week. She snuggled her cute little body up next to me at the bar when making the request and, yeah, I've got a few good dance

183

moves in me, so I agreed...regretting it every minute since then. Today was to be our first dance instruction with our partnered dance professional, who was going to teach me the Samba, whatever the hell that was.

"Karen, I'm sorry. I'm not going to be able to make it at four. I completely forgot about it, and something's come up I must take care of."

She looked at me, her expression crestfallen. "Brian...."

"I know. Next week, for sure. It's this whole Ken thing, Karen. I have to do a couple of things."

That did it. She smiled in understanding.

"Okay. I'll let you off the hook this time. But you better be there next week."

I crossed my heart and held up my hand toward her in a three-fingered pledge. "Scout's honor. With bells on my toes, I promise. By the way, what exactly is the Samba?"

She laughed. "Oh, you'll find out next week, don't worry."

I heard my name being called, and I turned to the faculty room door. Sam Shapiro, the head of Security, stood at the entrance, his face flushed in excitement.

"Trouble in the cafeteria," he said loudly. "Come quickly, Brian. We need you!"

EIGHTEEN

YA GOTTA KNOW WHEN TO HOLD 'EM,

KNOW WHEN TO FOLD 'EM

We do not have gangs at Central High School. Ask any Empty Suit in the Central administration building or any school board member. They'll tell you...right after they extract their heads from the sand. However, those of us who are on the front lines and in the trenches – and believe me, the Central High Cafeteria is definitely the trenches – know the truth.

And, trust me, the days of Jets and Sharks, with guys snapping their fingers as they whistle and dance their way down the street are long gone, not that they ever existed except in musical theater. The gang members at Central High definitely do not dance, unless they're strung out on lines of coke, that is, and swaying to rap rhymes of violence.

These days, gang members peddle drugs and violence, not show tunes, and they have worked their way from the inner city streets of the Big Apple right out and into the hallowed bedroom communities of Long Island, where everyone fled to get away from such inner city horribleness. This just goes to show for the umpteenth time that it is better to try to solve bad situations than run from them. And, at Central High, we had attempted to at least keep in check the cafeteria chaos frequently brought on by the gang underbelly of drug commerce that loved to ply its trade there.

John Arthur Long

First of all, there is no duty that is more dreaded by teachers than cafeteria duty. It is probably one of the most thankless jobs that exists within a high school. Teachers hate it!

After being pent up in classes for hours, students are hungry, rowdy, and looking to cause trouble, just to add a little excitement to their boring, routine-filled days. Teachers are looking to avoid such trouble at all costs and hide in the corners of the noise-filled, food-flying cafeteria, reading and grading papers and pretending not to see anything that might force them to actually perform the duty to which they have been assigned. It is, or rather was, a horror show until the solution to the chaos was found at Central High in the personage of one Greta Gruber, who became Central's very own Zoo Czar.

Greta Gruber is another member of the Language department who used to teach German, but had since relinquished her teaching duties to take on the assignment of Cafeteria Management. Greta is one tough cookie. She is huge, but in a stocky rather than plump sort of way. She speaks in a very heavy accent, having come to the United States from Germany as a young adult. She struts around the cafeteria with a push broom in thick-heeled work shoes that clunk loudly against the floor tiles as she walks. Most importantly, she takes no shit from anyone, students, teachers, and Security included. And to the delight of Central Administration, Greta Gruber, the Cafeteria Czar, as those

186

caged within her domain refer to her, has brought things under control. In other words, under Greta's rules of cafeteria conduct and her iron broom-pushing hand, the students of Central High cafeteria had shaped up.

Except for one thing: Texas Hold 'Em poker.

Her one concession to student requests was to allow card playing after they finished eating. Her reasoning was sound. The kids loved to play cards, and it kept them occupied. The naïve aspect of her decision was that they were allowed to play cards as long as there was no gambling, and, of course, all students agreed.

Yeah, right.

The truth was they secretly gambled with pencils, pieces of paper, and anything else they could get their hands on that they could throw into the game's pot in the center of the table. Greta, no dummy that they adolescently assumed, let it happen because as long as there was no money on the table, there was no proof of gambling and, most importantly, they were QUIET. At the end of the game or the bell, whichever came first, they then divided up the spoils in hard cash on their way out with Greta the Cafeteria Czar quote-unquote supposedly none the wiser.

Unfortunately, as has been the case since Wild Bill Hickok held the dead man's hand of aces and eights on that fateful day in Deadwood, and was shot by a disgruntled card player, occasionally the card playing did not keep students occupied as intended, but instead went horribly awry.

And that was the reason for Sam's "trouble in the cafeteria" call for help.

Even worse, the card game had been between rival gang members and, by the time I arrived, the cafeteria was in an uproar. The head of the gang known as The Vipers was out for blood against a member of a rival gang known as the Tongs, who had been accused of cheating.

One gang member kept Greta at bay, his tattooed arms holding the woman back with the broom he had ripped out of her hand. Other members had scattered themselves among the bunches of hollering students, holding the various groups back. Meanwhile, Laurence Pugh, sweat pouring off of him, was shouting cries of "LET'S ALL SIT DOWN, PLEASE" from the cafeteria's far entrance to countering cries of "Pee-U, Pee-U, Pee-U!" that exploded anonymously from within the surging groups of students.

At the opposite end of the cafeteria, several Vipers were blocking the two Security guards from advancing, and in the middle of all this, near an overturned table that had sent cards and food in all directions, stood the leader of The Vipers whose name was Spit. His real name was Brendan, but if you're the leader of a gang called The Vipers, a name like Brendan doesn't really cut it. Actually, I don't think the handle of Spit has much of an impact either, but that's not really important. What is important is that Spit held a glistening single-edged box cutter to the throat of the supposed card-cheating Tong member.

English teacher Tanya Seaford struggled to her feet. She held her knee and grimaced in pain as she leaned back against the cafeteria wall. Where she had fallen, I could see a carelessly tossed open packet of salad dressing smeared across the floor that Tanya had obviously slipped on.

Not hesitating at the barrier of Viper members, I yelled for them to get out of the way, which upon seeing me they did and, with a motion for Sam to hang back momentarily with his Security team, I moved into the cafeteria alone. I advanced quickly, climbing from a chair seat to the top of a cafeteria table and raised my arms, with a loud cry of, "QUUUIIIIEEEETTTTT!"

The first shout had very little effect, so I screamed it again even louder and, this time, the cafeteria uproar slowly eased to a tension-filled muffled silence. The reason was because students began to realize that Assistant Principal Scarlucci had arrived, and everyone in the cafeteria knew that Brian Scarlucci had once been – drum roll, please -- a Navy SEAL.

Not only that, but every impressionable male student in high school knows that a Navy SEAL can kill a human being in a matter of seconds with his bare hands, and probably in my Navy SEAL days I had done that very thing, so, when Brian Scarlucci spoke, students listened.

All right, the truth is I have never been a Navy SEAL.

However, they thought that I had been, and that was the only thing that mattered.

The whole Navy SEAL thing was another little favor that I owed to my good friend, Ken Valentine. Several years earlier, before I had accepted the job of Assistant Principal and was still a teacher among the English staff, Ken had been substituting for me while I handled a student squabble in the Dean's Office, and probably to amuse himself as much as anything, he told the class that if they would do their work quietly and not cause any trouble, he would tell them something about Mr. Scarlucci that no one knew.

Naturally, the kids shut up immediately, and Ken told them to keep it to themselves and not tell anyone else, but before becoming a teacher, Mr. Scarlucci had trained and served a tour in the armed forces as a Navy SEAL. At first, the students expressed their doubt, but totally into the joke at this point, Ken continued to explain my exploits with tales of derring-do until he had them convinced. With a further request to tell no one, my good friend released the class when the bell rang, and, to Ken Valentine's amused delight, the news that I was a former Navy SEAL spread through the school immediately.

I couldn't believe it. Navy SEAL? Are you shitting me? I didn't know a scuba tank from a snorkel. I couldn't even swim all that well. Forget the breast stroke. I was lucky if I could dog paddle my way across the kiddie pool at the golf club. And about the only thing I knew about self-defense when threatened was: *run, run, as fast as you can. You can't catch me, I'm the Scarlucci Man.*

At first, with the class he had told and others, I attempted to deny it, but students wanted so much to believe the mystique of such a tale that they thought I was just being modest. As word continued to spread and other members of the staff discovered the ruse, they started calling me SEAL and saluting in amusement and on and on. But the interesting thing was that I noticed a change in the male students of the school in terms of their attitudes toward me. There was a sort of awe in their demeanor when I approached. It was as if they didn't really believe it, and yet a part of them did believe it because they wanted it to be true. Trouble would just seem to dissolve when I came on the scene, and I could see in their faces why: *Hey, Scarlucci's a SEAL, Dude. Don't mess with him.*

Out of the corner of my eye, I saw Mary J., her expression etched with concern, reach the entrance of the cafeteria near where Pugh stood blocked behind the masses of students. I climbed down from the table and walked slowly toward where Spit held the member of the Tongs.

"Let him go, Spit," I said. "Whatever is wrong, we'll solve it. You know me, and you know I'm as good as my word. So, let him go. Right now. If you don't, I'll have to handle it, and you know I can, and it could go very badly for all of us." Spit stared at me, not moving. The cutter against the other kid's throat eased ever so slightly as he considered the options, which clearly were not in his favor. "You're a smart card player, Spit. How many cards you holding right now? That's right. None, Spit. It's a bad hand. You know what they say, 'You got to know when to hold 'em, know when to fold 'em, know when to walk away.' Play it smart. This is no time to gamble, Spit. Walk away. Throw the cutter down and let him go! Now! Do it! I will not ask you twice, and if I start to move, I will not stop!"

And Spit did just that. After a couple more beats of indecision, his mouth curled in disgust, he dropped the cutter to the floor, and shoved the Tong member away from him, the released Tong falling forward in a sprawl onto the cafeteria floor as the jarring sound of the bell ending the period filled the air within the now-quiet cafeteria.

Behind me, I heard murmurs of disapproval and I turned to see a slight forward surge of various Tong gang members as Security rushed forward and surrounded Spit.

"IT'S OVER," I said loudly. "THE PERIOD IS OVER. PLAY IT SMART. GO TO CLASS, RIGHT NOW." The groups of students began to disperse, heading toward the two cafeteria exits, though Tongs and Vipers did not move. Outside a siren sounded. "HEAR THAT? YOU'VE GOT ABOUT TEN SECONDS TO MAKE UP YOUR MINDS! YOUR CHOICE! CLASS OR THE POLICE! WHAT'LL IT BE?"

It took several more beats of tension, but then the Viper holding Gerta's broom handed it back to her, and that did it. Slowly the gang members dissolved into the departing crowd and it was over.

I crossed to where Security had hustled in to pick up the box cutter, and held Spit and the Tong member who had been involved in the altercation.

"As soon as the halls clear, take them to the Dean's Office, and start filling out the forms. Five day external suspension to both for fighting, and a concealed weapon charge for Spit which means a police report." Spit looked at me, his eyes narrowing. "Put in the report that Spit cooperated. We'll see how it goes."

Spit's eyes opened again, Sam nodded with a look of approval coated with respect toward me, gestured to the Security crew, and away they went, Viper and Tong in tow. Greta Gruber, holding her broom over her shoulder like a rifle, her other arm around a struggling-to-walk Tanya Seaford, came up as Security departed. She was still white with fear.

"Sank you, Brian," the German woman said with a shaky accented voice. "It hoppened zo fast. I sink a new rrrule is rrrequired. No more carrrds. You agrrree?"

"Good call," I said. "What do you think, Sam?"

Sam nodded his agreement.

Greta sighed in relief, and a grimacing Tanya added her own suggestion.

"I tried to go for help, but slipped on some crap the kids had thrown on the floor, Brian. Jesus, we should get hazard pay for this duty. Look at my knee. I can't even walk now, for God's sake."

Tanya was a runner. I knew she ran every morning on the beach to stay in shape. Looking down at her knee, I could see it was swelling badly, and I sympathized with her.

"I know, Tanya," I said. "Greta, could you help Tanya to the nurse. She needs to get some cold packs on that knee as soon as possible.

"Of course," Greta said. "Come, Tanya, vee vill see to you." The two walked away, Greta supporting a limping Tanya and shoving discarded food and trash ahead of them with her push broom as they moved across the cafeteria floor.

When I turned, Mary J. was beside me.

"Good job, Brian," she said. "Thank God you got here when you did."

"The police would have dealt with it," I said, sloughing off the compliment.

Mary J. shook her head. "It escalated so fast, no one had called the police yet. That siren sound outside was just a passing ambulance."

"I see," I answered, wiping the perspiration from my face with what I noticed was a shaking hand. I tried to smile through the danger of the sequence that had finally begun to catch up with me. "Does that mean you're not still angry with me for losing control at the meeting this morning?"

"I'd say you've earned your keep for the day." Then it was Mary J.'s turn to smile in relief with an empty threat of amusement. "But don't push your luck." She pointed a hand toward the cafeteria entrance. "I think you're wanted."

Turning, I saw Betty at the cafeteria entrance, beckoning me.

"What now?" I said, leaving Mary J. to talk with Sam and hurrying to where my secretary stood.

"There's a man from Dent Wizard here, Brian. I told him your Volvo is in the corner of the parking lot, but he needs your okay to begin."

A wave of released tension swept over me. Ahhh, yes, finally there was a bright spot in the day. Dent Wizard had arrived to fix the ding in my car. It's the little things in life that make you happy.

However, as I hurried off to see the Wizard, a random element from the cafeteria scene surfaced in my mind. I had taken it in as I swept my gaze over the cafeteria, but the crisis had prevented it from registering.

Now, however, the out-of-place element surfaced at the end of the tension release, demanding my attention. It was the figure of a lone student, standing against the wall on the opposite side of the cafeteria near the food line entrance, away from the groups of shouting students and threatening gang members. iPhone ear buds were in, and a random hand brushed back his wavy unwashed dark hair as steady intense eyes watched...taking it all in.

Tyler Karidae.

And the thing that struck me about the watchful, motionless figure was that the new Central High student from Queens was not caught up in the surging excitement of the moment. Rather, it looked to me as if he were objectively watching, judging and assessing the strengths and weaknesses of all those around him.

Hmmmm.

NINETEEN

ANALYZE THIS!

The high school auditorium was dark later that afternoon, house lights dimmed and stage lights up full, rehearsal already well underway as I slipped into the back row and sat down unnoticed in a theater seat. On stage, Todd Hershborne was in his Willy Loman costume, spouting Arthur Miller's famous lines from *Death of a Salesman* to Lois Sheffield, the female student playing Willy's wife, Linda, about what a loser slash winner his kid Biff was. As I watched the scene play out, I had to admit, Hershborne was pretty good. Once you forgot you were watching a student, it was possible to suspend your disbelief and go with it. Though only eighteen, Todd had the older washed-up salesman movements down, the little ticks of emotional doubt, the ranting rise and fall of the voice. I mean it was no Dustin Hoffman on stage, but it looked like it was going to be a good show. If it were not discovered that Todd and his faculty director were doing the nasty after rehearsals, that is.

Maggie Madison came out of the darkness at the front of the auditorium, and hurried up the side steps to the stage, stopping the action. I sat up, watching her give the actors instructions. She had decided to change the direction of Willy's cross from the abstract doorway of the set that served as the entrance to the house. Originally, she had blocked Willie coming in and moving absentmindedly to the stairs. Now, to give the lines more focus, she wanted Willie's stage

197

cross to be directly to the table where his wife Linda sat. I nodded to myself in the dark, an armchair director agreeing with the change.

Then I frowned as I watched Maggie go to Todd and move him to the entrance spot at the door. It was the way she touched him as they moved together, her caress on his arm as she directed him to the designated spot that caught my attention. It was the closeness of her body to him as they moved. It was the little squeeze of affection she gave him as they stopped. It was the look on her face as their eyes met, and even more telling, it was the look on the kid's face.

Shit.

In any other situation, had it been any other female, I wouldn't have been so sure. However, this was not any other female. This was Maggie Madison, and I had been there, as the saying goes. I knew that little squeeze of affection, that closeness of her body when she moved with you, that look on her face…that touch. Oh, yes, I knew those many splendored things all too well because I had been Maggie Madison's lover in days of yore. And that was why, watching them together as Maggie re-blocked the scene, I got the very bad feeling that Maggie Madison's latest lover was standing on stage right next to her playing Willie Loman.

Shit.

Then again, maybe I was wrong. After all, there was no proof. Maybe I was imagining the whole thing. Maybe I was attributing more to Maggie's behavior than I should. Maybe it was just the way she was, with the movements and touch and all. Yeah, and maybe bears don't shit in the woods either.

Damn.

I watched Maggie hurry back down the stairs as the action began again, and shoved myself out of my seat. She had stopped halfway down the right aisle, her attention riveted to the stage, and I moved quietly down the aisle, stopping next to her.

"Oh, Brian," she said, her body doing a little jump of surprise. "I didn't see you come in."

I nodded to her in the darkness. "Rehearsal had started. I didn't want to interrupt so I slipped in quietly. Looks good. I'm impressed. These kids are pretty good."

She beamed, loving the compliment. "I know. And we still have two and half weeks before we open."

Her body moved closer to mine, and her hand found my arm, squeezing softly, the old familiar touch.

Hmmmm.

"Listen, I'm sorry about yesterday," she said, her voice coated with a sensuality that always seemed to be such a natural part of her. "God, I was being such an ass. I didn't know anything about Ken, yelling at you the way I did. I feel terrible." Her body moved closer, pressing lightly against me. "And I kicked your car. My God, can you forgive me?"

Another squeeze of affection caused images of the two us moving together, naked, Maggie on top, to flash into my mind as I stood beside her in the darkened auditorium, and I forced the memories out of my mind, edging away from her slightly. Her body stayed right with my movement, her touch edged with promise, her voice warm and softly inviting.

"Well, can you? Forgive me?"

"The car's already fixed, Maggie," I responded. "Dent Wizard came this afternoon. They used a little suction cup contraption to pop the dent. It's good as new...like it never happened. And Galli's gone, thanks to Mary J.'s transfer. So, see, problems solved," I snapped the fingers of my right hand. "Just like that."

"And the video?" she said quietly after a moment.

"The video shows nothing, Maggie. And why should it? There's nothing to see, right?"

It was a loaded question, of course. I'd slipped it in casually, testing her reaction, and I wasn't disappointed. Or maybe I was, depending on your viewpoint, because the subtle changes I didn't want to happen happened.

Maggie's body stiffened ever so slightly, and she eased back from me. There was a slight catch in her voice as she answered. "Right."

Come on, Maggie. You're an actress, for Christ's sake. You can do better than that. Or maybe not, considering....

"Well," I said, slipping my arm around her waist and giving her a return squeeze of my own, "right now my concern is about Ken. Even though they impounded his school email, they won't find anything. Apparently, Central School district email histories are stored somewhere in Central storage and
200

they can check all emails that anyone has ever written. I didn't even know they could do that. Did you?"

"No" was her answer after a few beats of hesitation. Her body had tensed once again beneath my grasp as I fed her the additional loaded information, and I filed that and the hesitation away on the negative side of my analysis. "Anyway, you don't have to ask for forgiveness. Not from me. You should know that."

Her head went against my shoulder and she came up on her tiptoes and gave me a quick cheek kiss in the dark.

"I do," she said.

Willy stopped moving on stage and peered out into the auditorium, his hand shading his eyes to see. "Ms. Madison. Do you want me to pick up the glass from the table here?"

Had he seen Maggie's little peck of affection to Assistant Principal Scarlucci and been taken aback? No way to tell.

I scooted her away from me with a gentle shove. "Back to work, Ms. Madison. I have to go anyway. I just wanted to stop in to see how you were doing. I'll talk to you later, okay?"

"Okay," came the answer, accompanied by a quick, cute Maggie-wave as she hurried up the stairs to the stage.

I backed up slowly, watching her instruct Todd about the stage business with the water glass, her body next to him, her hand squeezing the student's arm.

Damn, maybe I was wrong. Maybe it was just Maggie's way, after all. Well, shit.

As I headed down the Art Wing to check out the backstage hallway where the Security camera was located, I almost missed seeing two students running around the corner. However, the Scarlucci instincts kicked in despite my mental distraction, and I called out with authority as I hurried around the corner where the bodies had bolted out of sight. I got to the hallway just before the two male students were able to hustle their way out the exit door at the far end of the hallway, and I called out again.

"I said hold it!"

The students stopped and reluctantly turned.

Lewis Grimley and Tyler Karidae stood waiting for me to reach them, their expressions blank and unreadable, which meant they had been up to their eyeballs in bad business, of course.

"Schools over, guys," I said, stopping in front of them. "I'd think you'd want to get out of here as soon as possible." Karidae met my gaze with a cold return stare of his own. Lewis Grimley refused to look my way.

"Wait a minute," I continued. "Aren't you suspended, Lewis? You do remember smashing Mr. Pugh's aquarium earlier today, don't you? Dean Latch told me you got a five-day external for that. What are you doing in the building?"

Lewis looked at the floor.

"Hello? I asked you a question, Lewis,"

"Maybe he doesn't feel like answering you," said the boy next to him.

I shifted my attention to Tyler Karidae, welcoming the chance to get acquainted. There wasn't even a hint of nervousness or fear in the eyes that met mine.

"I don't think we've met."

"I know who you are," Karidae said, holding my gaze.

"Then we're even because I know who you are too, Tyler," I said. "So what's going on here? Lewis showing you around, getting you acquainted with all the areas of the school, is that it? Actually, he may be leading you astray because they don't hold any classes in this back hallway behind the stage."

Karidae smirked. "You think you're a real funny guy, don't you?

"Hello, Mr. 'Carlucci," a female voice said behind me. The second I heard Angel Jehmar's voice and saw Tyler Karidae take a quick little involuntary intake of breath as he saw her beyond me, it all came into focus. Of course. Karidae had been waiting for Angel to come out of the Music Wing where the girl's ensemble had choral rehearsal after school. That's why he and Grimley were in the back hallway.

I turned toward Angel, pleasantly surprised to see her dressed in a top that was neck high...cute and cut a tad short at the waist, but in no way revealing.

Good job, Scarlucci.

Seeing who stood beyond me, a short cry of alarm came from the girl.

"Keep him away from me," Angel said, leaving the two friends with her to stand and stare from the main Art Wing hall as she moved toward us. She was glaring at Karidae, but speaking to me. "He threatened me on the phone last night, Mr. 'Carlucci. Said no one refuses him. That I'd be sorry! He'd make me sorry!"

Then coming to beside me, she shifted in anger toward Karidae, the words spilling out of her, eyes clouding with tears.

"YOU STAY AWAY FROM ME!" Angel screamed. "LEAVE ME ALONE, GODDAMN YOU, OR YOU'RE THE ONE WHO'LL BE SORRY. YOU HEAR ME? LEAVE ME ALONE!"

I moved to her, put my arm on her shoulder, and gently turned Angel around.

"Okay, that's enough, Angel. You go along with your friends now. I'll take care of this. I'm sure Tyler understands the situation, don't you, Tyler?"

Karidae said nothing, his cold eyes moving from me to Angel and back again.

Angel nodded to me, mouthed a quick "thank you," and hurried away, meeting her friends and disappearing around the corner.

"You heard her," I said, moving past the two and pushing open the exit door. "Enough. Leave Angel Jehmar alone or you'll be answering to me, and that's a promise."

Karidae said nothing, but his eyes held me, hard hostility radiating from them.

"You don't scare us, Scarlucci," Lewis Grimley said, picking up the pissed-off adolescent ball and running with it. "Think you scare us? We'll see about that."

I gestured to the open door. "Out, Lewis. You're suspended. And that means I do not want to see you anywhere near this school again until that five-day external suspension is up, and then it better be in my office at seven a.m. Got that?"

Lewis gave a hand signal to Karidae and, without another word or glance in my direction, the two of them moved past me and out the door, which I released, allowing it to slam shut after them.

Sam Shapiro came rushing around the corner.

"Got a call from the Security room that Lewis Grimley was in the building back here," he said.

I nodded. "They just left. Better go out and make sure they're off school property. If not, call it in, and we'll alert the police."

"You got it." Sam pushed the door open, hesitating before rushing outside. "Good job in the cafeteria today, by the way."

"Go check on them, Sam," I said.

He nodded and hurried out as I closed the door, making sure it locked behind him.

Then, standing by myself for a moment in the hallway, I looked first up at the Security camera mounted in the ceiling and then to the backstage door which stood slightly ajar. I pushed the door slowly open, half-expecting to see Maggie and her star locked in an embrace as it swung open.

There was nothing there, of course. Just stacks of stage scenery inside the opening. I shook my head, closed the stage door, and headed for the faculty parking lot.

Enough with the Maggie Madison analysis for the time being. There just wasn't enough hard evidence for me to make any kind of concrete decision. Not only that, but I had more than a full plate of problems at the moment.

It was time to pick up Ken Valentine.

TWENTY

OUTSIDE THE WAKE

Ken was waiting for me on the stoop as I pulled up to the apartment's entrance. He came down the steps and got in the Volvo.

"You mind driving?" he asked.

"I'm behind the wheel," I said. "Where to?"

"It's at the Ferguson-Whittler Funeral Home off of Old Country Road. You know the way."

"Yes I do," I answered, pulling away from the curb.

We rode in silence for a while.

It's a guy thing. There were huge amounts of things to talk about, so, of course, we said nothing and just rode along.

"I heard about the cafeteria incident," Ken said finally.

"Just another day in the life of a SEAL," I answered.

He grinned, then chuckled. "One of my best, don't you think."

I nodded. "Your absolute best, old buddy. I could never top the SEAL thing. That's why I haven't even tried."

"Who was The Viper with the cutter? Spit?"

"Yeah. Don't you think he should consider a name change? I mean, really. Spit just doesn't have it if you're the leader of The Vipers. What do you think?"

"You think it should be something like Fang or Forked Tongue?"

"Hey, those names are better than Spit. At least you don't think of saliva," I said.

We rode on in silence again until, finally, I decided it was time to bring a little focus to the catchy banter we had been exchanging.

"So, what do you think is going to happen when you walk into Laura's wake? I only ask because the idea of it is giving me a Mr. Pee U-vian case of severe diarrhea, you understand."

Ken's expression became very serious. "I know what's going to happen."

"Well, would you like to let me in on it, or were you saving it for a surprise?"

"I'm going to be arrested. The police will be waiting for me when I come out of the funeral home."

"And how do you know that?"

"J. D. Booker set it up. Someone will call the authorities after I enter the funeral home, and they'll meet me outside when I exit...and take me away. Booker will then meet me at the jail, and after I'm booked or whatever the hell is going to happen, he'll get me released." Then, in an attempt to re-capture the lighter exchange mode, he added, "And, I want you to know, I'm pretty impressed. Man, when you say you're going to check into getting a lawyer, you don't mess around."

"Yeah, well, I had to call in a few favors," I said. "But honestly, Ken, John Hill seems to be on your side. I mean he put Booker through to you, so I'd say it's looking pretty good, considering."

"Really. You want to go to the jail for me and see how good it looks from there?" he asked.

"Well, everything is relative. I think I'll pass on jail, if it's all the same to you."

"Some friend, you are," he said with a shake of his head. "When the going gets tough, you punk out. It's so hard to find a friend you can really rely on these days."

I pulled into the parking lot of the funeral home. Several students, a couple of Central High teachers, and assorted people I did not know were milling around the entrance. And there were two uniformed police officers.

Uh, ohhh.

I shut off the car, and looked over at my friend.

"Ready?"

Ken sighed. "Ready as I'll ever be," he said.

We never made it into the funeral home.

As we stepped from the Volvo, a group of students who had been standing in front of the funeral home moved quickly from the entrance and gathered around us. Joey Mordento spoke for the assemblage of Central students as they surrounded us, and I realized the students must be the meditation group Joey had told me about: the newly-named Valentine Vigilantes.

"We'll take you in, Mr. Valentine," Joey said, coming to beside Ken.

"Thank you, Joey, but I think it's better if I go in by myself. I want no trouble because of my coming here."

Joey pointed to the entrance where an aging blonde woman was smoking a cigarette next to the two uniformed police officers who stood in front of the door. "Too late for that. Silverman's got the cops here. Someone tipped her you were coming."

Ken stopped moving, and the group stopped with him.

"The best laid plans…," I said to Ken as we exchanged a look.

"Joey," Ken said, his face filled with fresh concern, "I appreciate what all of you are trying to do, but this is something I have to do alone. Please, I'm asking you to stay here while I go into Laura's wake. I know you also want pay your respects, but I'd like you to wait until after I leave. It'll be better that way, okay?"

Without a word, Joey nodded, and motioned for the others to step aside and let us pass. The group parted with murmurs of caring encouragement to Mr. Valentine, and Ken and I walked on, leaving them to stare after us as we moved forward.

By the time we reached the entrance of the sedate funeral home, any faculty members who had been outside the building had disappeared, and we were met by uniformed police and a couple of guys who, by the suits and attitude, I knew had to be a second set of cops in plain clothes. Laura Silverman's mother stood with the others in dark sunglasses that hid her

210

eyes, the two large men at her side. My guess was that the two guys accompanying her were family. At the curb behind us, I caught a glimpse of a Channel 10 News van screeching to a halt, a camera man and female news reporter with mike in hand, leaping from the van.

"Mr. Valentine...," one of the plainclothes officers said as we stopped at the entrance.

Ken cut him off. "I'll go with you when I come out. But first, I am going to pay my respects to Laura and express my condolences."

The blonde woman hurled her cigarette to the pavement, and stepped in front of the cop. Behind me, I heard the reporter talking loudly and I knew the camera was rolling.

"Why, it isn't enough that you killed my daughter? You have to come here to gloat?" Sheila Silverman hissed at Ken. She turned to the officer. "Get this sick son-of-a-bitch the fuck out of here so I can mourn the loss of my daughter in peace."

No one moved, and it got very quiet. Even the reporter behind us abruptly stopped talking, but I knew the camera hadn't stopped. Oh, no, that digital camera would keep right on humming silently along, taking in this hot-breaking News Watch story for the Six O'clock Evening News.

"Mrs. Silverman," Ken said quietly. "I cannot express to you how sorry I am about what has happened to your daughter. She was a wonderful young woman. I wish I had been able to help her realize that."

Silverman said nothing. The only sound in the air came from the traffic moving by on the main thoroughfare beyond the side street where we stood.

Sheila Silverman leaned forward and spit into Ken Valentine's face.

"FUCK YOU, YOU BLACK BASTARD!" she shrieked.

Then she turned and, supported by the two dark-suited men on each side, one of whom opened the door in front of her, she disappeared inside the funeral home, the door closing with a quiet hiss behind her.

Ken stood there, saliva running down his face, his eyes clouded with sorrow.

From the parking lot, I saw Joey Mordento headed our way.

The cop made a move toward Ken, but I put out my hand, fast and hard, and he stopped.

"What do you want to do, Ken? I said. "It's your call. If you want to go in and pay your respects to Laura Silverman, we're going in. I'll do my best to make it happen."

The uniformed police officers at the entrance glanced from where I stood with Ken to each other nervously.

Several tense moments passed.

Ken made no move to wipe off the spittle that trickled down his face, and it dribbled onto the collar of the suit jacket he wore, leaving a wet mark.

Finally, he lifted his arms and stuck out his hands to the plainclothes officer beside him.

When he spoke, his voice was barely above a whisper.

"Let's go," Ken said.

"The cuffs won't be necessary, Mr. Valentine. You can put your hands down," the cop said, taking Ken's arm. The plainclothes officer nodded to the man with him, who took Ken's other arm, and they led him forward toward the cruiser that was parked at the curb in front of the news van.

The reporter started toward us, but a hustling Joey Mordento stepped in front of her, stopping her.

"I don't think so, lady," I heard Joey say as I moved along with Ken. "Mr. Valentine does not wish to speak to you."

"Get out of my way," the reporter said.

"You know who I am?" Joey asked. The cameraman whispered to her, and she stared back at Joey.

He smiled and repeated the phrase.

"I don't think so," he said.

And the reporter stood there, not saying a word while we all walked past her to the police cruiser.

"I'll meet you at the police station," I said hurriedly to Ken as they opened the cruiser's back door.

He shook his head. "No, I don't want you there. Booker promised me he's got it covered. I'll be in touch with you later. It'll be okay."

I watched in disbelief, unable to comprehend that it was actually happening, as the almost surreal scene that I had seen in a dozen movies took place in front of me.

The cop's hand went to the top of my friend's head, making sure it didn't hit the car doorframe, as they put him into the back seat of the police cruiser. Then the officer slammed the door shut, blocking Ken from view. The cop climbed into the front and, siren wailing, the cruiser sped away, turning off the side street and disappearing down Old Country Road.

TWENTY-ONE

PARENTS NIGHT

I was tired. I mean really tired, and the day was far from over. I jammed down the first half of a sandwich while sipping some soup in the kitchen before changing my clothes to go back to the school building for Parent/Teacher Conference Night, my attention glued to the Six O'clock Evening News on the kitchen counter television.

The female reporter I had seen at the funeral home was on the screen for the introduction of the News Watch segment, and then, suddenly, there we all were in high definition color that caught every drop of the Silverman-hurled spittle dribbling down Ken's face. There was no audio, but you could lip-read her racial slur loud and clear.

Jesus Christ.

Not only that, but Mr. Hot Shot lawyer had been wrong also. Ken was not being immediately released, but, in spite of J. D. Booker's protests and threats, would be held overnight for further questioning.

"SHIT!" I yelled as I hurled the remainder of my ham sandwich into the kitchen trash basket, dumped the bowl of soup into the sink and went to change.

Joyce was sitting in the bedroom next to the bed where Evelyn was already sleeping – an unusual occurrence that was also causing me a nagging concern – and after showering and climbing into my suit in the spare bedroom where I frequently spent the night and kept my clothes so that my early morning departures for work would not disturb my wife – I stopped at the our bedroom doorway. Responding to my gesture, Joyce rose and stepped out of the room.

"Everything all right?" I asked softly.

"I'm not sure," Joyce answered, saying precisely what I did not want to hear. "She seemed very tired when I arrived for my three o'clock shift. When I asked if she'd like to lie down in the bedroom, she agreed immediately, so I brought her in. She's been asleep since then. That's a little abnormal."

It was a more than a bit abnormal. Unless she knew I was not coming because I called to say I would be in late, Evelyn always waited up for me to take her into the bedroom. It was a ritual with us, and very important to her.

"Should I stay home?" I asked.

Joyce shook her head. "No, I don't think so. These things happen. She probably didn't sleep well last night, and needs to catch up. She's so thin and vulnerable, anything like that can throw her rhythms off. Let's let her sleep. I'm sure she'll be fine."

I hesitated, trying to read any doubt behind the nurse's words, but seeing none, nodded and moved quietly into the bedroom. Evelyn was sleeping peacefully, just as Joyce had indicated. I kissed her tenderly, stroking her head gently with my gesture of affection, and headed back out of the bedroom.

"My cell is always on," I said as I passed Joyce. "Call me immediately if there's even the hint of a problem."

216

"Of course," Joyce said. "How about you? How are you doing?"

I gave her a weak smile. "Great."

"You go deal with Parents Night at the school, Mr. Scarlucci. I'll take care of things here."

I nodded, my hand up to my ear in the phone sign as I headed to the front door.

"Call me," I mouthed.

Surprisingly, the Ken Valentine business did not cause the disturbance at Parents Night that I had anticipated. Oh, there were plenty of stares as Mary J., Pugh and I stood in the main lobby to welcome people. And large numbers gathered at the memorial display that now had flowers around it and an abundance of messages, poems, and song lyrics fastened to it. Several candles had been placed at the memorial's base, but they were unlit because of school fire regulations.

Once seven-thirty arrived, Mary J. stepped into the main office to welcome parents via the P.A. system, listing Ken Valentine's name along with three others as teachers who were unable to attend and should be contacted by phone or email.

And the evening went on.

I walked around the building, praying people would leave me alone and, much to my amazement, they did. Of course, the fact that probably all of them had seen me on television with the police in front of the funeral home might have been a deterrent to casual early evening conversation. I mean, what were they going to say?

Oh, hi, Mr. Scarlucci. Saw you on TV when Mrs. Silverman spit in your friend's face, calling him a black bastard, and the police took him away.

I don't think so. Clearly, some things are better left unsaid.

I was headed down the main corridor to check in with Sherri on how the night was going, and I was almost to Wing C when I saw none other than Dr. Francis Farnsworth, accompanied by several parents, headed toward me from the opposite direction. It was too late to cut and run, pretending I hadn't seen him, so I girded up the old loins and walked steadily forward.

Seeing me, Farnsworth excused himself to the parents, and crossed to me. Without a word, he pointed to a nearby storage room door, and I walked to it, opened it, switched on the wall light switch and moved inside. Farnsworth followed me in, closing the door after him.

The room was the storage center for the English department, and full of books. Shelves and shelves of nicely-arranged books lined the walls in easily identifiable alphabetical order. Thanks to Sherri Walsh's solution, each wall of shelves was actually made up of several tall individual carts of books on wheels, metal push handles mounted on the two sides of each cart. This made it possible for teachers to move the books to English classrooms by simply separating a

218

loaded cart of say Shakespearean plays from the rest, and wheeling the cart to rooms in the English wing. It was a great innovation that incorporated both logical organization and easy transportation for hundreds of hardcover books. What can I say? She's one smart lady.

Farnsworth's hands went into his suit pants pocket as he looked at me.

My cell phone rang. I gave him an index finger of momentary apologetic necessity and answered it.

It was Joyce.

"Brian...."

"Yes, Joyce. What is it?"

"It's nothing. I just knew you were worried, and wanted to tell you we're fine here. Evelyn has not awakened and appears to have settled in for the night. Everything is fine. I just thought you'd want to know."

A wave of tension eased inside me. I thanked Joyce, clicked off, and pocketed the phone, turning my attention back to Farnsworth.

"The nurse at my home. Sorry."

It was an underhanded ploy to put Farnsworth off if he had been in the mood to do a little Scarlucci ass chewing, but I didn't much give a shit. Whatever works, as they say.

As expected, his forehead wrinkled in concern. "Everything all right?"

"Yes, thanks."

He nodded.

"Not the easiest of days for you, Brian. Or any of us, for that matter."

He moved around the room, looking at the book titles that lined the walls as he grasped one of the cart handles.

"You know, this shelf/cart combination idea that Sherri came up with is such a good one, I've requested that the Board approve having these specially-designed book carts put in all the schools," He continued. Then he dropped his hand from the cart handle and turned back to me. "The lawyer, J. D. Booker called me."

I waited, saying nothing.

"He wants to go over the emails with me personally. Says legally I have no choice and must comply."

I waited, saying nothing.

He shook his head. "Damn it, what a mess! I...I see now what you were trying to point out this morning. This Silverman woman is a damned lunatic of the first order. What the hell was she thinking, screaming out a racial slur like that? My God, talk about unwanted publicity. Arnold Federly tells me the national news wires have picked up on it."

I waited, saying nothing.

"In any case, I want you to know that I'm not going to just stand by and let a member of this district be treated in such a horrific manner as took place this afternoon in front of that funeral home. J. D. Booker and I will go through the emails together sometime tomorrow, and I'll do everything I can to get Mr. Valentine back in the classroom as soon as possible."

I almost said, *Yeah, better late than never,* but I didn't, waiting, saying nothing.

"I heard about the cafeteria incident today," Farnsworth continued. "We all owe you a debt of thanks for handling that so well. This could have been a pretty mean day for the district if you hadn't been able to calm that one down so quickly." He paused a moment. "I owe you my thanks. I value your presence in this high school, Brian, and I'm going to do what I can to help make the situation right with your friend. Despite what some may think, I not only care about what happens in this district, I also care about the staff members who serve it."

His hand came out of his pants pocket, and he offered it to me.

"I'm not just an empty suit, you know." Dr. Farnsworth said with a knowing smile. "Will you keep me informed about how things are going with Ken?"

I shook his hand.

Maybe there was something inside that suit, after all.

"I'll keep you informed," I said.

Sherri Walsh was seething as she exited the women's faculty room at the end of Wing C. I had seen her go in as I approached the Wing, and was waiting for her when she came out.

"Hey, what's up?" I said.

"Oh, it's nothing."

I opened the door and stepped quickly back into the room with her, holding my foot against the closed doorframe so no one would enter.

"Sherri...what's wrong?"

She shook her head angrily. "It's A. J. Gotz. He played a recording in front of the classroom instead of talking to the parents to save his voice because he was *hoarse from teaching all day*. Can you imagine? Jesus, why does he do shit like that? The parents went bug-fuck, of course. About twenty have either called or came storming down to my office so far, and the evening is only half over."

I gave her a quick kiss, pulling her to me. "Now don't you feel better, getting that off your chest."

She hugged me. "Sorry. I know you don't need to hear my complaints right now. I saw the television. Unbelievable."

"You could say that."

"Any news?"

I shook my head. "It looks like nothing's going to happen until morning. I would have gone to the station house, but Ken didn't want me there. He's the boss on this one. Farnsworth just stopped me and said he'll do what he can for Ken, though, so that's a nice change of tune."

She nodded. "I better get back out there. Are you going to The Horse afterwards?" A few drinks to unwind at The Black Horse Tavern was always a staff tradition after a Parents Night. I hesitated. "Come on, just one drink. We could both use it."

"We'll see," I said.   Sherri gave me a quick hug, I removed my foot from blocking the door, and we slipped back out into the hallway to face the remainder of the evening.

And what a remainder of an evening it turned out to be.

TWENTY-TWO
HORSING AROUND

The evening's teacher conferences had ended, and parents, with more than an occasional glance at where I stood leaning against the corridor wall, were slowly leaving the building.

Sherri came up beside me. She stood next to me for a moment, smiling and nodding to parents as they passed.

"Did you hear the news?" she asked, looking not at me, but at the passing parents.

"Don't tell me."

"Okay."

"Tell me."

"Salvatore Mordento died of a sudden massive heart attack earlier this evening."

"What!"

She nodded, still not looking at me. "You heard me. Sal The Gimp is dead, Brian. The Media students had the television playing in the cafeteria when the story broke on Fox News a few minutes ago."

"He's dead?" I said, repeating the information needlessly as I absorbed the shock of it.

She looked my way with the slightest of nods and then out to the corridor again.

"The Black Horse Tavern is definitely on," I said. "I need a drink."

224

"Well, I happen to know you've come into quite a sum of money, so you're buying," she said.

The good thing about The Black Horse Tavern was that it was not that far from the school, which made it an easy stopover before we all headed home, not too loaded to drive, of course. The bad thing about the place was that it was very popular and therefore packed most nights of the week, which meant you had to either shout to be heard, or stand very close to each other as you talked.

We'd been there a while, and I was finally beginning to unwind. At the moment, Karen Wuant was standing very close to me, wine glass in hand, as I sipped my Johnny Walker.

"Excuse me while I get another Chardonnay," she said.

I took her glass. "Allow me. I need a refresher anyway."

"Okay. I've got to pee. I'll meet you right here."

"I'll be here, drinks in hand," I said.

Karen disappeared and I worked my way through various faculty members and assorted regulars to the bar, reaching over Suzy Shiftlet and Sherri, where they sat next to each other on the padded red bar stools. I waved to Barry behind the bar.

"Two more, Barry. Johnny and a Chardonnay."

His shaved head gleaming from the light of the bulbs that lined the mirror behind the bar, Barry gave the briefest of nods, took the glasses and moved on without a word, but I knew he had the order. Barry always had the order. That's why we came to The Black Horse and left big tips.

"Hi, Brian," Suzy said, flicking her long, black hair as she turned to me. "It is true what I hear?"

I smiled, squeezing in between Suzy and Sherri. "That depends. What do you hear?"

Lifting her arms, Suzy Shiftlet shifted her long lean sultry self sexily on her bar stool. "The Samba!"

Barry placed the drinks in front of me, and I threw a twenty down on the bar. He made change with astonishing speed and moved on, taking several orders at once.

"Well, we'll see," I said. "The first lesson was today, and I had to miss it, so I don't know. As you and the entire town are aware, I was otherwise occupied this afternoon."

Sherri took a pull on her beer and shook her head at me. "Oh no, we're not going to go there, Brian. We're talking about the dance. There's not a damn thing we can do for Ken 'til tomorrow, so let's talk about something else. It'll do you good. Doesn't mean you don't care. Just take a break for a while. That's an order."

I took a full swig of Johnny Walker and lifted it to Sherri.

"Whatever you say. Gee, I didn't realize my mother was here to tell me how to behave."

Sherri made a face, shook her head, and turned to Molly Kirkland on the opposite side of her. I shifted around to beside Kirkland.

"Molly, I had to leave before I had a chance to compliment you on the lesson today," I said.

Molly frowned, her hand to her ear. "What?"

I lifted my glass again and shouted. "Great job today! I loved the lesson!"

Molly clicked my glass with her own long-stemmed glass containing an Apple Martini. "Thanks, Brian. You didn't happen to see my keys anywhere when you were in the classroom, did you?"

"You are shitting me, I hope."

She laughed. "Yes, I am."

Karen came up behind me. "Where's my drink?"

I reached past Sherri and handed it to her. "Right here. And Sherri says I should talk about the dance, so lay it on me. What is the Samba?"

Eyes widening in delight, Karen grabbed my hand and led me away from the bar, bumping into people. "Give us room here, please. Dance time. Room, please."

Bodies moved to clear a space, laughing and applauding, and I stopped, pulling back in protest. "I didn't mean now."

"Better when you're drunk than sober, right?" She dropped my hand and grabbed a nearby Theresa Deckel by the waist, spinning the blonde, svelte-bodied math teacher around. "Come on, Terry. Brian needs to learn the Samba. Let's show him some moves."

Laughing, the ladies turned and twisted as partners, their bodies swaying and moving sensually. People applauded, me included. Then real Samba music came on from somewhere, blasting out of the speakers above the bar and more people started dancing.

Barry again, on top of it, as usual. The guy is good. Several people tossed loose thank-you money on the bar as even more bodies danced and swayed.

Suddenly, I was between the ladies, trying to move with them, my drink sloshing over the sides of the glass. Suzy Shiftlet got up from her bar stool, grabbed Molly by the hand, and, laughing and clapping, the two sashayed into the dance space people had created beyond the bar.

"Good, Brian," Karen said, taking my hand and shifting against me, "Step slightly back. Toe first, slide your right foot back and change weight onto the right foot. Good. Don't move your left foot!"

I was listening to none of this, of course, just twisting and dancing away, spinning from one woman's grasp and churning body to the next and loving it. Suzy spun me toward the bar, and I ended up bumping into Sherri.

"I'm learning the Samba," I said with a grin.

"I see that. You're such a fast learner too," she said, laughing and pushing me back onto the floor.

And on and on we danced and drank.

And then, within the sounds of the laugher and the music, I heard a cell phone ringing. Once. Then again. Then again. And I realized it was mine.

I stopped, the women clapping as they laughed and spun around me.

I squinted in the dim lighting beyond the bar, checking the number on the phone.

It was Joyce.

Knowing there was no way she was calling me again to tell me everything was all right, I pushed my way through the dancing bodies and laughing crowd. Once outside, I punched in the number, glancing back at the large plate glass window that covered the front of the bar, the black outline of a huge stallion rearing on its hind legs etched into the glass. Sherri was standing on the opposite side of the window, near the horse's flaring mane, staring out at me.

"Yes, Joyce," I said. "I'm here."

It was very bad news.

Sherri must have read my reaction because, as I listened and nodded to what was said on the other end of the phone, she came out the entrance doorway of the bar and moved to where I stood.

"Okay," I said into the cell. "I'll be right there."

I punched off and shoved the phone into my pocket.

"It's Evelyn. They've taken her to the hospital," I said, starting to turn toward the car. "Joyce tried to call me before, but I didn't hear the phone. I guess because of all the noise. Goddamn it. I should have gone home."

"Brian...," Sherri said.

"I've got to go, Sherri," I said.

"I know."

She said nothing more, but the words were in her eyes: *I care so much about you and your pain. Please let me say goodbye. One last kiss....*

I glanced toward the bar's window. Of course, people were looking. They were attempting to appear casual and occupied, but they were looking.

"They're watching, Sherri," I said.

She took my hand.

"I don't care."

I pulled her to me and kissed her strong and hard, emotion rushing between us as we held each other. When I backed away, she was crying soft tears, but there was no sound.

"I...I've got to go," I said.

And I left her there, standing in front of The Black Horse Tavern, crying quietly and watching me run frantically to my car so that I could get to the hospital where the ambulance had taken my wife.

TWENTY-THREE
AS I LAY DYING

They had taken Evelyn directly to the ICU at Brookdale General Hospital.

When I arrived, she was already totally unresponsive and in a stage two comatose state. There are four stages altogether, they informed me. Apparently, she had not been sleeping at home, but rather slipping quietly away. However, our knowing that would not have made a difference, they assured me. Her body had simply decided it was time to shut down.

It was the machine which registers brain activity – I don't know the name and I don't care -- that had told Joyce something was wrong. Apparently, at eleven when she went in to check on Evelyn, she had seen the drop in brain activity. A similar machine in the ICU now told them Evelyn's chances of recovering and functioning on a conscious level were very slim indeed.

I had been there only a few moments when Dr. Janice Greenwald entered and told me my options.

They were not good, and they involved only two choices. The first was to wait a few days to see if there was a response. However, considering the amount her body had deteriorated, Dr. Greenwald was not hopeful. She reminded me that we had always known this day would come, and that we had been fortunate that Evelyn had been able to enjoy her level of existence for as long as she had.

And the other option?

Turn off the machine.

A very short time after the machine was shut down, her body would do the same.

I chose option number one, Dr. Greenwald left, and I started to settle into the chair next to Evelyn's bed for the night. God knows, I should have been tired, but, of course, I wasn't. Wide awake didn't come close to how I felt. Emotional crisis: nature's maximum strength NoDoz.

Then a thought came to me, and I opened my briefcase. I looked at the iPad Ken had given me, tucked in among the school papers.

Sure, why not. 'I have promises to keep and miles to go before I sleep, and miles to go before I sleep.'

Going to the bed and checking on Evelyn, I glanced at the machines on the opposite side of the bed. The ventilator signs were steady as the machine breathed for her. And I wasn't a doctor, but even I could see the brain wave indicator was low or dim or whatever the fuck it was called when the goddamned line didn't spike the way it was supposed to anymore.

I petted Evelyn's head, straightening the thin wisps of hair, humming our special tune of *Where Have All The Flowers Gone* softly as I always did when I comforted her. She looked so peaceful, but then she always did when she was asleep. If it weren't for the brain wave indicator – I would find out the name tomorrow so I could refer to the goddamned thing correctly – I'd think everything was the same as always.

Except, I knew it wasn't.

"Good night, Evelyn. I will always love you," I whispered to my wife, kissing the top of her head once more. "Sleep well. God knows you deserve it."

In the quiet, the machine beeped.

And beeped. And beeped. And beeped.

The brain wave lines remaining the same, tiny little bumps as the pulsating line moved across the screen.

How long would I wait?

I shook my head at the thought. No, not now. I'd think about that tomorrow.

Standing by my briefcase, I bent down and picked up the iPad. I wondered how Ken's night was going. Though I hadn't anticipated it, jail was probably the better option to sitting and waiting to see if your wife was going to die.

Tomorrow I'd order some flowers for the room. Lots of flowers.

I'd put my cell phone on vibrate, and felt it buzzing in my pocket. I pulled out the phone and switched it to off without looking at it.

No, no more intrusions. This was *our* time.

I hit the wall switch. The lights in the hospital room dimmed, the only light coming from the outside hall and the low-wattage light above Evelyn's bed that bathed where she lay in a soft oval glow of warmth.

A nurse appeared at the doorway, but I waved her off.

"I'll call you if you are needed," I said, and closed the door partially, leaving it open only a crack so that the outside hallway light pierced through the opening, creating a line of light that led to where Evelyn lay in her bed and spreading sideways, creating a glowing cross.

I sat down by the hospital bed. I picked up the iPad, put the ear buds on, and clicked: Music; then iTunes – play list; then - Valentine; then - Tibetan Balls - came on the screen. I went to settings and tapped repeat, and then back to Tibetan Balls. I settled back in the chair and tapped the play arrow.

The sounds were rich and full. More pleasing to my senses than I'd remembered.

Gong…gong…gong…gong….

I raised the volume, finding comfort in the sound, wanting to fill my head with it, blocking out all else. The gongs came in even sequences, louder now, with a deeper richness that seemed to vibrate into my consciousness. I raised the volume yet again as thoughts tried to force their way into my mind.

No.

Not now.

Not here.

Tomorrow I would face it all, but not now.

Now I would listen as I had promised.

And I would listen and do nothing else.

Think of nothing else.

Only listen.

And I did.

Over, and over, and over, and over.

Later, the little battery sign on the iPad began to flash, and I reached into my briefcase without pausing the sound that filled my being. I plugged in the AC cord to both iPad and outlet on the wall next to me, and the Tibetan Balls gonged on.

And on.

And on.

And on.

And on.

And on.

And on.

I played the audio track all night long.

I may have dozed. I'm not sure. I only know that sometime just before dawn, the gongs still playing in my head, my mind suddenly spoke to me.

I started at the command and sat up.

"Go to Evelyn," my mind said.

I did.

I lifted my body out of the chair, crossed to the bed, and stood over her, watching her as she lay there in the soft light.

In the warm streams of light that surrounded her, she had changed.

She was beautiful.

And then, as I stood by the bed, her eyes opened and she looked at me.

I cannot describe the sensation that went through my body, and I know even now that what I experienced in that moment is not possible, and yet I know just as positively that it did happen.

I know it, for as our eyes met, Evelyn's voice spoke to me within my mind.

"*I must go now, Brian,*" she said. "*It is time. I must say goodbye, but only for now. All is well, my love. I promise you. All is well.*"

And her eyes closed once more.

"*Goodbye, my love,*" her voice whispered in my mind, so very softly and suddenly from so very far away.

And the pulsating line on the brain wave indicator machine became an even line.

And she was gone.

BOOK THREE

DEATH COMES TO CENTRAL HIGH

John Arthur Long

PROLOGUE

In spite of how carefully all their clandestine movement had been so precisely executed, the leader was still somewhat amazed at how easily they had been able to enter the United States.

Using the forged documents that had been provided, they had crossed the border from Canada, coming down into the country through upstate New York. Now they were in a safe house in what was called Queens, one of the outer communities beyond Manhattan. It appeared they had arrived without even a ripple of suspicion anywhere along the myriad of safeguards implemented by the great, sophisticated channels of America's Homeland Security.

The leader felt an inner satisfaction that his instructions had been followed with such obedience. The instruction that was not to be broken under penalty of death: Absolutely no Internet activity of any kind! He knew this was the great mistake made by so many, those who thought they were clever and that the encrypted messages could not be traced. There was only one way to avoid such mistakes. Remain totally anonymous, moving in the shadows of secrecy and dealing only with those who could be trusted like family. Do this and you would succeed. And now they were here.

They had not brought the nerve gas, the Sarin. That would arrive in an anonymously-labeled carton of industrial air conditioning supplies at the docks of Manhattan by an entirely different route which could not be traced or in any way identified with them.

Once the crate had arrived, it would be brought to them at their location in Queens where others would soon be arriving with the additional supplies of explosives and the weapons.

And then?

The leader smiled to himself.

Then it would be time to go to school.

TWENTY-FOUR
DEALING WITH IT

Ken Valentine was released by law enforcement the following morning at eight a.m. I saw it on the news that seemed to hammer at me from the counter television as I wandered into the kitchen after walking around the house, bumping into things and having not the slightest idea what the hell I was supposed to do with myself.

The arrangements were all taken care of and in process. Ken had helped me put all that in place years before. It didn't make it any easier necessarily, but at least I knew it was happening. People would be arriving later in the day to remove the medical equipment and hospital bed that Evelyn had used. The wake was scheduled for tomorrow at the Mahoney Funeral Home in Middle Island, funeral to follow the next day in the Mahoney Chapel, gathering for the mourners immediately following the gravesite visit back in the reception dining area.

Mahoney was a huge operation where several services were taken care of simultaneously in various sections of the complex. After researching the matter thoroughly a couple of years earlier, I had specifically chosen it because of that. I wanted lots of activity and people around, having no intention of going through it all in some isolated funeral home where family members, who have become masters at looking mournful, bullshit you through the process as they sell you gilded caskets and assorted crap that is designed to take you for everything you've got while you're so *vulnerable and will agree to anything.*

Sorry, mournful looking gold-diggers. Not this time.

Except for the flowers.

That was one area where the florist was going to make a small fortune. I'd already placed an order before I came to my senses, and the more I thought about it, the more I loved it.

Evelyn loved flowers, and she was going to get flowers, by God.

Sherri had called, of course, but I had insisted she go to work and not come over. I knew she wasn't happy about it, but what could I do? There would be time. It just couldn't be right now. I knew that in retrospect she would understand. Anyway, I hoped she would.

There was a knock at the front door and I moved to the kitchen doorway to see who stood behind the house entrance at the end of the hall.

It was Ken.

"How the hell did you get here so fast?" I said, pulling open the door and gesturing him inside.

"J. D. Booker dropped me off. You can pick up that tab. At his hourly rate, I figure the ride over here will cost you about a thousand dollars. You look like shit, by the way. Have you slept at all?"

We moved into the kitchen.

"Nice talk, coming from a man who spent the night in the slammer."

He moved to the counter and started making coffee. I didn't have to show Ken Valentine where anything was. "Not a bad place, actually. Nicely colored walls of pale green. Shower facilities. I made sure not to drop the soap, of course. You want some coffee?"

"Yeah, I guess. And could you make me some eggs, while you're at it since you had such a nice time last night, 'cause mine didn't go so well."

Ken dropped what he was doing, and turned and pulled me to him as I suddenly began to cry, unable to stop. He held me like that for a while until I got it somewhat together.

I pulled away, grabbing at tissues from the box I always left on the counter next to the sink.

"I'm so sorry, my friend," he said, wiping the wetness from his own eyes.

"I know...I know," I said, blowing my nose. "Where the hell are my eggs? I don't function very well without breakfast, ya know."

He moved to the stove, taking down a skillet from the overhead rack.

"Comin' right up." he said. "Shiiiiit, I might even have some eggs and sausages today, too. And grits, of course. Musn't fowgit the grits. You got any grits for this nigga, Bri?"

"Holy shit," I said, unable to express how happy I was that my friend had arrived to help erase my sorrow. "You *are* human, after all. Sheila Silverman actually pissed you off, didn't she."

"Can you believe that woman? Callin' me a black bastard? What the fuck was that all about? You're damned right I'm pissed. She betta watch herself. Next time I see her, I'm gonna whomp her motherfuckin' ass 'cause that was bullshit, man." He opened a silverware drawer next to the stove. "Where the hell you keep the motherfuckin' spatula anyway?"

I laughed through my sorrow, and he made breakfast, and we talked and I cried some more, and they came for the hospital equipment, and Ken answered phone calls and when needed passed the phone to me, and I listened to friends and family express their condolences, and somehow, with the help of my friend, I made it through the day.

The wake? Well, that was something else again.

I had ordered a closed casket. There was no way I was going to have people see the way Evelyn's crippled body looked and how it had deteriorated by the time of her death. Instead, I had a pre-framed picture of her taken right before our wedding in front of a beautiful bed of roses placed on the closed casket, which was surrounded by flowers, and I do mean surrounded by flowers.

I had gotten a little carried away. Even I had to admit there were a hell of lot of flowers around. That's what had people talking. I had ordered so many flowers that I was a shoo-in for the *Guinness Book of World Records*.

Enjoy the view, Evelyn, with my love.

Each new face brought different swells of emotion and responses to the surface, of course. Sherri squeezed my hand and met my eyes with meaning that only the two of us could share, dabbed her eyes and moved away to stand with fellow English teachers as the line eased forward and others greeted me: fellow teachers, Mary J., Pugh, Sam with others from Security, Betty Orche, my secretary with other secretaries, other staff members from various sections of the building and the district, School Board President Alice Levy and Board Member Joseph Burson, Farnsworth and Federly, other friends, family members, and on and on.

I watched people talk as the greeting line moved on...like Dr. Farnsworth and Ken Valentine as they walked out of the viewing room together. I wondered what that was about, but didn't have time to dwell on it, as others came up to express their condolences, and so I moved on.

After a while, a kind of numbness took over, and I just sort of floated through it all, greeting and meeting, and saying the same responses, doing my best to deal with it all.

It was Joey Mordento coming into the packed room of well-wishers during the evening viewing period of the wake that brought me out of my daze in which I had been functioning. I realized as I watched him approach in the line that he shouldn't be here. He should be at his own father's wake. And it turned out he was.

TWENTY-FIVE
AN OFFER YOU CAN'T REFUSE

"Joey," I said, taking his hand as he came up to me. "You didn't have to come. You have your own sorrows to deal with. I was sorry to hear about your father."

Joey shook my hand, looking very mature and together in his black suit. "That's okay, Mr. Scarlucci. We're over in the Georgian wing down the hall and to the left, and I wanted to drop by and express my condolences for your loss. I'm sorry about your wife."

I paused, grasping, after a moment, what he was saying. "You're here? I mean, the viewing for your father is here?"

"Yeah, down the hall."

"I'll be right back," I said to those around me. "I need to visit the restroom."

"Of course," was the response, heads nodding with quiet understanding.

I took Joey by the arm and guided him from the viewing room. Outside, to my left, Farnsworth was talking to Ken by the water fountain. Ken caught my eye and smiled, but continued talking to Farnsworth, the two of them discussing matters of import that I would find out about soon enough.

"Come on," I said to Joey, "is it this way?"

"Mr. Scarlucci, you don't have to...."

"Wrong, Joey," I said. "I do have to. Lead the way."

There is a certain anticipation as to how it's going to be when you walk into the wake of a person who has been the head of an organized crime family. And you know what? That's exactly the way it was.

I couldn't believe it! Sammy "Bod-A-Bing" Goombotch standing around with Pauly "Bod-A-Boom" Goombatch, and assorted other sordid-looking types. I mean, not everyone there was like that, of course. There were family members and regular probably-on-the-take society types, not to mention a few undercover G-men, but still, there was definitely a smell of we-take-no-shit-and-can-kill-you in the air of Salvatore Mordento's wake.

Sal "No-Longer-The-Gimp-Because-He's-Dead" Mordento *was* in an open casket. It was very ornate and a *large* casket, and as I stepped up to it and kneeled to pay my respects, I couldn't help but being thankful that I wasn't one of the pallbearers who had to lift and carry this baby.

Stepping back, I turned to Joey, speaking very quietly and quickly.

"So, who's in charge now, Joey," I said.

Joey frowned. "What do you mean, Mr. Scarlucci?"

"Cut the shit, Joey. You know what I mean. Who's in charge?"

Joey nodded. "Oh, you mean Uncle Tony."

"Introduce me, okay?"

"Sure." Shrugging, he led the way to a rotund balding figure who stood off to one side of the casket. Size Extra

246

Large definitely ran in the Mordento genes. Good thing Joey liked working out, 'cause when middle age kicked in, he was in trouble, if he lived that long, of course. In the Mordento family, there was a tendency to buy the farm before reaching old age.

"Uncle Tony, I'd like you to meet Mr. Scarlucci. He's a principal at my school," Joey said.

"Actually, Assistant Principal," I said, taking Tony Mordento's thick hand. "I'm sorry for your loss."

Tony's jowls moved as he nodded a little. "Yeah. Sal mentioned he'd met youse."

"Would it be possible for me to speak with you for a moment, Mr. Mordento?" I asked, releasing his hand. "In private."

Tony "The Jowls" looked at Joey, then, motioning for the two goons who stood near him to stay put, he gestured for me to follow him.

I did.

In the next-door anteroom, Tony stopped and looked at me. I recognized the family resemblance in the eyes: nothing there but vacant threat.

"So?" Tony Mordento said.

The urge to start off with a "How *you* doin'?" surfaced within me, but I suppressed it and went right for the gold.

I cleared my throat. "Suppose a certain party were given some money and didn't really want it or know what to do with it?" I said.

Tony took a labored breath. "You mean like a supposed fifty grand, fer instance?"

Okay, that took care of that little suspicion. I mean, let's face it. Nobody gives away fifty thousand dollars without someone else knowing about the money. Now all I had to do was get rid of it without getting killed.

Thank God I hadn't stained it.

I pursed my lips and shrugged my shoulders like I'd seen them do on *The Sopranos.* "Yeah, like that."

Tony sucked at his teeth for a moment, which, though a little uncouth, was certainly preferable to having one of his goons come in and fasten electrically-charged clamps to my balls.

"I'd say he should give it back to the rightful owners if he knows what's good for him." He paused for a beat, and then continued, staring at me with those dead eyes. "Can I level wit' youse?"

"Please," I said.

Oh, and also, please don't kill me.

"Sal, God rest his soul, was a little off as of late. The supposed funds you mention? It wasn't his to give. Certain people are upset about it. It's good you came to me."

"I want to do what's right," I said.

Tony grunted. "I'm sure you do, Mr. Spuducci."

"Uh, that's Scarlucci."

"Whatever. Where's the money?"

"Where ever you want it to be, Mr. Mordento," I said.

248

And to that, Tony Mordento chuckled, his jowls bouncing. "Sal said you were all right. I think we're going to be okay here. What do you think?"

"I certainly hope so," I said.

Sherri and Ken were waiting for me as I hurried back down the hallway to Evelyn's viewing room. Ken motioned for me to hurry as I approached.

"Where have you been? People are looking all over for you," he said.

"Taking care of business," I answered. "I stopped in at the Mordento wake. I wasn't gone that long, was I?"

Sherri's eyes widened. "You went to the Mordento wake?"

"That's correct. Fate offered me an opportunity, and I took it. The money problem is solved, thank God." I turned to Ken. "What happened in your talk with Dr. Farnsworth."

"Things are moving along. I'll fill you in later." Ken said. "But by money, I hope you don't mean the money that I found in your apartment." He grinned to Sherri. "Because I spent that, old Buddy. Got myself a new Beemer convertible. I figured I deserved it after all the shit I'm being put through."

"Great," I said, going with it. "Because I just made a deal with Tony "The Jowls" Mordento to give it back, so you can drive your new Beemer to the drop off point and tell him you've already spent the money. I suggest you take a large bazooka with you. Put the top down so you can get it in the car."

"You mean as in *say hello to my little friends*," Ken answered, doing a decent Pacino.

"Bigger," I said. "Much bigger."

Sherri interjected. "We really should get back in there, you know."

"He's been gone this long. Another minute won't matter," Ken said. "Seriously, now, Bri. What did he offer you for the money? I mean it's business. He must have offered you something."

"You know that old Bee Gees song?" I asked.

"Could it be you mean *Stayin' Alive*?"

"That's the one," I said.

Damn it.

Yeah, we'd been doing our thing in an effort to tread just above the sorrow that awaited me as I went back into the room to sit with the mourners while the priest spoke, but as Ken said it, going with the joke for my sake, I saw the little tick of hesitation in his response. I had led us down the wrong humorous path and knew it immediately, grabbing from within to take it back…but it was too late.

You don't joke about *Stayin' Alive* with a man who has told you he has incurable cancer.

In the midst of my sorrow, I was slipping, goddamn it. What the hell was I thinking with a remark like that?

Yes, you deserve to be messed up right now, but this is your best friend. Get a handle on it, Scarlucci. Don't let shit like that happen again.

250

Sherri was totally unaware of anything amiss, because she had not even been told yet, one more little matter of difficulty that would have to be dealt with sooner or later. I hadn't meant it, of course, and Ken would know that. Still, it was there.

And as I moved back into the viewing room, the sorrow that hovered over me like a dark storm cloud thickened once again in my awareness that the mean days in which I found myself were far from over.

The funeral the next day was beautiful and horrible, as one would expect. As the guitar player did his rendition of Pete Seeger's *Where Have All The Flowers Gone?*, I thought my head was going to explode in agony, and the gravesite ceremony wasn't much better, but somehow I got through it all.

Rest in peace, my love.

It was later near the conclusion of the required post-funeral feed that I finally had a moment to stop and reflect about what had happened in the hospital room when Evelyn had passed away. Ken and I were standing alone in a far corner of the dining hall, and people were leaving us alone for a change.

"Could we discuss the audio track for a second?" I asked him. "There's something I need to talk to you about."

"Sure," he said, pleased as punch with my topic suggestion.

"The thing is," I continued, "I didn't tell you this, but at the hospital that night, I listened to it. I thought it might calm me down, you know...."

"And...?"

"And after listening to the Tibetan Balls all night, I thought I heard a voice in my head. Does that sound reasonable to you?"

"Go on. Let me hear the rest before I answer," he said.

"She spoke to me, Ken," I said, not believing it myself as I said the words aloud. "As I stood over Evelyn's bed just before she passed, she opened her eyes and it sounded to me like she spoke to me inside my head."

A light of excitement came into Ken's face. "No fooling around now, Brian. I mean it. Are you telling me that Evelyn communicated to you just before she died after you spent the night listening to the Tibetan Balls audio track?"

"Well, yes. I mean I know I was pretty screwed up, and needed sleep and all. But, it seemed so real. I don't know. What do you think?"

"I think you don't know how happy you've made me, Brian," he said, smiling broadly. "I knew it."

"But it can't be true. I mean seriously now, Ken. Evelyn did not *really* speak to me. It can't be true, can it?"

Ken wrapped his arm around my shoulder.

"Just keep listening, old buddy," he said. "Just keep listening."

TWENTY-SIX
DUDE, WHERE'S MY CAR?

In the passing days, everything started looking up a little, actually. On Saturday, as I watched the local cable channel from the safety of my kitchen, Central High won the big playoff football game:

...seconds left as Bobby Weiss goes to the line. This is it, folks. Central must make this play. Weiss looks both ways. Set. Hutt...Hutt. And HE KEEPS THE BALL. Look at that, folks. It's a quarterback sneak! What a chancy call from Coach Hite with only seconds left in the game!

Weiss moves to left, cuts back, dodges the right tackle, and leaps into the air. TOUCHDOWN! CENTRAL WINS THE GAME!

YAAYYYYYYYYYYYYYYY!!

Pom Pom lift: Gimme a C, gimme an E, gimme a BLAH, BLAH, BLAH, ...WHAT'S THAT SPELL? CEENNNTTTRRAALLLL! YEHHHHHHHHHHHHH! Shake Pom-Poms and leap around like a lunatic as the football players jump up and down, hugging each other and smacking each other's asses and The Q-Man's marching band members swing their instruments and play "Ya Gotta Be A Football Hero" as loud as they possibly can, ...YAAYYYYYYYYYYYYY!....

Oh yeah...and our thanks to Mr. Scarlucci for not suspending Bobby Weiss because the kid was screwing around during bio and putting leaches on the neck of a hemophiliac to impress his girlfriend, Dawn, who is the one going apeshit with the Pom-Poms in front of the bleachers....Yeah, right.

The other piece of what looked like really good positive change came from Channel Ten later that same day in the form of breaking news by Pamela Shutter, the young lock-jawed newscaster I'd seen clam up in front of Joey at Laura Silverman's wake:

"...according to our sources, lawyer J. D. Booker and Dr. Francis Farnsworth, after a careful review of the email communications between Central High School teacher Ken Valentine and the deceased female Central High student, Laura Silverman, have reached a decision that there were absolutely no improper communications between the two. Based on further analysis of the circumstances surrounding the girl's death and an agreement by the authorities, in an announcement which should be forthcoming by tomorrow or early Monday, it appears that there is a good chance that Mr. Valentine will be allowed to return to the classroom within the next few days. Superintendent Farnsworth is quoted as saying he is pleased with the decision, and looks forward to Mr. Valentine's return to his teaching assignment. Mr. Booker promises that his client will make a full public statement as soon as the authorities have reached their decision. Mrs.

Silverman, the mother of the deceased Central High student is in seclusion and could not be reached for comment. I'm Pamela Shutter, inviting you to stay tuned for the latest developments right here at Channel Ten, where when the latest in news breaks, you see it right here on Channel Ten...."

Ms. Shutter's announcement merely confirmed what Ken had told me in a phone call earlier that morning, but still, it was good to hear the words said in a public news statement.

Everyone from Farnsworth to Mary J. had told me to take a few days off, of course. However, by Sunday night, after answering "How are you doing, Brain?" phone calls for three days and eating small portions of the seventeen tons of food that had been delivered hour by hour to my house, I was getting a little stir crazy.

I had only left the house once, and that was to go to the apartment on a secret mission. I picked up the money that I had enclosed within a large sealed Inter-office envelope, and had driven to an undisclosed location where I was met by Sammy "Bod-A-Bing" Goombotch, who *took it off my hands*. Other than the fact that, as I drove back to my house, the feeling of relief was very satisfying, that's all I can tell you about that because if I told you any more,....well, you know.

The truth is that the only other relief I was able to attain during those first days after Evelyn's passing came from listening to Ken Valentine's audio track. Perhaps because of what happened, it gave me a feeling of closeness to my departed wife, or maybe it was simply that it allowed me to go away to la-la land for a while, where billions of thoughts could not continue to speed through my mind, begging for attention. Whatever the reason, I had listened to the Tibetan recording on the iPad regularly in both morning and evening sessions over the days following the funeral, and it gave me a wonderful feeling of comfort and peace.

Still, in between those meditation sessions, I was getting more and more antsy, and by Monday morning, it was either bang my head against the wall or go to work.

I decided to go to work.

Returning to the job after any sad occasion is always difficult. People want to be supportive, but don't know what to say. You dread the fact that every single person you encounter will feel compelled to say something, and, though it is appreciated, you will have to respond to these condolences over and over. After the first day, everything gets back to normal. It's that first return to work that's difficult. Fortunately for me, I had a nice little distraction waiting for me when I walked into Central High School which broke the ice…or rather the wall.

Betty Orche stood and hurried over to me as I came into the main office. Other secretary heads came up from where they were typing away at their stations.

"Brian." she said, "What a surprise."

I understood she wouldn't be expecting me, but she seemed not only surprised, but anxious.

"I know, but I figured getting back to work would distract me."

"I'm sure that's true, but...."

"I know, Betty. People said stay home, but this is best for me."

"That's fine, except...."

Uh ohhh. Bad Betty behavior. Something was wrong.

"Except what," I said with a wary frown.

"Except that...there's a car in your office," Betty said.

Of course there was a car in my office. What would a day at Central High be like without some kind of unexpected bullshit coming at me from all directions the minute I stepped though the door, not that I had any idea what *a car in my office* really meant. I mean, there couldn't really be a *car in my office*.

Oh, yes there was.

Mary J. emerged from her office, started forward and saw me.

"Brian...."

I walked quickly to greet her. "Yeah, I decided to come in. Betty tells me there's a car in my office?"

Saying nothing more, Mary J. gestured with a curl of her index finger for me to follow and led me to my office door. She took out her key, slipping it into the opening below the door knob, then shoved back the bolt of a new locking hasp that had been installed shoulder high to the door frame, releasing the locked door, and opened it with a flourish.

It was incredible. An old rusted-out black Chevy sat in the middle of the room. It sat in the space backwards, having smashed through the side wall, taking out the radiator along that wall, the video stand and equipment, the lamp that stood by my desk, and a portion of the side of the desk itself. Dust, cement, plaster, books, papers, and all sorts of crap was scattered everywhere. There was a huge ragged hole that led to the outside of the school where the wall should have been and flies buzzed around the room. "Tally Ho" figures had been scrawled all over the remaining three walls and one huge particularly obscene "Tally Ho" rendering glared from the car's hood.

I shook my head as flies buzzed near where we stood, and she closed the door. "There really is a car in my office."

"Yes," she said. "And a rather large deposit of human feces in the exact spot on the driver's seat where the driver *should* be."

"That explains the flies. The phantom strikes again. Listen, I know this is my office, but I want you to know those cartoon drawings were not there when I left."

Mary J. was not amused. "I have a feeling that if we can just find the culprit to this, it will *all* stop. And I'm making it my mission, damn it. This has happened for the last time. I mean it. I'll triple security, paying out of my own pocket, if I have to. I'll add more cameras, whatever it takes, but this has to stop. The police were here, of course, dusting for prints and taking down information. It happened Friday. Someone should be here later to tow the car away. I was hoping to have it cleaned up a little before you got here, but here you are."

I nodded. "Yes, here I am. How did he accomplish it?"

"Lock on the steering wheel and a brick on the accelerator. The car was stolen, of course. Taken off a side street. Apparently, sometime in the pre-dawn hours of Thursday night the perpetrator...."

"Known to us as the phantom shitter," I added.

Mary J. shook her head, unable to keep the tiniest trace of a smile off her face. "Nice to have you back with us once more, Brian," she said. "Anyway, according to the police explanation, he must have parked the car on the grassy slope outside and, after locking the steering in the right position, revved the engine as high as possible, fastened a brick against it so that it would continue revving, put the car in reverse gear, and leaped out. Worked perfectly. As you can see, it came smashing right through the wall, just as he had planned."

"This could be a good thing, you know." Mary J. frowned. "I'm just trying to see the cup half full rather than half empty. Maybe he made a mistake and left a clue that the police can use. I mean this isn't just an angry kid taking a dump somewhere. This is auto theft and destruction of public property. Our phantom has entered the big time of real criminals here. Any leads?"

"They found a partial print on the steering wheel. No matches yet."

"Tell them to run Lewis Grimley's prints."

She nodded. "Already done. The partial print is not enough to be conclusive."

"OOOkkkaay then," I said. "Well, I'll salvage what I can from here to deal with my needs of the immediate future. Where should I set up shop?"

She looked around. "I guess you'll have to share Larry's office for the time being until I can get something worked out."

Yeah, right. Like that's going to happen.

"Where should I set up shop?" I said.

Mary J. sighed. "All right. Use the Guidance conference room for now. I'll tell them it's off limits until we can find you a more permanent space."

Sam Shapiro's flushed face appeared at the end of the hallway as he came hurrying around the corner, talking as he moved. "I need someone."

"What is it, Sam?"

"Mitch Bright just hit a kid during his Global class. He's got the kid outside the room trying to calm him down."

"I'll take it, Mary," I said. "Mitch will listen to me. Knickerbocker free?"

Mary was already headed the other direction toward her main office secretary's desk. "I'll check. If not, I'll get someone else there to watch the class."

I nodded. "Let's go, Sam."

TWENTY-SEVEN
GOOD TO BE BACK

Mitchell Bright was standing outside his closed classroom door in Wing C, having a heated discussion with a male student when Sam and I got there. Mitch appeared to be trying to deal with the irate teen, but it wasn't happening. And it wasn't happening because Mr. Bright had gotten into a confrontation with the boy. Rule number one of teaching: Never get into a confrontation with a student. It always escalates and it always turns out badly.

The kid continued to shout back at Mitch.

Sam stepped a few paces back, and let me handle things.

"What's the problem here, Mr. Bright?" Assistant Principal Scarlucci said, casually inquisitive, but with an air of authority.

"He hit me," the student yelled, pointing at Mitch.

"I did not hit you," Mitch countered. "I hit the desk as a warning. The desk hit you."

"Same goddamned thing," the enraged student said.

Mitch exploded, spit spewing from his mouth as he stood straight, his huge body lifting to its full height in his rage.

"WHAT? HOW DARE YOU USE THE LORD'S NAME IN VAIN! THAT'S *MY GOD YOU ARE BLASPHEMING, YOUNG MAN, AND THAT'S WHY I HIT YOUR DESK! YOU WILL NOT USE THE LORD'S NAME IN VAIN IN MY CLASS! 'HEED MY WARNING, SAITH THE LORD'!*"

The student backed away, his anger transforming into genuine fright.

"See," the student sputtered. "I told you. He's crazy!"

Sherri came rushing down the hall, sans Gene Knickerbocker. I had forgotten that Knickerbocker had been assigned to cover Ken Valentine's classes in his absence.

"May I help out here?" she said.

"Yes, Ms. Walsh," Assistant Principal Scarlucci answered. "Why don't you step in and watch Mr. Bright's class for a moment while we work this out."

Sherri nodded and went through the door, closing it after her.

"What's your name?" I asked the boy.

"Charlie Fena," he answered, having moved to behind me to avoid the wrath of God's self-appointed servant.

"Well, Charlie, maybe you can help clear this up for me. What did you say in Mr. Bright's class?"

Charlie Fena shrugged and looked at the floor. "I don't know...."

"Yes you do, Charlie!" Mitchell Bright said, his finger pointing down at the kid like Moses to the worshipers of the Golden Calf.

"Let's let Charlie tell me, Mitch," I said, my eyes meeting his in warning.

Mitch crossed his arms, standing firm.

"Did you swear in class, Charlie?"

"And don't lie, Charlie," Mitch put in. "This God you're so fond of blaspheming sees all!"

"So what if I did?" Charlie said, his anger getting the better of him. "Bright's crazy and everybody knows it. I'm getting transferred out anyway. My mom's already called Guidance and everything."

"Tell you what, Charlie," I said. "I'm going to send you along with Mr. Shapiro to the Dean's office. " I turned to Sam. "Mr. Shapiro, have Dean Latch assist Charlie in filling out an insubordination form." I turned back to the student. "Charlie, I want you to go to Guidance after the forms are filled out, and see what may or may not have happened with a change in your schedule. Then go to my office...."

No, I don't think so....

"Rather...then go to the Guidance conference room and I'll be along to help you straighten things out in a few minutes."

Sam led the student away, and I turned to Mitch Bright.

"Did you hit him? And don't lie to me, Mitch!"

"I hit the desk, and it moved. As God is my witness. I do not lie, Brian, and I resent the fact that you would think such a thing. I'm also sorry for your loss. God be with her."

"Thank you, Mitch, but we're talking about you right now."

"I only meant she's better off now that she's with God. Her suffering is over. She did seek the forgiveness of our Lord before she died, I assume, for otherwise she could not take her rightful place in the Kingdom of Heaven."

I felt a dull ache begin in the back of my head. Maybe I *had* come back too soon.

"Mitch, I don't want to talk about my wife. Listen to me. This is very serious. If this kid files charges against you, you've got a problem. Now I may have to send him back in here for tomorrow's class. There can be no more problems. Do you hear me? There have been too many incidents, Mitch. It may be taken out of my hands. No more problems. Do you understand?"

"God will take care of me," Mitch said.

"Yeah, well in case he's a tad busy, you better start looking after yourself. All right?"

His eyebrow arched. Mitch stood tall once more. "Do you blaspheme, Brian?"

The bell rang, ending the period. The classroom door opened and students poured out.

"I have to go upstairs to my next class," Mitch said. "As you have warned me, I mustn't be late. May I go?"

I nodded, and Mitch strutted away. Sherri came out of the room and stood next to me.

"Hi," she said. "Welcome back. I take it you've seen your office."

"You know, we've only talked on the phone about seven hundred times in the last few days. You could have told me."

"Well, Mary said you and Larry are going to be roommates. I didn't want to ruin the surprise."

"Very thoughtful of you. I didn't mean for you to have to cover Mitch's class, by the way," I said. "I forgot Gene was taking Ken's classes."

"Actually I borrowed Monica Smith, the Language substitute, to cover Ken's classes for now. She's better at control than Gene, and I wasn't sure how long the Ken coverage would be needed. Gene Knickerbocker is covering Maggie Madison's class at the moment," she said. "Maggie seems to be missing from the school building...."

I looked at her. "Don't tell me...."

"I don't know anything for sure. But I did look up Todd Hershborne's schedule and go to the classroom to check."

"No suspense, please. I'm too vulnerable. I have no office, you know," I said.

"Todd was not in his math class. Could be absent from school, of course. I was about to check on that when I got the call that Mitch's class needed coverage so I came straight here."

"Okay, I'll check on it," I said.

"I missed you," Sherri said, as she walked away.

"Same here," I called after her, a genuine smile on my face. It was good to be back.

TWENTY-EIGHT
ANSWER ME THIS

After calming Charlie Fena down enough to make sure no charges would be brought against Mitchell Bright, I spent the rest of the morning trying to bring some kind of order to the stuff I hauled out of my office. While I was moving things, the tow truck came and removed the car. This left my office just one big mess with a blue tarp stretched over the hole where the wall had been.

Oh, and also, the word came into the main office that Maggie Madison had gotten a flat tire while out getting coffee at the nearby Starbucks, and would be back as soon as possible. I had checked with Attendance while in Guidance and discovered that Todd Hershborne was indeed out, having gone to the doctor to get medication for a sore throat, but planned to be back in school by noon so that he could still be at rehearsal for the play that afternoon.

You see what rumors and innuendoes can do to the mind. I made a mental note to myself to let the Maggie suspicions go. Enough was enough. Let someone else be the hanging judge on that one.

Finally tired of collecting materials from among the rubble and sorting it out on the round table in the Guidance conference room, I headed for some lunch. Maggie Madison came rushing in the front entrance from outside, and I stopped her as we met in the main lobby.

"Everything okay, Maggie?" I asked.

"Brian...," she said in surprise. "You're back."

"Yeah, couldn't stay away. How's the tire?"

"Not tire...TIRES!" she responded, her face coloring in rage. "Someone slashed all four of the tires on my car in the parking lot while I was in getting coffee at Starbucks. I should have gone to the drive-thru window, but I needed to go to the bathroom, so I parked and went inside. Then I had to wait until a tow truck came for my car. Unbelievable."

"Well, it's okay here. Knickbocker is covering your classes. Relax."

"Relax!" Maggie shot back. "How can I relax? That bastard Galli slashed my tires, Brian!"

"We don't know that. Did you actually see him do it?"

"Who the hell else would do such a thing while I run in for coffee, for Christ's sake."

"All right. Tell you what. I'll make a call over to the middle school later. See if he left the building during the morning. Okay? We'll take it from there."

She sighed. "Okay. I better get going."

I took her arm. "Maggie, take a deep breath, and relax. It'll be all right. Okay?"

"Okay," she said, trying to smile; then Maggie hurried on down the hall.

Considering the ramifications of that new little development, I continued on my way to lunch. And I almost made it, too. However, just as I walked past the library

267

doorway on the way to the faculty room, who to my wandering eyes should appear, but Harold Billings, the Answer Man, also on his way to lunch.

"Hello, Harold," I said, stepping up beside him.

"Hello, Brian," he said, head looking straight ahead. "I'm sorry for your loss."

I squinted at him. "That's it. Don't you have a question for me, maybe?"

"I don't find that amusing, Brian."

I stopped. "Wait a minute. Okay, look, I'm sorry I yelled at you. There was a lot going on the other morning. Come on, ask me a question?"

"I wouldn't want to bother you," Billings said, though I noticed he had stopped with me rather than moving ahead to the lunchroom.

"Come on, Harold, you know you want to. Let me make it up to you. Ask me a question. Let's see if I know the answer. I actually used that one about the cat that you told me the other day. Thanks to you, people are lifting cat's tails all over my neighborhood."

Billings smiled and took a deep appreciative breath. He just couldn't resist. "All right, if you insist, I might have a question or two that need answers."

I opened my arms, palms up. "Lay it on me, Answer Man."

I had just been placating Billings, trying to make up for the way I had treated him the other day, but when he asked the question, to my own amazement, I knew the answer.

268

"Where are Panama hats made?"

"Ecuador," I said, the answer rolling out of me. "They're called Panama Hats because they were distributed through Panama."

Billings looked at me, a little taken aback. "That's right. How did you know that?"

"I don't know," I said with a shrug, "I must have heard it somewhere. I'm glad we talked, though. Come on. Let's get lunch."

Oh, no. Not yet, Brian. Fool that I was, I had opened Pandora's box. When would I ever learn?

"Wait a minute," was the Billings response. "Here's another one. On *Star Trek*, what was Captain James T. Kirk's middle name?

"Tiberius," I said, a little astounded I actually knew the answer, since I didn't give a good flying shit about *Star Trek* and never had.

"That's right," Billings said, with the slightest edge of irritation. "Which dog bites the least?"

"Golden retriever."

"Come on, Brian. How are you doing this? It's some kind of trick, isn't it? That's why you asked me. So you could do this to me."

"Do what? No, Harold, I swear to you. I just got lucky. Come on, let's eat."

"Oh, no. Let's just see what's really going on here. How many stars can you see on a clear night?"

269

The number *2,500* came into my mind.

"I don't know. I guess around 10,000, maybe more," I told Billings.

The Answer Man beamed. "Wrong...the correct number is 2,500."

Hmmmm.

"Okay, good," I said. "See, it was just luck. Let's eat."

"One more," Billings said. "Who was the founder of Detroit?"

The answer came in, loud and clear within my head: *Antoine de la Mothe Cadillac, a French explorer.*

I shrugged. "Henry Ford?"

"Wrong. Antoine de la Mothe Cadillac. The Cadillac automobile is named after him. Maybe you *were* just lucky. Let's do one more just to be sure. Why is a swan song a farewell?"

The swan, silent its entire life, sings aloud just before it dies, came the answer, and my chest tightened.

"I don't know," I said.

"Because," Billings replied, all proud of himself, "according to legend, the swan never makes a sound until its final moments of life when it sings out loud."

"I think I'm finished for now, Harold," I said. "I really don't want to talk about death."

His hand went to his mouth in shocked realization. "Oh, good Lord, I'm sorry, Brian. I'm so sorry. I didn't mean to...."

"I know you didn't," I said. "Enjoy your lunch."

And as Harold Billings, the Answer Man, scooted away down the hall on the fleeting soles of embarrassed regret as quickly as he could without actually running, disappearing into the faculty dining room, I stood there for a moment...dealing with a question of my own.

Answer me this, Brian Scarlucci, you smart ass, you. *YOU DIDN'T MISS A SINGLE QUESTION FROM THE* *ANSWER MAN. How the hell did you know all those answers?*

But mysteriously, the Answer Man inside Brian Scarlucci's head had vanished.

I had no idea.

TWENTY-NINE
GOOD NEWS

"Brian," Karen Wuant called as I left the lunch line with my tray of chicken salad and a bottle of Poland Spring. I saw her scoot over, leaving me a seat next to her. "Come sit with us."

"Hello, ladies," I said, sliding in my chair and nodding hello.

"You decided to come back right away, huh," Karen said. "That's probably for the best. Keep busy."

"That's what I thought," I said.

Suddenly, Sherri Walsh came hurrying into the dining room. She instructed the food server to turn on the television that the Media squad had mounted near the ceiling beyond the serving counter to Channel Ten News. We barely ever watched it, wanting a break from the day's happenings while we ate, so I knew if Sherri wanted it on, it was about something important.

It's Ken, my mind said to me.

"There's been a decision," Sherri said, glancing to me with a twinkle in her eye. "J. D. Booker and Ken Valentine are holding a news conference."

The picture snapped on, and sure enough, the news conference was in progress. Facing the cameras in a tight group in front of multiple microphones were Ken, of course, along with J. D. Booker, County Executive Winslow Pickington, the Chief of Police for Nassau County, and our very own Dr. Francis Farnsworth of the Central School District.

"...And we could not be more pleased with the outcome," Dr. Farnsworth was saying. "This is a gratifying moment for us all. Yes, it has been a difficult time. But it has also shown what we in education try to teach our boys and girls. Follow the due process of the law, and truth will win out." Farnsworth turned and offered his hand to Ken. "Welcome back, Mr. Valentine."

Applause broke from those gathered in the faculty room. Several rose from their seats and crossed to me to shake my hand and pat me on the back.

On television, Pamela "Lockjaw" Shutter of Channel Ten News was asking Ken a question, and the faculty room noise settled so we could hear him answer.

"What will be the topic of your lesson when you return to class tomorrow, Mr. Valentine?" Ms. Shutter asked.

Ken looked into the camera, and the lens zoomed to a close-up, his handsome features filling the television screen.

"Well, I been thinking about that one," he said. "I believe I'll do some teaching from *To Kill A Mockingbird*. Not the newly published draft, *Go Set A Watchman*, that someone found in the author's archives, but the original book by Harper Lee where a black man is wrongly accused and is still found guilty. Fortunately for me...and for us all...today we live in a society and school district where prejudice and hate do not win the day, but rather can be defeated when the true facts are considered and justice is allowed to prevail. Here, all men *are* created equal."

As more applause accompanied by whistles and shouts of approval resounded both within the faculty room and from those gathered at the press conference we watched, I caught Sherri's tear-filled eyes of joy and smiled back, sharing her happiness.

Yes, there *was* Ken's illness that only I knew about, but this moment certainly lit things up with a shining beacon of hope. I mean, he'd turned a horrific racially-tainted accusation into a moment of prideful meaning, hadn't he? Maybe he'd beat the disease within his body also. Why not? Weren't we told the mind was capable of doing anything, including healing the body? If anybody could make the mind work for him, wasn't Ken Valentine that person?

I watched his smiling face beaming with happiness on the television screen. Damn it, maybe it was true. Maybe Ken Valentine really had discovered a way to open student minds for the better. If he could do that, anything was possible.

As I sat there, considering it all, and watching my friend's smiling face, a new feeling of calm that I hadn't experienced for some time settled into my being.

Maybe it was going to be all right, after all.

THIRTY

THE CALM BEFORE THE STORM

A victory celebration was called for, and celebrate, we did. I'd seen The Black Horse Tavern packed and rockin' before, but this night was something special. Barry the barkeep of The Horse was at his best, taking orders, serving drinks, and keeping the sounds blasting from the speakers over the bar. *Celebration* by Kool & the Gang was the song choice for the evening. Every time things settled down a little, Barry hit it again; *"Celebrate good times, come on!"* came blasting from the speakers once more and people went nuts all over again.

Here's a sight no one would ever want to miss: Larry Pugh and A. J. Gotz, both still in suits and ties, dancing to Kool & the Gang. But dance they did, perspiration dripping off of *both* as Suzy Shiftlet and Karen Wuant spun them in circles. Even Mary J. showed up for a few moments to offer her congratulations to Ken. Though, she didn't dance. I mean, everything has Its limits. And, ever the Principal, she did leave us before the shank of the evening with a reminder that there was school the next day. So, of course, ever the obedient staff, we all stopped dancing and drinking immediately, and went straight home.

Yeah, right.

Though, next morning, I'm sure many wished that they had. Ken was the one who finally called things to a halt, reminding us that the news media would probably be present

275

upon his arrival the next day, and that an entire high school staff that was hung over and badly in need of sleep might not make the best impression. So, after everyone hugged Ken until I'm sure his arms ached, we all went our separate ways home.

Except for Sherri Walsh and Brian Scarlucci, who went to the apartment.

Sherri was more hesitant than I had ever seen her as she lay down next to me in the queen-sized bed and pulled up the covers.

"Are you sure this is all right?" she asked. "I know it's soon, Brian. I'm here for you however you want me to be, okay?"

How could I have been lucky enough to have found a woman who knew just what to say and when to say it? I moved next to her, curling up against the softness of her body.

"Could you just hold me?" I said, a heavy tiredness spreading through me. "I think I need to be held, Sherri."

"Of course," came the quiet answer, her arms going around me. "For as long as you want."

We fell asleep like that, our arms around each other and, finally, I actually slept for what seemed like the first time in days.

I had never seen Mary J. Talley as jubilantly happy as she was when I walked into the main office the next morning.

"WE GOT HIM!" she cried as I came up to her. "I told you I would do it! The phantom is no more!"

276

I actually leaned in and gave her a hug for the first time that I could remember in our entire relationship.

"Wow, that's great. Is it Grimley?"

She nodded happily. "You were right, as always, Brian. Lewis Grimley is presently on his way to the police station."

I escorted her down the hallway. "And it's not even seven o'clock yet. Pretty damned impressive, Principal Talley. Well, come on, out with it. How'd you do it?"

"I set a trap," she said proudly. "Before I left, I told Sam to make sure the stage door to the outside was left ajar so that anyone looking for the opportunity, would see it. And, sure enough, the little shit went for it."

"No pun intended," I added, astounded that Mary J. Talley had actually called a student of Central High a *little shit.*

"Exactly," she said with a smile, not even caring that she'd uttered the words. "I got here very early as planned, and Sam and I waited out of sight, watching the stage door from behind the curtains. We knew when he was coming in, of course, because Sam had Carl Delby in the Security room watching the exterior camera feed."

"Just like in *Mission Impossible.* This is good stuff," I said.

Mary J. beamed. "He came sneaking through the door and went right to the middle of the stage. Knowing we had to have proof, I made Sam wait to make sure he would...you know."

I nodded. "Either shit or get off the stage."

She ignored my lame attempt at humor and hurried on, excitedly. "Grimley was squatting with his pants down when Sam leaped out and told him to hold it right there!"

"Amazing. He must have just shit!" I should have resisted that last one, and Mary J.'s look told me as much, so I hurried quickly on. "Was anyone with him?"

She shook her head. "Only Grimley. Why?"

"I just wondered. There's a new kid named Tyler Karidae who's been hanging with Grimley. I thought maybe he might be involved."

"Not that I know of," Mary J. answered. "Grimley was alone this morning."

"Okay, well congratulations again," I said, turning to go in my office.

"Ah, Brian...," Mary J. said.

I looked at the locked door, and nodded back to her. "Oh, right. I'll be in Guidance if you need me," I said.

It would be almost the end of the day before Mary J. would need to take me up on that offer.

Meanwhile, Ken Valentine had arrived to the applause of his vigilant meditation group. Representative Joey Mordento, just recently back in school himself, gave Mr. Valentine a welcoming handshake on behalf of the group, media and handheld cameras clicking and whirling with flashes exploding. It truly was amazing when you thought about it; the son of a recently-deceased crime figure was welcoming the accused and racially-slurred teacher back to his assignment. *The times*

278

they are definitely *a-changin'* as Robert Zimmerman aka Noble Prize winning Bob Dylan reminded us in one of those songs that never grow old.

Next, Superintendent Farnsworth offered his greetings on behalf of the school district, and Mary J. led Ken into the school as the students applauded and followed them inside. That matter concluded, the news vans departed, a pleased Farnsworth returned to the Central administration building, and the day progressed pretty much like a normal school day...whatever that is.

As I had promised Maggie, I checked with Security at the middle school, and, sure enough, Anthony Galli had left the building to *get some coffee* the previous morning. It was not a good sign, and I made a note – on a pad at the Guidance table where crap was scattered all over the place - to follow up on that one.

In addition, speaking of ominous signs, when I ran into Angel Jehmar later that day, once again dressed appropriately I might add, and asked her how things were going, she was a little unsure. Apparently, not only had Tyler Karidae's harassment suddenly vanished, but so had Tyler Karidae. After she had spotted him standing outside her home while harassing her with threatening phone calls over the weekend, he was suddenly nowhere to be seen. Though still very anxious, keeping an ever-vigilant Joey Mordento's number at the ready on her cell phone's speed dial, Angel didn't know what to make of it. Just in case, she informed me, her mother was going to pick her up after school in the front waiting area. I nodded with approval at her precaution, and I went to check with Attendance. Tyler Karidae was not in school, and had indeed been absent since the previous Thursday. Calls to the number on file had gone unanswered.

Hmmmm.

Then Sam Shapiro came bursting in through the door of my quote unquote *office* with the message that Mary J. needed me immediately, and the day, which should have been winding down, went into high gear.

There was trouble in the Music wing.

That was all Sam knew. But he knew it must be bad because Mary J. had also alerted her secretary to find Gene Knickbocker and send him to the Music Wing immediately for coverage, and she had instructed Sam to bring two additional Security people with him.

Uh ohhh.

"What's up," I said to Mary J. as we met her in the lobby and headed down the Music wing corridor.

Mary J.'s face was flushed to scarlet. "It's Quentin Bellerio," she said. "He's suddenly gone crazy or something. I just got a call that he's holding the band members hostage and won't let them proceed to ninth period in spite of the fact that eighth period ended over half an hour ago."

For once, I kept my mouth shut. Whatever was going on didn't sound good. We hurried down the hall.

On Mary's signal, we paused at the wide windows in the two doors that opened into the band room. We peered inside. Quentin Bellerio stood on the raised conductor's podium in front of the band. He had the outer hollow casing of a trombone slide in one hand, shaking it threateningly at the band members near him, who were mute with fear.

Gene Knickerbocker, all gangly and unkempt with tie askew as always, came hurrying down the hall behind us. Mary nodded to Sam, who opened the door for her, and we stepped inside the room.

"Yeah, yeah,...now see what you done," the Q-Man shouted, looking our way as we entered and waving the long curved empty trombone slide casing threateningly overhead. "You made the Principal come 'cause you couldn't shut up! What, you think the princ-e-*pal* is your *PAL*? Well, she isn't. Not for this gig, man! And I'm not either, ya dig? Not any more!"

"What's the problem here, Mr. Bellerio," Mary J. said, her voice firm and hard as she moved forward into the room.

"WHAT'S IT LOOK LIKE?" the Q-Man hollered. "THEY WON'T SHUT UP! I'VE ASKED THEM OVER, AND OVER, AND OVER, AND OVER. BUT NOOOOO, THEY NEED TO TALK. TALK AND RUIN THIS GIG FOR ME. Well, it's not happening, baby, 'cause the Q-Man will take it *no more!*"

Bellerio swung the metal trombone slide in the direction of the band, and the members sitting in the clarinet and flute sections in the front flinched.

"Mr. Bellerio...," Mary J. said.

"No!" he countered, cutting her off. "They need to know why! Don't you? Huh? You're curious musicians, right? You want to know why *Mr. Q.* is so angry with *y-o-u!*" Bellerio jumped off the podium and ran to the chalkboard behind him, grabbing a piece of chalk in his free hand.

Sam looked at Mary J., but she held out her hand, palm down with a "wait and see," gesture.

"Okay," Bellerio said, scribbling with the chalk. He drew a large circle at one end of the board and then ran to the opposite end and drew a second very small circle.

"You know what this is?" he snarled, running back to the first circle and tapping the chalk angrily against it. "This, kids, is a hole in the ground!" He ran to the second circle, the chalk hitting loudly against the board. "And this...this is *YOUR ASSHOLE!* AND THE PROBLEM IS YOU DUDES DON'T KNOW YOUR ASS FROM A HOLE IN THE GROUND!"

And with that, the Q-Man hurled the empty slide casing he held in his hand over the tops of the seated students' heads. It sailed past the percussion section and smashed with a loud clang against the painted blue cinderblocks that formed the back wall of the room.

"Okay, that's it," Mary J. said to Sam.

As one, Security and I moved to the front of the room, grabbed Bellerio and dragged him out screaming.

"NO, WAIT," Bellerio bellowed. "I'M NOT FINISHED!"

"Oh, yesss you are," I hissed quietly in his ear, and out the door we went.

As we exited, I saw Mary J. move to the front of the band room and step up onto the podium, a very nervous Gene Knickerbocker standing behind her.

"What the hell is the matter with you, Quint?" I said, moving with him as Security marched him down the hall. "Get it together, for Christ's sake."

"ME? Hey, Brian, it's not me, man. It's them! I warned them time and time again to shut up. I tried to tell them they were ruining the gig. But noooooooooo! They wouldn't listen. So, too fuckin' bad, man. Nobody ruins the Q-Man's gig. Nobody!"

"Except the Q-Man himself," I said, as we reached the main lobby. Then the end of the period bell rang, which meant the school day was over, and I knew the halls would be instantly filled with students rushing to their lockers and the waiting buses to leave school. I pointed to the auditorium doors behind me. "Take him in there, Sam. And keep him quiet, for God's sake. Maggie's drama rehearsal won't start for a few minutes. Once the school is clear, bring him to Mary's office."

Sam nodded, and hustled Bellerio away and out of sight through the auditorium entrance, the doors closing behind them.

Muttering a quiet "damn" to myself, I headed down the main corridor to place myself at my usual station near the exit at Wing C, where I usually stood for the dismissal of school. Just ahead of me, I saw Ken approaching from the opposite direction and waved, giving him a smile.

"*Look at the door!*" my mind said, as I passed the outside exit to Wing A.

I glanced sideways.

A hooded figure hovered just outside the open door. There was something in his grasp, held tightly up against his body.

"*It's a gun!*" my mind said. "*Stop him!*"

The figure I was looking at saw me turn, and sprinted from the doorframe toward the outside of the school.

It was Tyler Karidae.

Instinct pulled me into motion, and I hurled my body toward the doorway.

THIRTY-ONE
GUNFIRE

Beyond the exit in the outside area along the curved drive at the entrance to Central High, it was the usual after-school pandemonium. To my right, buses were lined up along the drive, waiting for students. To the left, parents and others waited in the designated pick-up area in their cars. Under the curve of the cement-column-supported overhang that covered the sidewalk in front of the school, stood A. J. Gotz, clipboard in hand, along with Blanche Turner. Gotz was in charge, and Blanche was his assistant for the week, which meant A. J. took care of getting students loaded and Blanche just stood there. Talking, running, strolling, shouting students exiting the building were everywhere.

Coming out the entrance of the building, my tracking vision caught site of Angel Jehmar accompanied by Joey Mordento heading toward the sidewalk that wound along the curved drive to where the pick-up cars were waiting. Above the upward sloping lawn on the opposite side of the entrance drive in the fenced-off student parking lot, sat a Channel Ten news van. The sliding side door of the van was open, and a cameraman and Pamela Shutter stood next to it, probably waiting to interview Ken about his first day back.

Ahead of me, the running figure stopped in the middle of the large expanse of front lawn between the building and the sidewalk. The hood dropped from his head and the object he held in his hands came away from his body.

Someone stepped beside me as I moved. It was Ken.

"He's got a gun," I said, unable to keep the panic out of my voice.

"I know," Ken answered, his hand coming to my shoulder, grabbing the cloth of the sport jacket I wore in a tight grasp.

Not breaking his running stride, Ken yanked my body to a stop and gave me a powerful shove that stopped my forward momentum. Off balance, I stumbled backwards, smashing against the Wing A exit doorframe as I watched my friend continue to move out into the lawn toward where Tyler Karidae had stopped.

As Ken approached the armed student from behind and I struggled to stay on my feet, I saw Tyler Karidae's left hand pull back a lever, cocking the automatic rifle he held in his grasp.

"AAAAANGEEEEL," Tyler Karidae screamed.

Mayhem replaced chaos.

Seeing the armed lone figure standing in the open expanse of lawn in front of the school, students screamed and ran for cover. At the sidewalk, Angel looked out, and a cry broke from her as Joey Mordento stopped, pulling her behind him, and moving in front of her body.

Blanche Turner screamed and ran behind a nearby cement pillar. A. J. Gotz dropped his clipboard, his head snapping sideways to glance at where his briefcase sat, leaning upright against the same pillar. I knew immediately why he was looking at it. There could only be one explanation. English grammarian and auxiliary police officer A. J. Gotz had broken the rules once more and there was a gun inside that briefcase.

"MOVE OUT OF THE WAY, JOEY," Tyler Karidae shouted, raising the weapon to his shoulder.

Joey's answer was loud and determined.

"I DON'T THINK SO!"

Joey's voice was determined, but I knew he would not have a weapon on him. Joey had learned his lesson. He was a good student now.

The movement and panting sounds he heard coming from behind him pulled Tyler Karidae's head around to where Ken Valentine's running figure came to a stop not more than four feet from where Karidae stood.

"Give me the weapon, young man," Ken said, his palms open and raised before him to show he was unarmed. "We'll work it out. But this is not the way. There are innocent people here who might get hurt. You don't want that. Give me the gun."

"FUCK YOU," Tyler Karidae screamed, and he spun, the automatic rifle kicking in his grasp as he opened fire.

The bullets caught Ken's body full, smacking into him, throwing him backwards as he crumbled to the ground.

I heard myself screaming "No," as I tried to rush forward, but Sam Shapiro's aging hands were on me, the grip surprisingly strong, pulling me back.

At the sidewalk, A. J. Gotz had the briefcase in his grasp, one hand holding it and the other opening the lid.

But Tyler Karidae was turning in that direction, his weapon continuing to fire. Students dropped to ground, screams filling the courtyard. A terrified Blanche Turner ran from behind the pillar, trying to climb into the open door of a nearby bus, but flying bullets caught her as she ran, smacking her back against the side of the bus.

A. J. dropped the briefcase, weapon in his hand, but Tyler Karidae's sweeping automatic continued to move, bullets catching Gotz's body as he attempted to raise the weapon, and he fell sideways against the pillar.

However, Joey Mordento was moving at the same time A. J. went down. Shoving Angel behind the pillar, Joey dove to where A. J.'s body was dropping. Tearing the pistol from Gotz's hand, Joey turned and fired the gun repeatedly in the direction of Tyler Karidae, getting off several shots before his own downward-falling body smashed against the cement sidewalk.

In the middle of the lawn, Tyler Karidae's body jerked spasmodically as bullets from the pistol Joey Mordento fired tore into his body, the automatic weapon Karidae held flying from his grasp to the ground beside him. With a cry, Tyler Karidae fell sideways, but as he hit the ground, he kept

288

moving, crawling frantically toward the weapon that had been knocked from his grasp.

Security personnel burst past where Sam held me, running onto the lawn toward Tyler Karidae, but Joey Mordento was already on his feet, his lean, muscled body moving, legs pumping, as he ran toward where Tyler Karidae crawled to the rifle.

Reaching the scrambling Tyler Karidae, Joey's white high-topped sneaker lashed out, streaks of blood from bullet wounds spreading across the whiteness as Joey kicked savagely again and again at Karidae's crawling body. Then the automatic rifle was in Joey's hands, and he fired.

Finally, the squirming body of the attacker was still. Joey hurled the weapon at the unmoving body as Security reached him, grabbing him.

"I SAID I DON'T THINK SO!" Joey screamed down at the body as Security pulled him back.

But I was not watching what happened around me anymore. Breaking from Sam Shapiro's grasp, I was running forward to where Ken Valentine's body lay in the bloodstained grass.

THIRTY-TWO
AS I LAY DYING

"I'm sorry, old buddy," Ken whispered hoarsely as I held his bleeding body to me. "It had to be me this time."

I was on my knees, my arms around him, lifting his head and shoulders slightly in an attempt to comfort him where he lay in the grass. Sirens wailed in the background. Bodies moved around me. Screams and sobbing surrounded me. But I was beyond it all, holding my friend. Trying to comfort him. Trying to save him with my words.

"You hang on, goddamn it, Ken," I said. "You hear that sound. The ambulance is coming. Just hold on, okay?"

"The way I stopped you. Not a bad move for someone who's not a SEAL like you, huh," Ken said, ending his words with a cough. Blood appeared at the edge of his lips.

"This is no joke. Ken. Please don't talk," I said.

"Is this Brian telling *me* not to joke around?" he said. "It's okay. You know that, Brian. That's why it had to be me. Don't you wonder how I knew?" he asked. "I was behind you coming down the hallway. Couldn't even see the doorway. How did I know the kid had a gun, Bri?"

"Ken, shut up. I mean it."

He shook his head. "Not 'til you answer me. How did I know?"

"All right," I said, cradling his head, watching in horror as the blood streamed out of the edge of his mouth. "It's the Tibetan Balls...is that what you want to hear?"

He smiled weakly and unable to suppress a groan, grimaced in pain, his eyes closing. "That's what I want to hear," he said, his voice suddenly hollow, almost a whisper. "And the opening is happening for you too, isn't it. No need to answer. I know it is."

"The ambulance is here, Brian," I heard Sam Shapiro say from where he stood above me.

"You promised me, remember," Ken's voice whispered. "Keep listening...."

And then his body went limp, his head falling to one side in my hands.

"No..." I cried, pulling at him. "You hang on, goddamn it. I can't lose you too, Ken. Please, you can't do this. Goddamn you. Why did you stop me? You've got to hang on. Please, Ken. Please."

Then Sam Shapiro was kneeling next to me, trying to help me stand, and the paramedics were around Ken, doing what they could. But I knew it was too little, too late.

My friend was gone.

BOOK FOUR

THE MEANEST DAY OF ALL

PROLOGUE

"...Tragedy struck at a public high school on Long Island today...."

The anchor for NBC was reporting the evening news. The leader had gathered them all into what was called the living room of the safe house in Queens where they were staying to watch the news program on the wall-mounted high definition flat-screen television. They had to agree, the clearness of the picture was truly lifelike. No one had ever seen anything like it, and they nodded to one another in amazement as they watched.

For several days now, all had been in readiness. Explosives and weapons had arrived with additional forces shortly after the supply of nerve gas was delivered. Several among them paced anxiously, with lack of understanding why, each day increasing the risk of discovery, the leader hesitated to act. Now, however, they understood. He had been waiting for a sign showing when such an act should be done. This became clear to all as they listened, and their faith in the leader was renewed, their own resolve also strengthened. Clearly, such a leader was one to follow in this deed of greatness.

The newscaster's words continued to explain the school tragedy as they watched, several of them nodding in recognition as the Jehmar name was announced.

"...though Angel Jehmar, the female student who was the object of the dead attacker's obsession, escaped unharmed, Blanche Turner and Ken Valentine, teachers at the school, were killed by automatic gunfire during the attack. Ken Valentine, who confronted the attacking student at the time of the shooting, was recently cleared in a controversial pedophile accusation with racial overtones involving the death of another Central High student who had taken her own life. Instrumental in stopping the attacker, a Tyler Karidae, who had only transferred weeks earlier from Queens to attend the high school, was Central High student Joseph Mordento, son of the recently-deceased organized crime figure Salvatore Mordento. Witnesses say...."

The leader held up the remote in his hand, pushing the off switch and the television screen blinked into blankness. He moved to the front of the dark flat screen where their attention had been focused.

"We have been blessed," he said, raising his arms and bringing his palms together with his head coming forward in the sign of sacred thanksgiving. They all moved as one, following his example. "We must give thanks for this sign that sanctifies our important mission in this land of the infidels. All of America is now focused on this school and our act will resound with meaning to all. Our responsibility is great. We must not fail.

"The time for our actions has also been made clear to me. Because his child was the target in the recent attack at the school, we now know that Abdul Jehmar returns to the United States where he will visit the school to give thanks to those involved in her rescue. On the day of his visit, we will act and be there to greet him.

"I will witness the disbelief in his eyes as he sees what his treachery has brought upon him and his children, and America will experience a renewed fear in the knowledge that it is not only in their great cities that they must watch in their fearful isolation, but also in their homes and in their schools, where not even their children are safe from the wrath of our holy purpose.

"We must move with precision and exactness on this day. When the gas is released within the hollow pipes to fill the building, all exits must be covered and secured, explosions assuring this. Then, wearing masks of protection, we will move through the school with our weapons, eliminating those who have escaped the deadly gas. No one must escape."

He gestured for them to follow him to what was called the home's dining room, where schematic drawings of the target called Central High School were laid out on the long table in the center of the room.

"Let us once more review the plan in all its detail," the leader said, "from the time we eliminate and replace those at the Winslow Air Conditioning Corporation to the time of the school occupation and assault. Only through such careful and exact preparation, can we know that we will not fail."

THIRTY-THREE
SO WHAT AM I SO AFRAID OF?

I gave the eulogy at Ken's funeral. Some asked me afterwards how I was able to do such a difficult thing, considering what I had been through. I said nothing. There was nothing to say. How could I not speak the words that paid tribute to the man who had been my longtime friend and, in a final act of self-sacrifice, had saved my life?

At the end of that same week, a memorial ceremony was held at the school, the day named in Ken's honor. It was called Valentine's Day with the theme being that of human love for one another. There were poems and memorial speeches read throughout the day in the auditorium for those who wished to attend, the day concluding with an assembly.

First, Blanche Turner was honored with a moment of silence in memory of her many years of service to the school, and I felt very sorry that her life had ended the way it had.

The remainder of the program was for Ken, during which musicians performed and students and staff gave witness to Ken's inspiration to them and his dedication to teaching and the uplifting of the human spirit. The ceremony ended with Ken's audio track of the Tibetan Balls being played. The reverberating sound of the hallowed gongs filled the auditorium while a large golden glowing *Phi* symbol shimmered on a screen at the center of the darkened stage. No one spoke as the rich sound vibrations rolled over them. Sherri held my hand tightly, as I sobbed silently in the front row. When the recording ended, no one spoke. They simply got to their feet and filed out quietly and reverently through the back doors of the auditorium.

It was quite a moment of personal and emotional reflection for all.

At the conclusion of the ceremony, I was asked by the meditation group if I would be their advisor for their weekly meetings and, of course, I agreed. They planned to meet in Ken's room, a different kind of classroom, as you might imagine.

I had joked about its physical setup when Sherri and I met with Ken days earlier, but in truth, my description was pretty accurate. The fountain in the corner was still there, as was the Buddha. There was a conversation sofa in the far corner of the room, with books covering all sorts of inspirational and New Age topics on the coffee table in front of it. And the desks themselves were in a circle for classroom instruction, the teacher sitting in a desk equal to the students so that they were as one for learning.

Ken had even refused to have the air conditioning duct vents added to his room, insisting that it created an artificial environment. Maintenance had gone nuts about it at the time, but Ken had held firm, so his room would be one of the few in the building without the benefit of air conditioning once the tests were run and the cooling system did in fact work, that is. The testing of that reconstructed system was one of the items on my agenda for the coming days, and I had placed the order for the Winslow Air Conditioning Corporation to come to the school and complete the final circulation test. It was scheduled to happen before week's end. I wasn't sure which day, of course. God forbid, anyone in the industrial sector should give you the actual firm date when anything was going to be completed.

I was back in my office, such as it was. There was still only plywood framing holding a thick blue plastic tarp covering the huge hole where the side wall had been destroyed, and the room was drafty, but I made do, making sure I locked the door when I left each day so the school could not be entered through such an insecure space. And slowly, time being the great healer, Central High School struggled back to some semblance of normalcy.

Quentin Bellerio, wearing a smart-looking tie on a daily basis, was back in front of the band after a letter of reprimand was placed in his permanent file and a stern warning was delivered to him personally from Dr. Farnsworth. Laurence Pugh had a brand new wall-mounted fish tank in his office, his multi-colored salt water fishies swimming their happy little fins off while Daddy watched in delight from his desk across the room.

And the days moved on.

I was driving toward home, the day having gone rather uneventfully, when my cell phone rang. It was Sherri.

"Are you driving?"

"Yes, why?"

"I just like to know because I'm aware of how anxious you feel when you are forced to break the law."

"Hey, at least I look around before I answer my cell while driving, which is more than I can say for most people in New York," I said, looking around for the first time since I answered.

"I wanted to let you know that I'm going to be out tomorrow."

"Okay. What's up?"

"My aunt in Brooklyn isn't feeling well."

"Oh, I'm sorry. Is there anything I can do?"

"Yes, you can call in and let them know you're going to be out tomorrow also, Mr. Naïve. We're going to play hookey."

I waited a beat. "Where are you?"

"I'm at the apartment."

Another pause. We hadn't been at the apartment together since the night before Ken died.

"What are you wearing?" I said.

"The sheet that's on the bed," she answered.

"Should I go home first?"

"Yes, get clothes for our post hookey return to work, but if you change out of your suit before you come over, don't take the time to put on any underwear. I have a surprise waiting for you."

"I love surprises," I said and, smiling, ended the call.

When I arrived at the apartment, Sherri was lying on the bed under the covers. I could make out delightful sections of her body against the sheet. I kicked my shoes off my sockless feet after closing and locking the door.

She giggled, the sheet tightly up against her neck. "Hi."

"Hi," I said, removing my shirt as I crossed the room. "What's the surprise?"

The sheet came back with a sweep of her hand, and she lay there naked, her right leg bent and crossed over her left. Under and around her there were many loose dollar bills all over the bed.

I nodded in appreciation, dropping my pants sans the boxers. Mr. Scarlucci Jr. was standing erect at military attention, awaiting orders.

"How much money ya got there," I asked, stopping at the edge of the bed.

"Only fifty dollars in one dollar bills. Are you disappointed?"

"Fifty or fifty thousand. Doesn't matter as long as you're the one in the money," I said.

"Good answer," she said, grabbing my hand and pulling me onto the bed. "Congratulations. You just won the grand prize."

The next day, Ms. Walsh and Mr. Scarlucci were absent from school without an absence note.

Following our day of cutting school, not sadder and definitely sexually wiser, I was adjusting my tie in the bathroom mirror when Sherri, already dressed and ready to leave for

John Arthur Long

work, came up from behind, her arms encircling me in a tight hug. I turned into her embrace.

"I think I love you," I said. Then after a beat, I finished the song lyric. "...So what am I so afraid of...?"

She looked at me. "Can I tell you something?"

"I think you're going to anyway."

"You are not going to lose me, Brian."

I pulled back slightly. "Sherri...."

She took my face in her hands and held it, holding my gaze.

"No, listen. I mean it. I know you've lost people you love and it hurts, but here's the deal. You're not getting rid of me. Because I love you too, by the way, and I refuse to be afraid of it. You and Evelyn shared something wonderful and even though the loss is painful, what you had makes it worth it. Ken was our friend and we loved him, and, yes, he's gone, but that friendship more than makes up for the pain. I wouldn't trade it for anything and neither would you."

"So what are you saying? You think you're worth it?"

"I know I am, Big Boy," she said. She kissed me with a tenderness and affection that made my heart sing.

"Nothing is going to happen to me, Brian," she said. "You better face it. You got me for the long haul. What do you think of that deal, Mr. Scarlucci?"

I kissed her back.

"I think it's a petty good deal," I said.

302

When we left, she went first and I followed ten minutes later so that we would not arrive at the school simultaneously...like we were fooling anyone with both of us being absent the previous day. Nevertheless, a ruse is a ruse is a ruse, and we played it out accordingly. For example, an hour after our separate arrivals at work, Sherri stepped into my office.

"Good morning, Mr. Scarlucci," she said.

"Why, good morning, Ms. Walsh. How's your aunt?"

She smiled, standing in the doorway, surveying the room. "She's improving, thanks. I like what you've done with your office. Who's your decorator?"

"Dumphole Interior Design," I said. "I'm thinking of checking with some other firms."

"Follow your instincts. Have a nice day, Mr. Scarlucci."

"You too, Ms. Walsh. You didn't park in the lot above the school, did you?"

"No, I didn't."

I nodded. "Just checking. The matinee performance of the play is today, and we've reserved that lot for the parents and guests. Since you were out yesterday, I wanted to make sure you knew about it."

"I got the memo," Sherri said.

"Very good. Well, have a nice day, Ms. Walsh."

"You too, Mr. Scarlucci," she said, blowing me a quick furtive kiss and disappearing.

So ridiculous. With a conversation like that, we couldn't even fool the likes of Larry Pugh if he happened to be listening from his office next door while he fed his fishies. However, I knew Laurence was not listening because moments later he entered my office and, with his usual Pugh proficiency, almost immediately soured my mood.

"Brian, did you ever put the information together on the Terrorist Intruder memo that needs to go out?"

I surveyed the disaster that made up what could be laughingly referred to as my organized desk.

"You are aware that a car plowed through my office recently, aren't you, Larry? I'm lucky I can find the daily morning announcements in this mess."

"I lost my fish tank also. I know what it is to have a mess in the office, but the needs of the day do not always wait until things are convenient, do they?"

Do not go for him, Brian. Remember, patience is a virtue.

"Except, you now have a shiny new tank mounted on your wall with fishies swimming merrily around while you work, and I still have a goddamned tarp across what's supposed to be a wall in here. Not quite the same, Larry. But I'll get right on it 'cause I'm sure Central High in the middle of Long Island is the number one target on some mad terrorist's list, and they'll be here any minute."

"No need to be sarcastic, Brian. I'm simply informing you that Arnold Federly was wondering why the memo hasn't been distributed, that's all."

304

"Yeah, well you can tell Federly that it's because I'm busy dealing with the air conditioning crap that you dumped on my desk when I wasn't looking."

"When is that test being done, by the way?" Pugh asked.

That's why harassing Mr. Pee U is not worth the effort. He doesn't even know it's happening.

"Sometime this week. That's all I know. They'll get back to me."

"Well, keep me informed,"

"No sweat," I said. He nodded and left. See? He doesn't even know you're dumping on him.

The little encounter with Pugh should have ruined my mood beyond repair. Surprisingly, however, it didn't. And as I sifted through the papers of my morning workload – purposely avoiding the completion of the Intruder Terrorist memo on general principles – I actually caught myself whistling while I worked.

The next significant encounter of the day was not a problem, but rather a nice resolution of a problem. Angel Jehmar came running up to me just as I headed for the auditorium. Mary J. was out of the building at a Nassau County principal's meeting, and my task for the afternoon was to be the administrator who would be in attendance for the matinee performance of the drama. This had caused a conflict for me because I was obligated to be present at the Valentine Meditation class in Ken's room, which was also taking place that afternoon. I'd informed Joey Mordento of my conflict, however, and he assured me they would be fine.

I knew Sherri had a budget expenditure meeting with Farnsworth, Federly and Pugh in her office sometime after one o'clock, so I'd asked her to look in on the group if possible. There were major worries that the school district budget was not going to pass in the spring, and the Central administration was looking for ways to cut costs. Sherri was not looking forward to the meeting because she knew it would mean losing staff and increasing class size. Still, since she'd be in the Wing, she promised me she'd check on the meditation class when she got a chance. We both knew it wouldn't be necessary. If Joey Mordento were the student in charge, he would handle things fine.

Since the shooting, the Joey Mordento change from troublesome teen to responsible, thoughtful scholar had been an amazing transformation. Joey now dedicated himself to humanitarian service and scholarly devotion in the name of Ken Valentine. The transition was truly a wonder to behold. Joey Mordento was rapidly becoming one of the nicest, most considerate human beings I had ever encountered.

And sweet, smiling Angel Jehmar, dressed very conservatively indeed, was more excited than I could ever remember seeing her.

"What's the big smile all about, Angel?" I asked, knowing full well not only why she had chosen such a conservative style of dress for the day, but also why she was so happy.

"My father is coming to school today!" she answered, so full of joy she literally jumped up and down as she spoke. "Isn't that wonderful! I'm so excited!" She looked at me, suddenly all serious. "Do I look all right, Mr. 'Carlucci? You *must* tell me the truth. You know about these things. Will my father be pleased with my appearance?"

I smiled in genuine happiness for her, suppressing a Scarlucci thought that it was a shame his daughter had to almost get herself killed to get him there. "He will be overjoyed with his daughter and the way she has been able to remain true to her upbringing, yet function within the American school environment."

She beamed in delight. "Thank you, Mr. 'Carlucci. I am so happy. I will tell you everything later. Now I must go to the Counseling Center and wait for him to arrive with my mother. Bye."

"Wait a minute." I reached in my pocket and withdrew a closed fist, opening my fingers as I waved them over her head. "Angel dust for the meeting with Dad. Now nothing can go wrong."

Bubbling with glee, Angel leaned forward, gave me a quick hug, and then rushed away in a half-skipping walk down the main corridor toward the Guidance lobby doors.

I was still smiling as I entered the auditorium and stood leaning against the back wall. However, something was bothering me that I couldn't quite put my finger on.

What was it?

John Arthur Long

The day was going pretty well. Still, I had this tiny grain of anxiety just beginning to nag at me, trying to get my attention for some unknown reason.   Maybe it was just all that had happened over the last couple of weeks.   Maybe the whole thing had made me a little gun-shy, to use a somewhat inappropriate reference.

Stop it, Scarlucci. You're being paranoid!

I pushed the feeling to the back of my mind and brought my attention back to the upcoming drama production. I told myself to relax and enjoy the show. Everything was fine. And I could almost make myself believe it. Except the old Scarlucci instinct refused to buy it. It insisted on staying in high alert mode, even though I could see no apparent reason for it. Everything seemed perfectly fine.

So what was I so afraid of…?

THIRTY-FOUR
THE BLAZING SHOULDERS OF HATRED

The auditorium was packed with senior citizens who always attended the matinee free of charge – a little get-out-the-vote ploy of Farnsworth's – guests, parents, and select Honors English students and classes that had been bused over from the middle school. In fact, I had never seen the auditorium so full for a matinee performance. Obviously, *Death of a Salesman*, not the easiest play for a group of high school students to perform, had stirred quite a bit of interest.

Maggie Madison came in through the back door as the house lights began to dim in preparation for the opening of the curtain, and I stopped her as she passed me, leaning in and giving her a quick cheek kiss.

"Break a leg, Maggie."

"Thanks, Brian," she said, slipping her arm around my waist and giving me a tight squeeze of affection. "It's been a tough couple of weeks. Thanks for being there with your support."

After another quick squeeze, she released me and looked up, giving her Tech crew in the balcony booth the *okay* sign. Then, as she walked down the aisle to her reserved seat, the house lights dimmed the rest of the way, and the show began.

I was standing in the dark, wrestling with the guilt of suspecting this woman who had just thanked me for my support, when, suddenly, the answer to the Maggie Madison quandary came to me.

Of course. She's a toucher! It's that simple!

I stood there amazed that I hadn't come up with the explanation for how she behaved long before this: Maggie Madison was a toucher.

What I mean by *toucher* is that some people can't talk to you without touching you. It's just part of the way people like that communicate: talk-touch-talk-talk-touch-touch-talk-touch. That's what it was with drama director, Maggie Madison. It didn't matter whether it was a student or a friend, or a colleague, or...a former lover, she just touched when she talked. I realized suddenly that it carried no inappropriate meanings with it whatsoever. It was just the way she communicated. The Anthony Galli accusations had aroused suspicions. And, yes, the fact that Maggie was a very sexy woman did give her talk-slash-touch behavior a little extra zing when it came to a member of the opposite sex she happened to be talking with while she touched. But did that make her guilty of inappropriate behavior with a student? Absolutely not! The jury inside my head reached a unanimous decision, and I nodded to myself in agreement.

Has the jury reached a verdict?

Yes we have, Your Honor. We find the defendant, Maggie "The Toucher" Madison, not guilty!

I smiled as I watched Todd Hershborne aka Willy Loman come on stage to the mournful strains of background music.

310

"Is that you, Willy?" his student-stage-wife Linda said.

"I couldn't make it, Linda," Todd's Willy Loman said on stage as he sat down with a deep sigh at the kitchen table across from his wife, his shoulders slumped in defeat. "I just couldn't make it...."

I nodded to myself in appreciation of the opening lines. Not only was she not guilty, Maggie was an excellent director. It was going to be a good play...a nice conclusion to a pleasant day.

Then, of course, the back door of the auditorium opened, and Sam Shapiro poked his head inside, gesturing in my direction.

Oops. Maybe not. When would I ever learn?

"Yeah, Sam," I said once outside the auditorium door, closing it quietly after me. "What is it?"

Sam shook his head, leading me across the lobby to the high plate glass windows that showed the outside entrance of the school. He pointed out toward the upper parking lot above the slope on the opposite side of the curved entrance drive.

"Ya gotta see this one. Words just won't do it justice."

I followed his lead. Above the slope of lawn in the parking lot that was filled with the cars of the people attending the matinee, I could see Security people running around in and out and around cars, in movements that looked like they were chasing something.

"What are they doing?"

Sam smiled in spite of himself and shook his head. "Chasing sheep."

"SHEEP?"

"You heard me correctly. Sheep! Against specific orders in today's school memo to faculty, Mitch Bright left his truck in the upper lot so he could watch it because the back flat bed of his truck was filled with sheep. Some kids must have opened the tailgate on the truck and let them out because the sheep are now running around all over the parking lot."

"You've got to be kidding me. Sheep? Mitchell Bright brought sheep to school? Why in God's name – *No pun intended, I might add* – would Mitch bring sheep to school with him?"

"You think I know?" Sam responded, all in a huff. "I guess because he's Mitch. I told you it had to be seen to be believed."

As we watched, a Security guard lifted a small kicking lamb into the back of Mitch's truck, slammed the back gate closed, and ran into the parking lot for more.

"Well, how many are there?"

"I don't know. I'm not counting sheep. I'm trying to get them back in the truck. They're running all over the damned parking lot, Brian," Sam responded, his face reddening. "Should I get Mitch?"

"NO!" I answered loudly. "You get out there and help your Security people. I'll get Mitchell Bright. It's about time someone made it clear to Mitch he can't just do whatever he wants to do around here. Give me one of your radios so I can get in touch with you if I have to."

Sam snapped one of the 2-way radios off his belt. "We're using…frequency 23 today," he said and hustled out the main entrance. Fuming, I spun and headed toward the front corridor leading to the lower wings of the school just as Betty opened the side door to the main office and called my name.

"Brian, the air conditioning people are here to run the test on the system. They came while you were in the auditorium. Security didn't alert any of us because there's some kind of problem in the parking lot."

I stopped in surprise. "What? You mean they want to test the air conditioning system now? No one called me."

"That's what they tell me," she said, shrugging and pointing to where the group of men stood inside the main office near the counter. "I had the metal detector shut off when they came in so all that equipment they've got wouldn't set off a blaring alarm sound and ruin the drama production. Should I give them a visitor's pass, and let them go to the vacuum pump station in the boiler room? They say they have to check there and turn on the system before going up on the roof for the ductwork inspection."

"*TELL THEM NO!*"

The words rang out so loudly in my head I almost jumped. I looked through the lobby window into the main office at where several men dressed in Winslow Air Conditioning Corp. outfits stood waiting, their arms filled with containers and other

313

equipment. Two of the men were carrying round metal canisters on their shoulders.

"Tell them no!"

The command inside my head was not as loud this time, but just as clear.

"No," I said to Betty. "Tell them no. They can't do it now. They should have called. I've got an auditorium full of people watching the play. School is still in session. No way are they running an air conditioning test now. Tell them the drama production will be over at 4:00. If they will come back around 4:30, the school will be relatively empty except for a few after-school activities. They can run the test then. I'll even stay and help, make sure it goes all right."

Betty shook her head slowly. "I don't think they're going to like it. They seem pretty insistent that it has to be now."

"I don't care. The answer is no, Betty. Go tell them. I've got to get Mitch because his sheep are running all over the damned parking lot or I'd tell them myself. At 4:30, they can run the air conditioning system until it's thirty degrees below zero in here, but not until then. Tell them!"

With a look of determination, Betty turned to go back into the main office.

"Oh, and Betty, call Richie and tell him to activate the switch that controls the automatic locks for all the exit doors. If these guys do run the test at 4:30, I'll have to make an announcement that no one should go out the doors during the test and engage the exit locks so that no one can come in.

314

Richie leaves at 3:00 when the evening crew comes in, and sometimes he forgets to activate the system. Tell him to do it right now so he won't forget. I'll throw the switch when the time comes. And tell the Air Conditioning technicians 4:30, okay? That's the best I can do."

"Got it, Brian," she said. Betty disappeared into the main office and I headed in a run down the main corridor toward Wing C to get Mitchell Bright.

Something is wrong.

As I moved the words kept sounding in my head.

Something is wrong.

But angry about the loose sheep and intent on getting to Mitch, I pushed the repeating words from my consciousness, turned the corner to Wing C and hurried down the hall.

When I reached the room of A. J. Gotz, I gave it a quick knock and opened the door. A. J., his right arm still in a sling from the gunshot wound he had received, was standing by the chalkboard, instructing a student beside him to write down the information of his lesson. On the board were definitions for predicate adjectives and predicate nouns with accompanying examples of how each followed a copulative rather than a transitive verb.

"Mr. Gotz, could you help me out and keep an eye on Mr. Bright's class next door. I need him for a moment."

"I'm teaching an important lesson," A. J. answered.

I could tell by the bewildered looks on the student faces that they did not have the faintest idea what Gotz was lecturing

315

about…and furthermore, they didn't care. "I think they'll survive. Just stand by the door so you can watch Mr. Bright's class and your own until he gets back. Your students' notes are thorough, I'm sure…*thorough* being a predicate adjective. They can study and review for a few minutes until Mitch gets back."

The predicate adjective usage did it. Never argue if you want to get your way. The secret to supervision is knowing when and where to stroke positively to get results.

"Good grammatical reference," A. J. said, beside himself with delight that someone on the staff other than A. J. Gotz not only knew the meaning of a predicate compliment, but could actually use it in reference. "I think I can keep an eye on both classes until Mitchell returns."

Look at the back of the room, my mind said, interrupting our exchange.

I looked. Spit, the leader of The Vipers, sat in the last seat in the back row. He met my gaze, but his eyes said nothing.

Remember he's there, my mind said.

Ignoring the mental chatter inside my head, I thanked A. J. and hurried next door.

Mitchell Bright came to the door as I knocked. "Yes, Brian?"

"Mitch, you brought sheep to school?"

His eyes widened. "WHAT'S HAPPENING TO MY LAMBS?"

"Mitch, what possessed you to bring sheep to school with you?"

"Lambs, not sheep, Brian," Mitch said, correcting me. "I need them for our services this evening, and I will not have time to go back to our communal farm to collect them. We are having our countywide Service of Sacrifice this evening, and the sacrificial lambs must be a part of it."

"Yeah, well I wish you'd parked in back like you were supposed to because some kids opened the rear gate on your truck, and right now your precious lambs are running all over the parking lot."

"Oh, they must not be hurt or marred in any way. They must be pure. I must get out there," he answered in genuine alarm.

"Great idea. Something tells me Security is not being overly careful with *their* sheep collection. We'll go out the Wing C exit. It's a faster way to the parking lot. A. J.'s going to keep an eye on your class." Telling Mitchell Bright's class to study for a few minutes and that Mr. Gotz from next door was watching them, I started back up the hall with Mitch, his last words suddenly registering. "What do you mean, *sacrificial lambs*? Please don't tell me that means you're going to kill these sheep, Mitch."

"It's in the Old Testament, Brian. Read your Bible. We are all sinners. Only through sacrifice on the altar of the Lord can we be made pure. The lamb of God takes on the sins of the world."

"Mitch, you cannot kill these sheep."

"The Lord giveth and the Lord taketh away. It is all in His name," was Mitchell Bright's answer to his planned evening's sheep slaughter.

The 2-way radio on my belt crackled with a beep. I pulled it off, and pushed the intercom. "Yeah, Sam. Ya got the sheep? I'm bringing Mitch to move the truck."

"Sheep are secure," Sam's voice said. "But do you know anything about the Air Conditioning van in the entrance drive?"

"Have them move it. I told them they should come back at 4:30."

"Well, they're not leaving," Sam's voice said. "The rear doors are open and they're taking things out. Why do they need gas masks?"

GAS MASKS?

SOMETHING IS WRONG!

I was moving faster now. Almost running as I approached the closed exit doors at the end of Wing C on the other side of the main corridor. Reaching them, I strained to see out the rectangular windows on the top half of the doors. Beyond the glass I could see the van parked in the curved circular drive at the school's entrance. Sam was right. Several of the men coming out of back of the van were carrying gas masks. Two of the men with gas masks carried metal canisters on their shoulders. Then I saw the weapons in the hands of the men next to them....

THIRTY-FIVE
GUNFIRE

"How's the play going, Brian?" I heard Dr. Francis Farnsworth's voice say from behind me. "I thought I'd stop in and have a look before we left."

I glanced behind me to see Farnsworth, Federly, and Pugh, their meeting with Sherri obviously completed, three-fourths of the way up the Wing C hallway as they approached.

Panic surged through my system.

My mind was racing, the words spilling into my head, beyond my control, feeding me information:

DO NOT QUESTION THE WORDS. USE THEM!

THE SCHOOL IS UNDER ATTACK.

Why? Why now? Why today? What is different today?

ABDUL JEHMAR, THE NEGOTIATOR IS IN THE SCHOOL! came the answer. *BRING HIM HERE NOW!*

"MITCH, WATCH WHAT'S HAPPENING OUTSIDE!" I shouted, shoving Mitchell Bright to the exit and running toward the approaching men. Everyone saw my alarm as I reached them.

"What's wrong," Farnsworth said.

"The school is under attack," I said.

"ATTACK?" Farnsworth responded, his voice cracking. "WHAT DO YOU MEAN, *ATTACK*?"

319

"I MEAN ATTACK. THERE ARE MEN WITH GAS MASKS AND WEAPONS AT THE FRONT OF THE SCHOOL," I said with all the force I could muster.

LOCK THE DOORS my mind screamed inside my head. LOCK THE DOORS NOW!

"Larry," I said to Pugh, the words continuing to pour out of me, "go to the Counseling Center. On the way, stop at the custodian's office. If Richie has not activated the automatic door lock system on the computer, he must do it right now! Do you know the location of the switch that sets the locks for the building's exit doors?"

"Yes..." Pugh answered, his voice shaking.

"Turn on that switch. YOU MUST LOCK THE DOORS SO THAT NO ONE CAN GET IN FROM THE OUTSIDE. THOSE DOORS MUST BE LOCKED IMMEDIATELY! Then, in the Counseling Center, find a parent named Abdul Jehmar. He is Angel Jehmar's father. I know he's there. Repeat the name."

"Ab...Ab dul Jeh...mar," Pugh stuttered.

"That's right. Abdul Jehmar. Tell him we are under attack! Bring him here as fast as you can! DO NOT ASK QUESTIONS. JUST GO! NOW! RUN!"

Pugh ran from us.

Farnsworth had his cell phone in his hand. Panic was at the edge of his voice as he spoke into it, but his words were firm and coated with authority.

I nodded. "Don't let them doubt what you're saying for an instant. This is really happening! Eye In The Sky Security probably would have missed it because it's an air conditioning van. But those men out there have guns. I just saw them. Get police here as fast as you can. Tell 'em we are under attack and need SWAT teams, helicopter coverage, anything they can give us. Tell them to get any kind of armed force here immediately, or people are going to die!"

MAKE AN ANNOUNCEMENT TO THE SCHOOL NOW! USE THE MEMO INFORMATION! STUDENTS MUST STAY IN THEIR ROOMS. DO NOT FORGET THE AUDITORIUM!

The commanding flow of words sounded in my mind. I followed what I heard without hesitation, turning to Federly.

"Arnold, get to the main office. Get on the intercom. Betty will turn it on for you. It reaches every room in this building.

The words were sounding in my head and I simply repeated them to him.

"Say this: THIS IS DR. FEDERLY, THE ASSISTANT SUPERINDENT OF SCHOOLS --THIS IS NOT A TEST -- THIS IS AN EMERGENCY -- EVERYONE IS TO FOLLOW MY INSTRUCTIONS WITHOUT HESITATION -- THE SITUATION IS VERY DANGEROUS AND INSTRUCTIONS MUST BE FOLLOWED TO THE LETTER WITHOUT QUESTION -- TEACHERS ARE TO LOCK THEIR CLASSROOM DOORS, TURN OUT THE LIGHTS, CLOSE THE WINDOWS AND BLINDS, AND MOVE STUDENTS OUT OF THE LINE OF SIGHT OF DOORS AND WINDOWS -- SHUT OFF ALL CELL PHONES -- TEACHERS ARE NOT ALLOWED TO OPEN THEIR DOORS FOR ANYONE AT ANY TIME UNDER ANY

321

CIRCUMSTANCES UNTIL INSTRUCTED TO DO SO -- ALL ACTIVITIES IN THIS SCHOOL WILL STOP IMMEDIATELY -- TEACHERS NOT ASSIGNED TO A CLASS AT THIS TIME MUST SWEEP THE HALLWAYS OF STUDENTS AND MOVE THEM TO THE NEAREST OFFICE OR ROOM. NO ONE IS ALLOWED IN THE HALLWAY!"

The next words came in an unstoppable rush, my mind racing ahead, issuing commands...and I hesitated in momentary doubt....

DO NOT HESITATE! SAY IT! my mind screamed at me.

And I said the words aloud....

"EXCEPT ADMINISTRATORS, QUENTIN BELLERIO, THE MEMBERS OF THE VIPERS, AND JOEY MORDENTO...."

Federly looked at me in alarm as the last words came flowing from me. He glanced at Farnsworth, but his boss was turned away, talking into his cell phone.

"Do not question me, Arnold, or people will die! Can you remember and repeat what I just said?"

"I think so...most of it."

"Do your best," I said. "Lives depend on it. GO!"

Arnold Federly turned and ran down the main corridor.

"Mitch," I said, shifting my attention momentarily to the exit. "What's happening?"

"They're moving from the van, Brian," Mitchell Bright said from the Wing C exit doors where, his back against the door frame so that he was as far out of view as possible, he looked out the windows. "They're,...they're splintering off in groups. Looks like they're going to head for several different entrances."

Farnsworth took his phone from his ear. "Police are on their way!"

"They're not going to make it in time!" I said, pushing back the panic, refusing to yield to it. "Call the band room office. Mr. Bellerio should be there. There's no band today because the sound would be heard in the auditorium and interfere with the performance of the play. Tell him to bring the marching band megaphone to the Wing C entrance right now! We'll give it to Abdul Jehmar as soon as he gets here. He's The Negotiator. There must be a connection. They may even know him. We'll see if he can negotiate for us and stall for time." Farnsworth nodded. I snapped on the 2-way radio. "Sam,..."

"Jesus, Brian. They have weapons. What the hell is going on?"

"Please just listen, Sam. Do not waste time with questions."

"The locks on the doors just snapped into place," Mitch called to me.

I went right on talking, throwing him a thumbs-up, as Sam's voice said, "I understand. I understand. Go ahead."

"Do any of the off-duty police on Security have weapons in their cars?"

I heard Sam's voice asking the question, and then his voice answering me.

"Two weapons. That's it, Brian."

"Okay, have them get them…extra ammo if they have it. We may need to draw the intruders' fire. Can they do that?"

"They're New York cops, Brian. They can do it. Just say when."

"All right. I'll call it. Release the sheep!"

"What?"

"Release the sheep and drive them bleating down the slope toward the intruders. It'll distract them! Maybe confuse them. As soon as you have the guns and shooters are in position, send the sheep down the slope! Get the sheep now!"

"Roger," came the answer.

Mitch had heard me, of course, and looked my way.

"Sacrificial lambs, Mitch," I said to him. "Don't say a word. Just keep watching for me."

Pugh came hurrying down the hall with a man I assumed was Ahdul Jehmar.

"Did the locks come on?" Pugh half-shouted as they approached.

Mitch threw Pugh a thumbs-up, imitating my response to him.

"You understand the situation?" I asked Abdul Jehmar as he and Pugh stopped next to me. The grey-haired man was panting, his expression strained as he stood before my in his dark tailored suit.

"Quentin's on his way with the megaphone," Farnsworth said. His cell rang and he answered as I nodded to him.

"I understand the situation," Abdul Jehmar said to me.

"Who is it? Do you know?"

"This is very serious," he said. "We have had reports of Sarin, the nerve agent, being sold to a terrorist group of which I am aware. There are reports they may be in this country. Critical negotiations with this group and others stalled because of lies from other factions. Some of their people died because of the lies. They believe I betrayed them. I am concerned that these may be the people outside your school...."

"Sarin," Farnsworth said, turning from his phone. "Oh, Christ. They have Sarin!" he repeated into the phone.

Bellerio came charging down the hall, stopping where we stood, the megaphone in his grasp.

"Here ya go, man," he said.

I handed the megaphone to Abdul Jehmar.

"You may be right, and you may not. It doesn't matter. What we need is time. We must somehow prevent them from entering this school until help arrives. You're the expert at negotiations, Mr. Jehmar. If you can't help us, people are going to die. Now will you attempt to negotiate with them to buy us time?" I asked.

"Yes," he said. "We must stop them. My daughter is here."

"Everyone's daughter is here, Mr. Jehmar," I said. "Go stand by the door next to that tall man watching the outside, and wait until I give you the word."

I thanked Bellerio, telling him to get back to the band room and stay there."

"No problem, man," he said, "You call me if you need anything else."

He ran off as Farnsworth finished his call.

"They'll be here as fast as they can," Farnsworth said, his eyes going to Jehmar. "Not only police, but also the military. They're sending in a Black Hawk helicopter. Looks like you may be right about this, Brian. Go with your instincts. What else would you like me to do?"

"Stay with me," I said, already moving back down the hall. My head was issuing commands, and I was following them.

GET SPIT! my mind commanded. I moved to the words. No more doubt. Just do it!

I stopped at the door of A. J. Gotz. He was standing at the open doorway, frowning. "What's going on?"

"I know what you were told about absolutely no weapons on the premises after the shooting incident, A. J., but I also know you believe you were right in having one in your briefcase, and that, because you had it, lives were saved. Do you still have a weapon locked and stored somewhere in this room?" I said. "And don't lie to me. Lives depend on it."

He only hesitated a moment. "Yes," he said.

"Get it," I said.   He looked at Farnsworth, and then nodded, crossing toward his desk.

"SPIT," I yelled into the room. "I need you!"

Frowning, the leader of The Vipers looked around at the other class members, got to his feet, and started for the door. I turned to Farnsworth, lowering my voice.

"If the intruders have nerve gas, they're going to go for the air conditioning system and pump it through the ducts into the school. That's why they have the company clothing and van. There's probably been an attack at the Winslow facility already. We just don't know it yet. I'm going to have The Vipers guard the boiler room entrance."

Farnsworth shook his head. "NO! Sorry, I have to override that one, Brian. I cannot condone putting a student's life in danger. We have to find another way."

Outside the school, we heard the first sounds of gunfire.

"There is no other way!" I said to my superior in a harsh whisper. "These guys are drug dealers and some may even be killers. Anyone else will hesitate when threatened. They won't! They'll react to the threat of force with force. We're using them!"

Spit stopped in front of me.

"The school is under attack by terrorists, Spit. You know me, and know I would not lie to you." Spit stared at me, his expression blank. "I need you and the other Vipers to protect the entrance to the boiler room in the middle of Wing A. The intruders may have a nerve gas called Sarin. They must not

327

be allowed to reach the air conditioning pump facility in the boiler room or everyone in this school could die. Will you help us?"

"This is America, Scarlucci," Spit said. "We fucking protect our own in America. You tell me what you need."

I looked at Farnsworth. He bit his lip and nodded.

"Thanks, Spit. You have any weapons you can get ahold of? Knives or guns?"

"Both," Spit said, looking at Farnsworth, daring him to say something. Farnsworth said nothing and Spit turned back to me.

"Get them, and get your guys. Go to the boiler room entrance as fast as you can." I turned to Farnsworth. "What's your cell number?"

Farnsworth gave his number to the leader of The Vipers.

"Call us the second anything happens on your end, okay, Spit?"

"You'll stop them, Scarlucci," Spit said. And then he spat at the floor, a signal of his determination, answering the question that I had wondered about since I first heard his name.

"Let's hope so, Spit,"

"No fucking doubt about it," he said, as he turned to hurry away. "You're a SEAL!"

Beyond us, I saw the door to Ken Valentine's room open. Joey Mordento stepped out through the doorway and into the hall. He closed the door behind him and headed toward us. A.

J. Gotz returned from his desk, carrying his briefcase, using a small key to unlock the latches.

Suddenly, Arnold Federly's voice sounded over the loudspeakers, filling the hall and the interior of the rooms in the wing, and the emergency announcements began.

Sherri suddenly came rushing out of her office at the end of the hall.

"My God. What is it?" she called down to us.

"Get back inside, Sherri! We'll call you if we need you," I answered. I saw Sherri was hesitating, and shouted down the hall, my words echoing through the empty corridor. "GET BACK IN THE OFFICE, SHERRI. NOW!

She stumbled backwards, yanking open her office door and disappearing back inside.

And stay there, my love. I will not lose you. Not now. Not ever. This I swear!

Joey Mordento did not need any announcement. He stopped in front of us. My gaze involuntarily went to a golden *Phi* symbol pinned to his chest, then up to meet his eyes.

"I know," Joey said to me. Then he turned to A. J. Gotz and said, "Give me your gun."

"Joey,..." I said.

His calm gaze met mine. "You worry about everything else, Mr. Scarlucci," Joey said, as A. J. Gotz opened his briefcase. "I'll take care of the nerve gas. If I can hit a canister before they get through an entrance, the gas exploding in their midst will stop most of them. Right? Just tell Security in the

329

upper lot to get into cars immediately if I hit a nerve gas container so they won't be affected by the gas."

Farnsworth's mouth opened in shock. "How,...how do you...know?"

Joey reached into the briefcase and withdrew the weapon, looking at A. J. Gotz.

"I understand you would do it if your arm was not wounded, Mr. Gotz, but it is," Joey said. "It has to be me."

"I cannot allow this," Farnsworth said sternly. "I'm ordering you to put that weapon back and stop this right now."

More gunfire erupted from outside the school.

"With all due respect, sir, I don't think so," Joey said. He turned to me. "I need Pugh to unlock your office, Mr. Scarlucci. I'll sneak out through the tarp hanging over the hole in the wall."

"But how will you know where to shoot? What container holds the nerve gas?" Farnsworth protested.

"I already know," Joey said. "I just hope I can hit one. It's a tough shot with a handgun."

My mind asked the question, but I said the words aloud. "Do you have the audio track, Joey?"

He nodded, and actually smiled with the knowledge that in ways I didn't even have time to try to comprehend, let alone understand, I was reading his mind.

"You know I do," he said. "I'll have someone put Mr. Valentine's audio track of the Tibetan Balls in the main office system and pump it through both the outside and the interior of the school before I go out through your office."

"As loud as they can play it," I said.

"As loud as they can play it," he answered.

We moved to the entrance where Abdul Jehmar stood waiting with his megaphone alongside Pugh and Mitchell Bright.

"They're shooting up into the parking lot...and shooting the sheep. And they've started a fire at the main entrance to block anyone leaving." Mitch said.

I nodded and clicked on the 2-Way. "Tell anyone with a weapon to defend themselves, Sam. Stay under cover and shoot back." I turned to Pugh. "Go with Joey and unlock my office door for him, then stay there with Dr. Federly and the others. Shut off the fire alarm so no one even thinks about leaving this building. And make sure no one comes out of that auditorium. Either you or Federly make sure of that."

More gunfire erupted outside the school, followed by what sounded like a loud denotation.

"They're hurling explosives at the parking lot area," Mitch cried.

"I've got a man down," Sam's voice cried. "Repeat. I have a man wounded out here."

"Do what you can for him, Sam," I responded. "Give someone else the gun and keep firing!"

"You can count on me, Brian," Laurence Pugh said. "I'll do whatever I can to save people."

"I know you will," I said, suddenly proud of my counterpart's show of courage. I shook his hand, then Joey's. Farnsworth repeated my actions.

"Good luck," said Farnsworth.

"God be with you," said Mitch.

Joey gave Mitch a smile.

"*She* is," Joey said.

"Go!" I said.

Joey Mordento and Pugh ran from us, down the main corridor. As they moved, six bodies passed them, coming toward us. They had red bands on their bare, muscled tattooed arms and held what looked like very modern and very lethal guns in their hands.

Vipers.

The one who spoke for the group was a short stocky gang member I had seen hanging with Spit who went by the name of Gutter. A huge knife was sticking out of his beltline, which I assumed explained the name. No one asked how the hell the Vipers had managed to get such weapons into the building.

"Spit said you might need some help, Scarlucci," Gutter said. "Even if you was a SEAL."

"How many stayed by the boiler room entrance with Spit?" Farnsworth asked, his eyes wide with disbelief as he stared at the weapons in their hands.

"Enough," Gutter replied, lips spreading wide to what was more of a sneer than a smile. "We'll stand by here, just in case. If they get through that fucking door, you get back fast, so we can take them out."

"They're coming, Brian!" Mitch shouted. "They're coming!"

"Okay, Mitch," I said. "Get back with your students. You've got to watch them and Ken Valentine's classroom. The meditation group is in there."

Mitch gave me another thumbs-up, and I watched his huge lumbering body run down the wing toward his room.

"All right," I said, turning to Abdul Jehmar, "I'm going to open this door just enough to try to let you speak to them with the megaphone. Hopefully, it will buy us some time. If it doesn't work, and I have to slam the door shut, be ready to jump back. The electric lock will re-set instantly." Sirens sounded in the distance. "Ready?"

Abdul Jehmar nodded.

Gutter signaled the other Vipers and they split into groups of three on the far sides of the exit, weapons ready.

I slowly pushed on the wide metal center door latch, disengaging the automatic lock, and slowly eased open the Wing C exit doorway.

THIRTY-SIX
BOOK 'EM

Bullets exploded around us as the door opened, and I scrambled back, hurriedly pulling Abdul Jehmar and the door after me until I heard the lock engage. The window in the upper half of the right door suddenly shattered from gunfire, glass flying in all directions.

Farnsworth was answering his cell. "It's Spit!" the superintendent cried. "They're smashing at the doors at the end of Wing A, attempting to enter."

"TELL HIM TO HOLD HIS FIRE. NO ONE IS TO USE A WEAPON UNLESS THE INTRUDERS GET INTO THE SCHOOL."

BOOKS! my mind commanded.

I frowned, not understanding.

BOOKS! GET THE BOOKS! BLOCK THE EXITS WITH BOOKS!

Of course. Books! We had thousands of books! And, thanks to Sherri, they were all on movable carts.

I ran for the storage room door in the main corridor next to the C Wing, grabbing Farnsworth and pulling him with me. At the doorway exit, I heard the bullhorn's electrical click and glanced back to see Abdul Jehmar shouting into the bullhorn through the open space of the shattered window. He screamed a name I did not understand over and over. The shout was answered with gunfire.

I pulled the storage room door open and screamed at The Vipers by the exit.

"Get the books!" I shouted, pointing at the walls that lined the room's interior. "They're all on wheeled carts. We'll block the doors with books! Take two carts at a time! Overturn them, smashing the books against the doors to block it! We'll take this exit. You get books to Wing A, Wing B and the main lobby doors. Hurry! We'll stop them with books, Goddamn it!"

With a shout of "Yes!" Farnsworth ran into the storage room, matching my actions, as I pushed the carts apart with a heave. The six Vipers jammed their weapons into their belts and moved into the room, following our example, and pulling the carts of books from the walls.

Using all the strength I could muster, the two carts rattling before me as I grasped the handles, I pushed them out of the storage room, into the corridor, and sent them hurtling to the exit doors.

Abdul Jehmar jumped back, his shouting interrupted momentarily as the carts crashed into the doorframe, dozens and dozens of hardcover books spilling from the carts against the doors. Then I heard Farnsworth's carts colliding with the metal also, but I was running back into the storage room, and moving two more carts ahead of me, passing Farnsworth as he also ran for more. Beyond me, the muscled bodies of The Vipers ran down the hall, an occasional book flying into the air as cart after cart of hundreds and hundreds of books rumbled down the main corridor and out of sight.

"THEY WILL NOT LISTEN!" Abdul shouted, gunfire exploding against the doorframe.

I pulled him away from the door and shoved him forcefully backwards as bullets ricocheted against the metal of the doors and my released carts smashed into the scattered book mounds. Then two more carts of books exploded against the doors, and Farnsworth stood next to me panting, staring and pointing.

"That will definitely slow them down. It would take a fork lift to move those books," Farnsworth said.

The doors were covered by hundreds of spilled hardcover books. Piles and piles of novels reached to above the windows, blocking the malicious intruders from reaching the youth and their teachers huddled together within this place of learning: Sophocles, Shakespeare, Orwell, Hemingway, Hesse, Tolstoy, Steinbeck, Salinger, Miller, Melville, Morrison, Lee, Dickens, Twain, Sinclair, Chaucer, Wilde, Crane, Huxley, and more. Book after book lay in front of the doors, a fortress of literature from all the ages, standing up against the assault of hatred that threatened to destroy us.

Then we were running. Running down Wing C as shouting figures could be heard firing weapons and smashing at the closed doors, not understanding why the doors would not yield, not knowing that great stacks of the best in literature blocked their hateful advance.

Farnsworth's cell phone rang, and he answered it as we ran from the gunfire and assault at the entrance.

336

"Spit says good fucking call with the books," Farnsworth repeated to me, speaking the words verbatim, not even realizing he had cursed. "The Vipers will make sure they block Wing A and Wing B. Spit also sent some carts to the front entrance. Apparently Pugh has already had the people in the main office stacking everything that is not nailed down in front of the main doors and windows, but Spit's having his boys hurl some carts of books onto the piles. He says the books carry so much weight, they'll protect us. Nobody can destroy them all."

Outside the school building in the distance, I could hear more sirens, louder and closer.

"We just might make it," I thought. *"We just might make it."*

Then the English office door opened and Sherri emerged. "Brian, it's Sam! He had Security call my office from a cell phone because you're not picking up! You must call him!"

Simultaneously, as Sherri spoke, armed intruders came rushing around the corner from the back hallway, weapons raised.

Oh, God, no! They had gone around the building and come in through a rear entrance. I had slipped up. I should have anticipated it....

"SHERRI, NO...." I screamed, running, watching the intruders stop and lift their weapons, pointing guns toward where she unwittingly stood, directly in the line of fire.

Then it happened:

John Arthur Long

GOOOOOOOOOOOOOOONNNGGGGGGGGG!
GOOOOOOOOOOOOOOONNNGGGGGGGGG!
GOOOOOOOOOOOOOOONNNGGGGGGGGG!

The sounds of Ken Valentine's Tibetan Balls filled the air with such an impact of sound that it shook the very air that surrounded us. On and on and on they gonged, the vibrations so strong our bodies froze in place, immobile from the shock of sound.

The startle of immobility lasted only a moment, but it was enough. Seeing the raised weapons of the oncoming intruders, Sherri screamed and dropped to the floor. Recovering from the sound shock, the attackers moved in our direction once more, intent on reaching us as their weapons began to fire and we scattered, diving against side walls and to the floor in a desperate attempt to find cover that was not there. Everywhere, the gongs filled the air.

Suddenly, bursting out of the room next to me charged the huge bounding figure of an enraged servant of the Lord named Mitchell Bright.

And Mitchell Bright was ready!

His mighty body was raised to its full height. His feet were bare so that he would not slip. In each hand, held high by his mighty muscled arms, was a student classroom desk/chair combination.

"VENGENCE IS MINE, SAITH THE LORD!" Mitchell cried, his voice thundering through the hallway, mixing with the shattering sounds of the Tibetan Balls. And his six-feet-eight-

338

inch, two hundred and eighty pound body of pure muscle and churning energy charged straight at the intruders, his arms swinging the desks in wide arcs as he charged.

Miraculously, though he hurled himself straight at them as the intruders fired, Mitchell Bright remained unharmed. Almost upon them, he hurled first one desk and then the other, each smashing into the attacker's bodies, sending them screaming in alarm as they tumbled beneath the hurled hard plastic and metal that came crashing down on them. Then we were all there, running forward, screaming, attacking, lost in the rage of combat.

Mitchell had a now-broken desk in hand again, smashing what was left of it at crawling bodies, while Farnsworth, Abdul Jehmar and I hit, punched, clawed at the fleeing, crippled figures. As I fought, I saw Sherri come to her feet, a weapon in her hand.

"GET THE HELL OUT OF OUR SCHOOL, YOU BASTARDS!" she screamed as the intruders turned to flee. Then the weapon came to her shoulder and Sherri fired, the automatic rifle kicking again and again against her shoulder, bullets smacking into walls and ceiling as the screaming wounded attackers ran, stumbling down the back hallway and out of view.

THIRTY-SEVEN
THE GOLDEN MEAN

"BRIAN!" a voice called.

I stopped, confused momentarily at hearing my name called amid the loud gonging of the Tibetan Balls; then I realized it was the amplified voice of Sam Shapiro, screaming for me, and I snapped the 2-way radio off my belt.

"Copy, Sam. Go ahead!"

"Someone fired a shot out here. It came from near the school," Sam's voice said, unable to contain his excitement. "Do you hear me? Someone shot and a canister that one of these bastards was carrying exploded! They're starting to run back toward the van! Who's shooting from the school building?"

"Sam, get everyone into cars and keep the doors and windows shut. Now! It's the gas. The container held nerve gas and now it's in the air out there! Get into cars and stay there. Do you copy?"

"Copy that." I heard Sam issuing the orders, then I heard a car door open and slam closed. Then he was back on the 2-way, talking from the protection of a vehicle. "You're right, Brian. Some are falling down in the entrance drive there. One fell and is vomiting."

"As soon as the authorities have control out there, send them in to sweep this building. We have to make sure more intruders did not get inside. Copy, Sam?"

"Copy, Brian."

"Call the police back," I shouted to Farnsworth. The Superintendent was sitting on the floor, leaning against a wall. He waved an exhausted hand to me and brought up his phone. "Tell them that nerve gas is in the air on the outside of the school. All personnel must wear masks to apprehend the intruders."

"That means Joey Mordento succeeded, doesn't it," Farnsworth said.

"It would appear that's what it means," I answered. "Sam couldn't see the shooter, but said the shot went right through the canister one was carrying and it shattered instantly."

Farnsworth nodded, already speaking into the phone. Abdul Jehmar crawled to his feet. "My daughter. I must go to my daughter."

I looked toward where Sherri stood, the automatic rifle hanging loosely in her hand, its muzzle touching the floor. I moved toward her. She dropped the weapon and ran into my arms.

"Go," I said, waving Abdul Jehmar forward, "Go find your Angel." And he hurried away from us, heading to where he belonged, at his frightened daughter's side.

I gathered Sherri to me, my arms squeezing her tightly, kissing the top of her head, her cheeks, her lips.

"Okay?" I whispered, my body shaking in aftershock against hers.

She held onto me tighter than I could ever remember. "I...I think so."

"How did you know how to fire that weapon?"

"I did a Scarlucci," she said, smiling weakly. "I just trusted my instincts."

"Can you call the main office for me?"

"Yes," she whispered hoarsely.

"Tell Larry to have Federly announce that no one is to leave the rooms until instructed to do so. Tell him to make sure it's Federly because he made the first announcement, and they'll listen to what he says. Under no circumstances, should anyone go to the outside of this school. Tell him to inform everyone a lethal gas has been released into the air outside, and anyone who is exposed to it might die. Tell him to inform them that the military will be sweeping through the school and not to be frightened when they see armed personnel pass by the classrooms. That everything is under control, but they must stay inside the rooms until told otherwise. We will make a general announcement when it is safe to leave the rooms."

Sherri shivered against me and then pulled away.

"It's over, right, Brian? We're safe now."

"Let's hope so," I answered.

"Can I come back out here after I make the call," she asked, crossing back toward the office, suddenly looking more unsure and vulnerable than I had ever seen her. "I...I need to be with you."

"I wouldn't have it any other way," I said. "I'll see you shortly. I'm just going to the end of the hall to check on things."

I started back down the hallway.

"Can I get my sheep soon, do you think?" Mitchell Bright said, pushing himself to his feet and moving with me as I passed.

"I don't think so, Mitch. There's nerve gas out there now. I don't know how that might affect their bodies, but probably they should just be disposed of when it's safe to do so."

"It's okay," Mitch said, stopping at his room door. "They've done God's work."

I extended my hand. "So have you, Mitch," I said. "Thank you."

"It's because I trained every day, you know. Running on the track. Lifting weights. Getting ready...."

"I know it is," I said. "The Lord works in strange ways, right?"

Mitch liked that.

"Right you are, Brian. God bless you!" he said, and smiled as he opened his classroom door and went inside.

My 2-way crackled, Sam's voice feeding me new information. "Brian, the Black Hawk helicopter is here...and the police. They've surrounded the building...and are taking captives. Many of the intruders are sick, it looks like. Falling and gagging. Looks like we're going to be okay. I'm sending the military inside. They want to sweep through the building. They already caught intruders going out the back entrance.

343

Who got to them? The Vipers? They looked pretty beat up. A couple of them even have gunshot wounds."

"Send in the sweep, Sam," I answered. "But, listen, be sure to tell them the students in red arm bands are ours. Do not harm any of The Vipers. They helped save us in here. Copy, Sam?"

"Copy that," Sam's voice answered.

Farnsworth waved to me. "Spit is awaiting orders. What should I tell him?"

"Tell him to take all The Vipers into the boiler room and wait there until the all-clear announcement. Let him know the army is sweeping the school, and I don't want there to be any problems. And tell him to lose the weapons before the army comes through, so there are no mistakes. And tell him thanks. I owe him. Tell him I may even let him play cards in the cafeteria again."

Farnsworth relayed the information, and called back to me once more as I started down the hall. "Spit says he'll even things up when he beats you bad in a game of Texas Hold 'Em."

"Tell him it's a deal," I said.

And then, I saw Joey Mordento come into view at the end of the hallway.

The audio track of the Tibetan Balls had never stopped playing, filling the air with vibrations of power, but the sound was softer now, more comforting, bringing a calmness to the interior around us, a cleansing to the air.

344

Beyond where Joey stood, I could see that the intruders had managed to smash their way through a small area in the pile of books that covered the shattered window at the exit doors, punching holes in the stacks. A glow poured into the window opening, streams of light passing through the random holes that existed among the books in glistening shafts of luminescence that radiated around Joey's body. He headed in my direction, moving out of the light that surrounded him, toward where I waited for him.

Yes, Joey, move this way. The window behind you is shattered. The gas..., I said.

The gas will not come this far. The air currents are pulling it away from us, he answered. *Do not worry. The gas is already dissipating. We are safe.*

You did it, Joey, I said.

We all did it, Mr. Scarlucci, Joey answered.

Then a chill ran through my body as I realized suddenly that it was my mind speaking.

I had not spoken aloud.

Look to your left, my mind said. *Look in Ken's room.*

I turned my body to the classroom entrance opposite me, and looked through the small window in the top part of the door into Ken's classroom, the vibrations of the Tibetan audio track playing ever-so-softly in the air around me.

The meditation group sat on the carpeted floor in a circle within. I saw that each student wore a golden *Phi* pin somewhere on his or her clothing. And I realized that through it all, the members had been like this, their legs crossed, upper arms resting on their knees, palms up, thumbs touching index fingers, meditating, not moving...not afraid.

And then their heads turned as one, and their voices spoke to me within my mind.

Join us, they said.

Joey had reached where I stood, and he stopped only for a moment, then moved to the door of Ken's classroom and opened it.

Join us, the voices said again.

You were here all this time, during it all. Weren't you afraid? I questioned.

There is no reason for fear, came the answer. *Fear is for the lost. We are not lost. We have found the way.*

And in that moment, the sound of the Tibetan Balls filling the air around me, I knew that Ken Valentine had not just saved me; he had saved all these wonderful students. A teacher had shown them the way. It was the way to the seed that was at the core of all learning. It was the way to the element that could be found buried within the basic fiber and fabric of all things in existence.

It was the way to the Golden Mean.

Joey smiled and opened the door.

Won't you join us? asked the voices within my head.

Sherri came to beside me.

"What's going on, Brian?" she asked. "What should we do now?"

346

I looked down the hall to where Farnsworth was standing, caught in the demands of the moment, talking into his cell phone, taking command.

"Let Farnsworth handle things," I said. "He's in charge."

Beyond us, I could hear voices shouting in distant halls, the clatter of boots running, bodies moving with the purpose of discovery, sweeping the school. Down the hall from where we stood, Farnsworth's muffled voice spoke into his cell phone. Outside the school, I could hear sirens and shouting. Within the closed classrooms in Wing C, the noise level was building as students and teachers began to speak. And above it all, the Tibetan Balls, the most powerful sound of all, continued to gong with a full rich vibrancy that seeped into my being, tingling against my senses, filling me with promise.

Inside Ken's classroom, I saw the small fountain in the corner where water poured down over rocks, the movement of nature in all its complex simplicity. The statue of Buddha sat on a pedestal in the opposite corner, content with all things, in a state of absolute peace. The students had returned to their meditation, and it seemed to me a soft blue light pulsated faintly around each of them.

I took Sherri's hand in mine.

"I need to go in here," I said. "Will you come with me?"

"I go where you go," she said with a smile as she leaned affectionately against me.

I turned to where Joey stood at the open doorway, waiting.

"I'd like to be a part of this," I said.

"I know," Joey said, gesturing us inside. "Welcome."

With Sherri at my side, I stepped into Ken Valentine's sanctuary of learning.

I was ready.

EPILOGUE

I am no longer one of the Assistant Principals at Central High School. I was ready for something more meaningful, and I believe I have found it. Actually, Sherri was offered my vacated position, and she took it, suffering no end of ribbing from me about having some pretty big shoes to fill. I would like to be able say that things are calmer at Central High than when I was there but, according to Sherri, who torments me with her tales of woe each evening prior to other fun activities, the school I left is still the same old Central High with all its good and bad points.

Except for one thing: It doesn't have any more gangs.

I've got all those at my school. Along with all the drug pushers, student criminals, and assorted volatile types that could be found within the Central School district. See, Dr. Francis Farnsworth was so impressed with the job I did of handling Spit and the boys during what is now referred to as *The Crisis*, he suggested that I work with them all the time. This is the classic educational ploy, of course. If the staff member is really good at something, as a reward, keep piling it on, higher and deeper.

Actually, I can't lie. I kind of like it. I am now the Principal of the Valentine Annex, made up of grades 6 through 12, that the Central School District has established for students who have trouble functioning in the regular educational system. The idea is to put them in a separate environment where these *problem students* will have a better chance of succeeding. As the Valentine Annex Principal, I had to shed my ego. I know it's a volatile and potentially explosive arrangement. I mean it's inevitable. You round up all the Spits and Gutters and younger Spit and Gutter trainees, and send them to an alternative school where Mr. Scarlucci can show them how much fun school and learning can be, and things are not going to go exactly what you would call…smoothly.

So, why would Brian Scarlucci, glutton for punishment that he is, take such a job?

Because during those devastating three weeks of loss and crisis that I experienced as Assistant Principal at Central High, something very deep inside of me changed. I found I could no longer just float sardonically along, taking care of business. It just wasn't enough. My dearest friend had taught me that. You have to take a stand. You have to try to make a difference. Whether you are really able to or not, you still have to try. That is what makes it all worthwhile.

And I believe I am making a difference. I'm no Ken Valentine, you understand. I haven't made any world-changing discovery about learning. But that's okay too. I'm happy to take it one day at a time.

Oh, trust me, I have discovered that running an alternative school is not easy, even for a SEAL. We're averaging about three fights a day, frequently a weapon or two surfacing…and that's on a good day. I made Spit one of the Student Deans. Those discipline sessions are something to behold. He does tend to get a little too worked up, and when I see him start to spit, I have to step in, but he's learning. And so am I.

I really *am* good with these kids. I'm irreverent, yet honest and tough enough with them to actually make it work...sometimes. And you know what else? Even when I am frustrated beyond belief with them, and ready to pull my hair out, I'm loving every minute of it. To see someone like Spit offer a younger trouble-maker positive behavioral advice gives me a feeling of satisfaction like I have never known.

I have not severed all my ties with Central High. I am still the advisor to the Ken Valentine Meditation group, which I think also helps balance out the stress of running the Annex. Each week, Sherri and I join the group for meditation as we did at the end of that horrific day of *The Crisis*. A wonderful calmness fills me during the sessions, and I think fondly of my friend, and when the meditation is finished, I feel better able to face the world somehow.

Sherri and I are living together now. I sold the house, dropped the lease on the apartment, and we've gotten a place of our own. And things between us just seem to get better and better.

So that just leaves one question to be answered, doesn't it?

Did listening to the audio track really increase my mental abilities and alter my mind to the point where I was reading the thoughts of others that day, or were my instincts just functioning at a higher level brought on by *The Crisis*?

John Arthur Long

Well, if this were a question from Harold Billings, The Answer Man, I'm afraid I would have to disappoint him because the cold hard truth is I just don't know. Sometimes, I believe I actually *did* hear the unspoken voices of those around me. Other times, I'm not so sure, and think considering the possibility of such a thing nothing short of insanity.

But when my friend was alive, I made a promise, and it's a promise I intend to keep for as long as I am able. That's why, every day, no matter how busy I am, I find a time to be by myself. I take out the iPad Ken gave me, put in the earbuds, and listen to the Tibetan Balls.

I truly believe listening to that audio track is changing me for the better, though I do not know what those changes will bring. What I do know is that my mind will remain open to the possibilities, and I will keep listening.

www.ingramcontent.com/pod-product-compliance
Lightning Source LLC
Chambersburg PA
CBHW050915250626
47155CB00001B/248